THE FOURTH COURIER

A Novel

TIMOTHY JAY SMITH

Arcade Publishing • New York

Arcade Publishing books may be purchased in bulk at special discounts for sales promotion, corporate gifts, fund-raising, or educational purposes. Special editions can also be created to specifications. For details, contact the Special Sales Department, Arcade Publishing, 307 West 36th Street, 11th Floor, New York, NY 10018 or arcade@skyhorsepublishing.com.

Arcade Publishing® is a registered trademark of Skyhorse Publishing, Inc.®, a Delaware corporation.

Visit our website at www.arcadepub.com.

10 9 8 7 6 5 4 3 2 1

Library of Congress Cataloging-in-Publication Data is available on file.

Cover design by Erin Seaward-Hiatt
Cover photo credit Michael S. Honegger

Print ISBN: 978-194892-410-8
Ebook ISBN: 978-194892-412-2

Printed in the United States of America

Everything is for Michael.

This book is especially dedicated to

Malgosha Gago
and
my many Polish friends who inspired me.

WARSAW, POLAND

1992

A SEAGULL FISHED THE GUNMETAL river.
Jay Porter paid his taxi driver and ducked under red-and-white incident tape to approach the sprawl of police cars. Their swirling blue lights bounced off the low gray sky. Basia Husarska got out of her own car—bright red and sporty—and tossed aside a cigarette. She looked like a bruise on the ice in her leather boots and black everything else. "*Dzien dobre*, Agent Porter," she said.

Jay shook her hand. "Good morning, Pani Husarska."

"Detective Kulski waits for you before moving the body."

He followed her down the riverbank.

Two bridges spanned the Vistula's sludgy water. Even at that early hour, their steel girders boomed thunderously from vehicles speeding overhead. It had snowed during the night, then rained, leaving an invisible crust. *Głodedź*. Was that the name for the thin ice that coated everything? The first word his tutor had taught him in a language short on vowels. With his feet crunching through it, Jay asked, "Is this *głodedź*?"

"*Gołoledź*," the director replied, her tone correcting everything: his spelling, his accent, the presumption that he could speak a word of Polish. "We have *gołoledź* only in winter. Now it is spring." Her voice, rough from smoking, made everything she said sound even more foreign.

Detective Kulski, standing next to a body on the riverbank, was finishing up with his police team. He switched to English at Jay's approach. "Remind the hospital not to accidentally burn his clothes this time," he instructed them. The detective took Jay's hand, pumped once, and let go. "I'm glad you were in your room."

"I am, too," Jay answered, wishing he were still in a warm hotel bed instead of bending over a body on the icy riverbank. He studied the dead man's face, not really seeing him but only the evidence of him: a slackened chin, blood smeared on the ears, lips blued by cold death. He hadn't shaved for four or five days, maybe a week. "Is he the fourth courier?"

Couriers, mules, runners. Smugglers. Post-communist Poland, with its porous borders to the East and West, had quickly become a freeway for unlawful trafficking. A native-born mafia was suspected of three execution-style murders in as many months. Each victim had a cheek ghoulishly slashed before a bullet to the heart killed him. From the looks of it, the dead man on the riverbank was the fourth victim.

"Some things are different this time," Kulski pointed out. "He was killed here, not someplace else and brought here."

The detective was right. There was too much blood, and dead men don't bleed. "That's a big difference. What more?"

"He fell here." The detective indicated where the victim had fallen facedown, his heart leaking into the snow. "The killer rolled him over to cut his face."

"So he was dead first and not tortured this time," Jay said.

He slipped on rubber gloves and squatted next to the body. The dead man's lacerated cheek revealed an almost full set of gold teeth. Blood matted his woolly hair to the snow, and his eyes were open, staring dully at—what? His last conscious moment? Jay wanted to develop his retina, make a print, see what he last saw.

Director Husarska pulled a pack of cigarettes out of her coat pocket. That morning she had shed her usual full-length fur for a shiny wet-look jacket that could not possibly have kept her warm, but perhaps, like Jay, she had been summoned to the crime scene at an awkward moment and had worn whatever was handy. Tapping out a cigarette, she slipped it between her lips, red like her car, and another rare spot of bright color in that blurry morning. She snapped open her lighter; its blue flame danced atop the silver case. "He is Russian," she said, so flatly that Jay halfway expected her to poke the body with her toe, as she might something washed up on the beach.

"What makes him Russian?" Jay asked.

The policewoman sucked on her cigarette so hard he could almost taste the tobacco. "Look at his teeth," she replied, the wind snatching smoke from her mouth. "Only Russians use so much gold."

The dead man's overcoat had fallen open, revealing a thinner jacket soaked in blood. Jay touched its flap. "May I?" he asked Detective Kulski.

"Of course."

Before he did, Jay paused for a last look at the undisturbed body. Director Husarska remarked, "The labels are removed."

"I thought the body had not been examined."

"It is only my conjecture. Or would you use the word guess?"

"Guess," he replied.

She smiled at the tease in his response.

Jay folded the man's jacket back. Heavy with blood, it clung to the shirt. They all looked for a label, and saw the clean cut in the lining where one had been cut away. Jay touched the razor-straight edge of what remained. The other victims' clothes had been cremated along with their bodies before Jay arrived, but the case files described how all the labels had been removed with a blade so sharp it never snagged a thread.

Remembering that Detective Kulski had described the other couriers' hands as soft—"not callused like a worker's hands"—Jay lifted the dead man's right one by its wrist. Even in death it felt light, fragile: an old man's hand. He looked to see if the victim had hair in his ears and he did. "He's older than the others. Almost seventy," Jay estimated.

"The Russians, they drink vodka, they look like this," Basia told him. "In Russia, you can be twenty or one hundred, and you look like this."

"You don't like Russians, do you, Pani Husarska?"

"It is not disliking them, Agent Porter. It is knowing them."

"His wedding ring is missing," Jay remarked, noticing the paler band on the man's already pale fingers. Then he saw something else: a pronounced bump next to the man's little finger. He turned the hand to look at it and pressed it. It felt like the writer's bump he'd had through high school, before he switched to an electric typewriter in college. He showed it to Kulski. "What would cause a bump like that?"

The detective shrugged. "I don't know."

Jay couldn't imagine a repetitive task that would create a callus in that spot. He lowered the man's arm to the ground, stood, and pulled off his rubber gloves. "Ask the pathologist about it. Will Dr. Nagorski do the autopsy again?"

"I can ask for him," Kulski said. "He is not always available."

"It would be a good idea. In cases with multiple murders, often the same pathologist makes a connection we overlook."

"I will guarantee that Dr. Nagorski is available." Director Husarska tossed aside her cigarette. Its butt, stained with red lipstick, rolled down the riverbank.

"Good," Jay said.

Across the river, a ray of sun, breaking through thinning clouds, reflected off the snow clinging to a church's twin copper spires. "The other victims were all found on the other side of the river," he said. "On the Praga side."

"It's nothing," the policewoman replied, lighting another cigarette. "So the courier comes from a different direction this time."

"But why?"

No one ventured a guess as they pondered the lifeless man on the ground. "Why does a man cut a face like that?" Basia finally asked.

"It's a signature," Jay said. "The killer wants us to know that it's him."

"But *why* does a man cut like that? What is inside him to do such a thing? We have no such experiences in Poland."

"You are certain it's a man?"

"Can a woman be so cruel?"

Jay thought about women he had seen in prison. Some he had put there. "You would be surprised," he said. "Any witnesses?"

"*Jeszcze nie,*" Kulski said. Not yet. By the way the detective shook his head, he didn't expect any to turn up.

"Polish people do not cooperate with the police. It is our tradition," Director Husarska said, and shivered from the cold. "Have you seen enough?"

"I'd like to take some pictures."

"Of course."

Jay pulled a Polaroid camera from his daypack, snapped the photos, and as they popped out of the camera, slipped them into a pocket without waiting for them to develop. When he'd shot what he wanted—face, close-ups on slashed cheek and odd callus, and setting—he rose.

Detective Kulski signaled for the ambulance crew. Two men hoisted a stretcher and stumbled down the riverbank, obliterating whatever forensic value remained. They heaved the dead man onto the stretcher and everyone plowed back up the hill behind them. The detective limped with difficulty on the icy slope. When they reached a service road running the length of the embankment, his gaze traveled back to the river. As a fellow cop, Jay knew he was engraving the scene in his memory for all the times he would try to reconstruct what happened there.

The stretcher-bearers shoved the body into the back of an ambulance, sounded a siren, and drove away.

"So, we shall wait for a report on the radiation from Dr. Nagorski," Basia said.

"I'd like to attend the autopsy," Jay said.

"Please arrange that, Leszek." Basia pressed a key fob that popped open the locks on her sporty car.

Jay was surprised by it. Electronic car locks were only beginning to appear in the States, and Poland, recently liberated from decades of stifling communism, had a long way to catch up. "Nice wheels," he said.

Director Husarska glanced at her tires.

"I mean, nice car. 'Nice wheels' is an American expression."

"I like nice things," she said, and got into the car, started the engine, and gave it gas. Her tires spun on the slippery cobblestones.

Jay tapped on her window. She lowered it.

"You call this spring, Pani Director?"

"The Poles are romantics, Agent Porter. It is already April. It should be spring." Her window glided back up.

Jay leaned on one fender, Kulski on the other, and her wheels gained enough traction to bolt up the ramp and disappear into traffic. Brushing off their hands, they walked to the detective's car. Along the embankment stood a row of kiosks with chairs chained to naked umbrella poles embedded in cement blocks. Beyond them, a houseboat strained at its dock lines. "What is this place?" Jay asked.

"A park," the detective told him. "It is very popular in the summer. Now, it is too cold except for young people."

Jay detected a wry note in what the detective said and asked, "Is it another lovers' lane?"

"We have the same name for it."

"Who lives in the houseboat?"

"No one is home, so we are checking. Are you going to the embassy?"

"I'll walk. It's not far."

"Another storm is coming."

"I'll run if it does."

"I will telephone you about the radiation test."

The men shook hands and the detective drove off.

A policeman was balling up the last of the incident tape as Jay turned into the strengthening wind. The plywood kiosks groaned under its assault. A sign nailed to the houseboat's side offered daily river tours, but judging by the trash in its lines, it hadn't moved for some time.

A light flickered in one of the deckhouse windows.

Had someone returned unnoticed?

The gangplank heaved as the boat rocked in the wind. Jay grabbed the ropes that served as rails and started up it. In a couple of steps, he slipped on the sheer ice, his feet going overboard before the ropes stopped his fall. He looked into the murky, unforgiving water swirling beneath him and pulled himself back on his feet.

When he looked up again, the light inside the houseboat went off.

PART ONE

FIVE DAYS EARLIER

CHAPTER ONE

THE SEISMIC FALL OF THE Berlin Wall opened more than one route to the West. Smugglers sprang from communism's ashes to form cross-border alliances that built a drug trail running from the opiatic hills of Asia to the ports of Europe. Not all routes led through Poland, but a disproportionate number did. In Warsaw, a series of grisly murders, initially attributed to a worrisome though ignorable war between rival mafias, suddenly became an international concern when an autopsy of the third body revealed traces of radiation on the victim's hands. In the illicit global economy, nuclear smuggling had become the fashionable high-stakes game. At FBI headquarters, it had always been assumed to be a question of when, not if, the world's illicit routes would turn atomic.

Apparently Poland's had.

The new Solidarity government had asked for help on the case and Jay had volunteered. His grandmother had worked on the Manhattan Project, his father was a physicist at the atomic labs in Los Alamos, and though Jay didn't follow in the family's scientific tradition, he was interested in any case involving anything nuclear. To learn some basic Polish, he hired a tutor, a graduate student as eager to make love to him as he was to her, which by their second session made for an interesting vocabulary lesson. When his clearance finally came through, the third victim had been dead over a month and his command of Polish physiology was outstanding. He pieced together his first complex sentence, telling his tutor that he would miss her and insisting on a final exam.

Now, after only a couple of hours in Warsaw, he barely had time for a quick shower—but no change of clothes because his suitcase was missing—before his first meeting with the Polish police. He passed through the hotel's breakfast buffet, downing two passable espressos

and a bowl of granola, before jumping into a taxi. After badly mispro-
nouncing his destination, he showed the address to the driver.

"Why don't you say you go to police?" the man asked.

"I thought I had."

Minutes later, the driver pulled up to a crossbar blocking a circular
driveway. Behind it loomed a building, foreboding in its drabness.
Jay paid the fare, flashed his passport at a guard, and started up the
building's sweeping steps, pausing to work out the Polish for National
Police Headquarters on a red-and-white plaque. At the top, he pushed
his way through a heavy wooden doorway into a cavernous lobby, as
brutally austere as he had always imagined official Eastern Europe to
be. Nothing softened the hard marble walls or muffled the sounds
ricocheting between them.

From inside a glass booth, a security guard demanded his ID.

Jay slipped his passport to her through a tray. "I have an appointment with Director Basia Husarska."

The guard examined his photo, checked it against his face, and
dialed a number on her telephone. Jay heard his accented name in the
woman's stream of words. She hung up, returned his passport, and
pointed to the foot of a grand staircase. "You wait there."

Jay crossed the room to wait in front of a kiosk beside the stairs. Its
window displayed everything from disposable razors to baby bottles
to panties. When he heard the clickity-clack of high heels, he glanced
up at a slender woman with purple hair coming down the stairs. "You
are Mr. Porter?"

"That's me."

"I am Pani Husarska's secretary. Please, you follow me."

He did, and asked, "Do you have a name?"

"Of course. Everybody has a name."

"I meant, what is *your* name?"

"Oh!" The young woman laughed at her mistake.

A man in street clothes, coming down the stairs with a pronounced
limp, said, "*Do widzenia*, Hanna."

"Goodbye, Detective."

"So your name is Hanna," Jay said.

"Yes!" she replied, and laughed again.

After another flight of stairs, they entered a long corridor lined with heavily padded doors. All of them were closed, and everything—walls, doors, ceiling—was the same dingy yellow. Hanna brought them to an office with the nameplate Basia Husarska, Director BPZ.

"BPZ?" Jay already knew what it stood for, but wanted to hear it pronounced correctly.

"*Biuro Przestępstwa Zorganizowanego*," Hanna told him. Bureau of Organized Crime.

They entered the office; she crossed to a second door and knocked on it. From the other side, they heard an annoyed "*Tak?*"

Hanna opened the door as Director Husarska, on the telephone in a high-backed leather chair, swiveled around to face them. On the wall behind her was a long red banner emblazoned with Poland's resurrected crowned eagle stitched in gold. With the telephone receiver pressed to her ear, she puckered her lips as if tasting something sour. "He is here just now," she said in English and hung up.

"This is Mr. Porter," Hanna said.

"James Porter. FBI." He flashed his badge.

"Yes, I know." Basia, a smile fixed to her face, stood to shake his hand. He had seen her photograph, but nothing had conveyed her exotic beauty, her feline movements, her eyes the green of a leopard's and equally calculating.

"You're not expecting me, are you?" Jay guessed.

"Only now your embassy calls to inform me."

"I was told I had an appointment. My apologies. I can return later."

"No, of course not, you are here. Please sit. Hanna, two coffees. Unless you prefer tea?"

"Definitely coffee."

Hanna slipped out, closing the door behind her.

"It is a pity, Agent Porter, that just now—"

Her office door swung open.

"—you missed Detective Kulski."

"He didn't miss me," said the detective. He was the man with a pronounced limp descending the stairs. "Are you Mr. Porter from the FBI?"

"Agent James Porter."

"Detective Leszek Kulski." They shook hands.

"Welcome. I asked the security guard who you were. You didn't look Polish, so I was curious. I didn't know you were coming today."

"Apparently only Agent Porter knew that he was coming today," Basia said. "Please sit, Detective."

Hanna, carrying a tray, backed her way through the door.

"Detective Kulski will need a coffee, too," Basia said.

"I already prepared three cups." The young secretary slid the tray onto the desk and left again.

The three chunky espresso cups formed a triangle, and in its middle was a bowl heaped with sugar cubes. Basia dropped three into her cup and Kulski took two.

"You look at me curiously, Agent Porter," Basia said.

"I look at everything curiously."

"It is your nature?"

"It's my job."

"The FBI must be a very curious job. Sometime I will ask you questions about it." Basia picked up her pack of cigarettes, tapped it until a couple popped up, and offered them to Jay.

He had to restrain himself from taking one.

Apparently it showed because Basia asked, "You are trying to quit, like all Americans?"

Jay plucked one from her pack. "I swear it's my last one."

"Of course it is."

She reached across her desk and flicked her lighter, and he leaned forward to catch his cigarette in the flame. He enjoyed the first rush of the tobacco and exhaled slowly. "It seems that everybody speaks English here," he said.

"We are capitalists now." Basia smiled wanly.

Exhausted from a night in economy class, Jay needed caffeine and sipped his coffee. No one had warned him about Polish coffee—made by boiling grounds without filtering them—and his teeth were suddenly covered with grit.

Director Husarska watched him running his tongue over them, and smiled sincerely for the first time. "You are not the first foreigner to be surprised by our national coffee. You must first wait and then drink it slowly." She took a sip. "So, Minister Brzeski tells me that you are coming to help."

Brzeski, her de facto boss, was head of the ministry responsible for law enforcement and security, who had requested the FBI's help when the case shifted from an investigation of serial murders to nuclear smuggling. "So how do you think I can help?"

"You must ask the minister." Basia tapped off an ash. "So, Leszek, show Agent Porter what you have."

The detective opened his briefcase and stacked three files on the desk. Each was clearly marked 1, 2, and 3. "It's lucky that I have these with me. Pani Husarska asked to see what I had prepared for you. There is a file for each victim." The detective flipped through one folder to reveal documents meticulously organized and labeled: Investigation, Pathology, Photos.

"You've been busy," Jay said.

Basia told him, "Leszek is very thorough."

"I tried to translate the reports, but I am not very successful with the technical words. What do you know about the case?"

Jay summarized what he knew. Three murders with traces of radiation on the third victim's hands. Worry that they might all have been nuclear smugglers. Witnesses, evidence, motive, victims' IDs: they had none of the above.

Kulski found a map and pointed to three red dots straggling the east bank of the Vistula River. "The first victim was here, the second here, and here, the third."

"I want to see each site. And still no clue to their identities?"

"They are Russians," Basia answered.

"Have the Russians reported any missing persons?"

"Many people are missing in Russia, Agent Porter. Many people *want* to be missing."

"What's your theory, Detective, on the radiation? Why did you even look for it?"

"Dr. Nagorski, who made the examination, was director of the committee to investigate the Chernobyl problem in Poland. By chance he examined the third victim."

"By chance?"

"We have more than one pathologist in Warsaw," Basia answered.

"Dr. Nagorski always tests for radiation to continue his study," Kulski elaborated.

"Did you go back and test the first two for radiation? It's been unclear to me if you have, or if not, why not?"

Basia stubbed out her cigarette. "The bodies have been eliminated."

"Eliminated?"

"Cremated. It is normal after thirty days."

"Even in murder cases?"

"In all cases. We have photographs and a report, and we have no space to keep every extra body. The third victim is also eliminated," Basia added.

"Even when you knew about the radiation on his hands? Why?"

"There was a mistake with the paperwork. It is a normal confusion with bureaucracy."

"I thought no more communists, no more bureaucracy?"

Basia smiled sincerely for a second time, and said, "We are the same people."

"So, these are copies for me?" Jay asked, looking at the files.

"Yes," answered the detective.

"Great. Thank you." Jay slipped them into his briefcase. "I'm sure I'll have questions. And how do you want me to operate? If the FBI can help, that's what I'm here to do."

Basia said, "Leszek is handling the investigation."

"Can we meet tomorrow?"

"Of course," Kulski replied.

They all stood and shook hands. "You can contact me at the Marriott."

Turning to leave, he noticed the poster hanging alongside Basia's door: a whitewashed village in a field of lavender running downhill to an azure sea. "It's beautiful. Where is it?"

"Hvar," Basia told him.

"Yugoslavia?"

"It is my dream to live there."

"Everyone dreams to live in such a place."

"I will, Agent Porter. I will live in such a place. I am certain of it."

"Then you'll be one of the lucky ones," he said, and walked out.

. . .

OUTSIDE POLICE HEADQUARTERS, JAY CONSULTED his map and decided the embassy was walking distance. He followed hectic Puławska Street under trees that poked knobby branches into the steely sky. It was neither raining nor drizzling, yet the sidewalk was wet as if water had seeped from the ground and formed inky puddles.

At the embassy, a Marine guard checked Jay's ID and smiled when he handed back his FBI badge. "Always like to see you guys around," he said, buzzing him through a security door. A receptionist steered him in the direction of the ambassador's office. On his way, he sniffed out an alcove that housed a coffeemaker. He looked for anything resembling a ceramic mug, and ended up filling a Styrofoam cup with coffee from the charred pot. He took a cautious sip and poured it out.

He found the ambassador's office. Outside it, Millie, the ambassador's secretary, scratched her head of thinning white hair while staring at a blank screen. "I will never figure out these confounded computers!" she complained.

"It helps to turn it on," Jay said, and reached over to press the button on the systems drive. Instantly her screen lit up.

"Oh, thank you! I know these new things aren't that complicated, but sometimes I can't remember what to do first."

"I'm James Porter. FBI. The ambassador is expecting me."

"Oh dear, is Carl in trouble?"

"No, not at all. But I am in a little bit of trouble myself. The airlines lost my suitcase. By any chance, did someone call? I gave them the embassy's telephone number as a backup to the hotel's."

"I don't think so," Millie said, fingering various slips of paper on her desk, "but I don't always remember to write things down."

The ambassador swung open his office door. "Millie, when that FBI fellow shows up— Oh, it looks like maybe he has. Are you Porter?"

"I am."

"Good. Come on in. I just received a phone call from Basia Husarska."

"Here's my boarding pass." Jay slipped it to Millie. "If you could check on my suitcase, I would appreciate it. Thanks."

"Millie, let Kurt Crawford know that we're meeting now," the ambassador said.

With a clap on his back, the ambassador propelled Jay into the room and strode back to his wide mahogany desk flanked by American and Polish flags. Behind him a picture window roiled with clouds the color of pencil lead. Carl Lerner had to become an ambassador: he had the looks—tall, amiably handsome and lantern-jawed, with cowboy boots and a pale rose handkerchief sprouting from the pocket of his charcoal suit. He had an affecting Texas drawl, too, and said, "I'm afraid, Porter, that Millie forgot to set up your appointment with the Organized Crime unit. We had it on our calendar, but she never put it on theirs, which is why you may have found the police a bit surprised to see you."

"They were."

"It didn't go well?"

"An awkward start, but salvageable."

"Well, I do apologize. Millie has worked for State since Waterloo, and unfortunately has a better memory for Napoleon than this morning's schedule. Also unfortunately, I am tasked with drop-kicking her butt into retirement, and it might take that."

There was a knock on the door. "Come in," the ambassador said.

A tall black man entered. He had crew-cut hair, and his face was peppered with shiny scars. His snug shirt revealed his muscular build. A tiny ruby pierced his ear.

"Good, you're here. Introduce yourselves," the ambassador said.

"James Porter. FBI."

"Kurt Crawford. Acting Regional Security Officer." They shook hands.

"Please sit." The ambassador waved them into leather seats that exhaled under their weight. "How much of a briefing did they give you in DC?" he asked Jay.

"I read the cable traffic, which was short on detail. Clearly Eastern Europe is a whole new game. I have a lot of questions."

"Do you want to start with your questions, or shall I have Kurt give you some background?"

Jay answered by asking Kurt, "What's your involvement in the case? I thought RSOs usually handled kidnappings and evacuations."

"Kurt works on jobs that don't fit into anyone else's job description," the ambassador said.

"That's clear," Jay said, instantly concluding that Kurt worked for the CIA. Wary of having his case hijacked, he added, "I didn't know Langley investigated murder cases."

"Ah, hell!" growled the ambassador. "Is there nothing confidential any more? You might as well go ahead, Kurt, and get into it."

"The murders are all yours," Kurt told Jay. "We're just glad for the extra eyes and ears. In case you've missed it, there's a war in the former Yugoslavia that's spreading. The Serbs are making expansionist moves, not to mention setting up concentration camps for Muslims. Last year the UN slapped an arms embargo on Yugoslavia, but that hasn't stopped the Serbs from acquiring weapons, and *Made in Poland* is stamped on most of them."

Jay asked, "What does this have to do with my case?"

"Right now, we don't know who the bad guys are. Who's buying, who's selling, and how the weapons are moving south. We're hoping you'll learn something useful from where you've landed in their system."

"I've landed in Organized Crime, not border patrol."

"Mafias control almost all the trucking in the country. We suspect that's how the weapons are being delivered. They're easy to conceal inside trucks, and it's a big enough operation that someone inside Husarska's unit has to know who is moving what to where."

"Do you suspect Husarska herself?"

"Let's not jump to conclusions," the ambassador interjected. "We don't know enough to suspect anyone."

"What we do know," Kurt said, "is that the weapons are coming from PENZIK. It's a state-owned factory that's been scrambling to survive ever since the Soviet Union crashed and burned. The Soviets used to be its biggest buyer."

"That sounds like something the new government could easily stop, if PENZIK is state-owned," Jay said.

"It's not as easy as that," the ambassador said. "Shutting it down would throw a lot of people out of work, and they don't want to abandon the equipment. The plan is to privatize the factory and retool it to make something useful, like refrigerators and car parts. Until then, they have to keep it operating, and for the moment they still have buyers for their arms."

"Embargoed buyers," Kurt pointed out. "It took the radiation on your third man's hands to convince them that they need to do something. The implications have everybody scared."

"The radiation wasn't a plant, was it?"

Kurt broke into a big grin. "Naw. Langley's good but not that good. What's the Bureau's take on the radiation?"

"We thought this stuff would start showing up. Too many underpaid Russian generals have keys to too many nuclear pantries. I have my assistant tracking down recent DOE inventory reports on uranium stocks in the former Soviet republics. It's a long shot, but we might see something that ties into the couriers. Basically, she'll be looking for missing fuel. If enough is unaccounted for, then we know we have a problem."

Ambassador Lerner tilted back in his chair. "Are you suggesting someone is trying to put together an atomic bomb?"

"Or more than one of them. You can blow up Manhattan with a soda can filled with plutonium, *if* you can deliver it." The fact was astonishing, and the men's expressions turned appropriately incredulous, which was why Jay always liked to tell it. "In reality, plutonium is literally too hot to handle and hard to deliver. In cases like this, we usually assume we're dealing with HEU-235. That's high-grade highly enriched uranium. With U-235, it takes about fifteen kilos to make a small bomb. That's only the fuel. The delivery mechanism is extra weight."

"Delivery mechanism?" the ambassador asked. "Do you mean the warhead?"

"I mean some way to set off the bomb where you want it to go off."

The ambassador's intercom buzzed. "Yes, Millie?"

"Please let Mr. Potter know that the airlines found his suitcase. He can pick it up at the airport."

"Can they deliver it to my hotel?" Jay asked into the speaker.

"You have to clear it personally through customs," the ambassador explained, and instructed Millie to have a car ready for him. "Now where were we?"

"You asked about a warhead," Jay reminded him, "and that's not something a courier can carry. Most smuggled uranium is headed for countries like Libya or Iran that have no way—yet—to deliver a bomb. What's more worrisome are low-tech terrorists who might use it in a dirty bomb."

"What's your next step?" the ambassador asked.

"I'll look over the files and forensics and get more background from Kulski. Basically, I'm investigating their investigation and look-ing for gaps until there's more to work with. How involved do you want to be?"

"It's your investigation. All I expect is that you two gentlemen share relevant information. I don't expect the usual competition between Langley and the Bureau to apply here."

Kurt grinned. "It's no competition."

The ambassador ignored him, and asked, "What do you need from us, Porter?"

"An office, a desk, an outside line, and someone who will take mes-sages." A blast of hail ricocheted off the window. "And a window," he remembered to include. He hated rooms without windows.

"For now, use Millie for your messages. We'll sort out an office for you by tomorrow."

Their business over, the three men stood and shook hands.

"Do you lift?" Kurt asked.

"The embassy has a gym?"

"In the basement."

"Let's work out sometime," Jay said.

On his way out, he saw Millie hang up the telephone. "Oh, Mr. Potter, the driver is waiting out front for you."

"My name is Porter," he reminded her.

"Oh, I wish I could remember the simple things!"

"Try clue-minders, Millie. Me? I'm the man with the lost baggage. So think baggage and porter. Mr. Porter."

"Clue-minders? What a clever idea. Now don't forget your passport."

He patted his coat pocket. "Got it."

"And your boarding pass."

"That too."

"You wouldn't believe what some people forget. Oh my, I could tell you stories!"

"Another time, I'd like to hear them."

He had started down the hall when she called after him, "Button up, Mr. Potter! It's cold outside!"

• • •

LILKA PUCKERED HER CHERRY-RED LIPS in the bathroom mirror. Carefully, she outlined them with black eyeliner, occasionally dabbing her pencil into Vaseline to imitate the glossy look of models she'd seen in fashion magazines. When she finished, she gave her thick hennaed curls a last toss. Her eyes were turquoise, her skin as smooth and unblemished as a porcelain doll, yet Lilka did not think herself beautiful. Even on those rare occasions when mood and light coalesced sufficiently to allow her a glimpse of her true beauty, she didn't trust herself a moment later. Men admired her, but she didn't trust them either, certainly not the paunchy businessmen in the airport's executive lounge where she worked, serving drinks to first-class passengers who always found excuses to touch her.

Jacek barged in. "I gotta piss. I can't wait."

"Lift the seat, Jacek!"

"Fuck off."

"And please refill the bucket."

"Who says I'm gonna flush?"

Lilka left the bathroom.

Jacek finished relieving himself and, grabbing his crotch, shouted through the open door. "You want some of this?"

She dropped her keys into her purse. "Go to hell."

He lunged at her and grabbed her arm. "Go to hell yourself!"

"Let go!"

He forced her hand to his crotch. "Tell me this isn't as good as your first-class tricks and I know you'll be lying. We were always good."

She squirmed. "Jacek, please, stop—"

He fell back on the couch and yanked off his muddy boots. "Fucking first-class whore."

Lilka rubbed her wrist. "Where's Aleks?"

"I don't know."

"Wasn't he with you last night?"

"I'm not his babysitter." Jacek flung a boot against the wall. "I'm sleeping in your room today."

"No, Jacek, please."

"*No, Jacek, please,*" he mimicked her. "I drive a fucking truck all night. I have a fucking right to a fucking bed."

"We have an agreement."

"Call the police."

"You're impossible." Grabbing her overcoat, she slipped into the hallway before his second boot could hit her.

It hit the door instead.

"*Kurva!*" he called after her. Whore!

Lilka fought back tears, not wanting to smudge her makeup. She headed for the stairwell—its door was missing—and smelled her neighbor's warm bread before she saw her. Agnieszka emerged a moment later, out of breath from climbing six flights. Two bread loaves protruded from a bag slung over her shoulder. To Lilka, they smelled like mornings, when families woke up, sipped coffee with toast, and talked of the day ahead. Her father had always gone out to buy the bread for breakfast. Agnieszka's yeasty loaves reminded Lilka of the happy family she didn't have herself. No one went out for bread; no one sipped coffee with toast. No one cared what she would do that day or any day. That unhappy realization brought on the tears she had struggled to hold back.

"What happened?" Agnieszka asked. She tried to look at the side of Lilka's face. "Did he hit you again?"

"He didn't hit me."

"Not this time."

"He was just being his usual mean self."

"They shoot mean dogs, don't they?"

Lilka dabbed her eyes. "He's not worth the bullet."

They both laughed, knowing their black humor was a cover-up for what they were really feeling. "Come in and have a coffee," her friend urged. "It might be your last chance to see Wojtek in his Mickey Mouse pajamas before he puts them away for summer."

Agnieszka had a repaired palate, and whatever she said had the comforting sound of shushing a baby to sleep. Her "Mickey Mouth pajamath" cheered Lilka, and she kissed her cheek. "I'd love to, but I can't be late for work."

She started down the stairs. The smell of fresh bread had already been overcome by the more familiar stench of old piss, to which no doubt her husband—*ex*-husband, she reminded herself—had contributed. They had been divorced over three years, in itself something close to a miracle in Catholic Poland. At least the secular communists had recognized that the sanctity of marriage could be sacrificed on the altar of wife abuse. Still, Lilka had been forced to remain in the same apartment with Jacek: the communists had a waiting list for housing longer than the Church's list of sinners.

She felt dirty by the time she reached the ground floor and pushed the bar on the door to let herself outside. A thin layer of virgin snow covered everything. She brushed it off her windshield, using the snow to wash Jacek off her hands. She pulled on her mittens and got into her old and dented Lada.

Lilka prayed the car would start. It had been acting up lately, and had stalled out the day before. She pulled out the choke, turned the key, and tapped the gas pedal.

As soon as the engine turned over, it sputtered and died.

She tried again and it died again.

The third time, it turned over, coughed, and stayed running. She let the engine warm up before backing out of her space. The sun shone through a break in the clouds, reflecting brightly off the new snow. She slipped on sunglasses and turned into the street.

◆ ◆ ◆

SNOWPLOWS HAD PILED MUDDY SLUDGE on the median dividing the road to the airport. Cars passed at hell-bent speeds, spraying the windshield with snowmelt and salt, which the wipers only managed to smear. Jay leaned over the front seat to peer into the muddy twilight.

The international terminal came into view. No doubt it had been a showpiece when it first opened, the communists wanting to prove that they were equal to the West with such a modern building: all glass in alternating clear and red-tinted horizontal bands, and a control tower shaped like a praying mantis perched over it. Over the decades, it had clearly suffered from neglect: where paint was needed, none had been applied, and broken windows had been replaced indiscriminately, making a hodgepodge of the linear design. Floodlights, blurred by a dusting of snow in the early twilight, added a touch of prison-yard ambiance.

The driver pulled to the curb.

Jay asked, "Where will you wait?"

The man pointed vaguely ahead. "There. How long?"

"Hopefully not long."

He entered the terminal through cracked glass doors repaired with packing tape. Birds nesting in the overhead rafters had splattered the floor with chalky droppings. Everything was the color of grit. Poles, it seemed, didn't so much argue as grumble, and there was a fair amount of that going on in the long lines. His airline's bright blue logo hung over an empty counter where a note had been taped: Mr. Porter please come to The Lounge.

"The Lounge," he muttered, and looked around. He headed in the direction of the gates and a minute later was ringing the bell on the lounge's door.

Lilka answered it. "You are Mr. James Porter?"

"Yes."

"Please, you come inside."

He followed Lilka into an empty lounge filled with upholstered chairs patterned with tropical birds. Next to each was a lamp in the shape of a flamingo. Jungle wallpaper surrounded them. "Boy, this is different," he remarked.

"Do you like it?"

"Like it? It's great. I'm sorry, I have to do this." Suddenly he beat his chest and bellowed like Tarzan.

Lilka laughed. "You are not the first man to make that joke, but you make it the best."

"Good, because I can't believe I just did that."

"I am sorry, Mr. Porter, about your suitcase."

"Do you have it?"

"Now there is a strike."

"A strike?"

"For suitcases."

"Ah, the baggage handlers," he said, guessing what she meant.

"It will finish in one hour."

"And there's no one else here? It's just you and me and the birds for an hour?"

"Until the next flight. Also in one hour."

"I'll take a drink." Jay gave a look at the bottles on the shelf behind the bar. "Do you have Black Label?"

"You are lucky, the plane from London is very late."

"Lucky?"

"We are allotted only one bottle a day."

"And the British drink it?"

"It is their last chance not to drink Polish vodka. Please, you sit?"

He slid onto a stool and watched her pour a hefty shot.

"Do you want ice or water?"

"Straight. I only ice Johnnie Red."

"You are an expert on scotch?"

"Only in airport lounges. I can't afford Black Label at home. Can I buy you a drink?"

"I am not permitted to drink when working."

"Not even a glass of *wino biały*?"

"*Pan movi po polsku?*" she asked, surprised at his Polish.

"Only *tak* and *nie,* and white wine. You sure no?"

"Yes, I am sure."

"Well, cheers." Jay raised his glass to her before taking a sip. He was warming to the situation. No longer just a beleaguered traveler in search of lost baggage in a gray and dreary city. Things were looking up. "You know my name but I don't know yours," he said.

"I am Lilka."

"And I'm Jay, not Mr. Porter."

"Ja-ay," she said, testing it, making it sound new. "You are first time, Ja-ay, in Warsaw?"

"Yeah, first time, and I know nothing about Warsaw. What's fun to do?"

She sipped her wine. "Do you like old things?"

"Old things?"

"Maybe castles?"

He wanted to be agreeable, but castles? Looking at her, he wasn't thinking about old things or castles. "Are there any good restaurants?"

"Oh yes! Now we have restaurants from French and Italian. You will like them."

"What's your favorite one?"

"There are so many," she said, and he knew she had been to none of them. "Do you go to Disneyland?"

"Only once."

"Tolek wants to go. Always he talks about Disneyland."

"Tolek?" Jay checked her hands: no ring. "Is Tolek your husband?"

"He is the husband of my sister, Alina. He has dreams for America."

"Don't we all?"

The lounge's buzzer interrupted them.

"Please excuse me one moment," Lilka said and disappeared into the entry. He heard her speaking to a man before reappearing to tell him, "Your driver has your suitcase."

The embassy driver stepped into the lounge, grinning and displaying the lost suitcase. "All finished," he said.

"All finished?" Jay didn't want it to be finished. He wanted to stay in the lounge with Lilka. "How did you finish it?"

The man flashed his embassy ID. "No problem with this."

"Five minutes, okay?"

"No problem."

When the driver stepped out, Jay asked Lilka, "Maybe we can go to a restaurant?"

"Go to a restaurant?"

"Yes. You and me. A date."

Her thoughts played across her face. She measured him with the same eyes that had assessed countless offers and come-ons. He wanted to think he was different, but he knew he wasn't, he was exactly what he was: a lonely guy talking her up because she was beautiful.

"Okay," she said.

"Okay?" He had passed her test! "That's great! What time do you get off work?"

"Midnight."

Six more hours. He would never make it. A tsunami of weariness already threatened to sweep over him. "I'll call you tomorrow, okay?"

"Yes, tomorrow is better. I will not be so late. You will telephone me here?"

He grabbed a napkin off the bar. "What's your number?" As he wrote it down, the ink bled into the soft tissue. "I'll call tomorrow," he promised and went out to join his driver.

• • •

THE STREETCAR CLAMORED TO A stop and the doors wheezed open. Alina stepped down, jostling cumbersome bags that rubbed against her legs. The wind tugged at her neck scarf. She pinned it with her chin as she crossed the tracks, remembering too late to look for an approaching tram—had there been one. Even in that weather, cars tooted their way down busy Aleje Jerozolimskie at reckless speeds. Pedestrians, shielding their faces from blowing snow, hurried along the sidewalk. Alina followed where they had tamped it down and soon turned into her neighborhood.

A long park ran between rows of dreary Soviet-style apartments. The fat, wet snowflakes landing on the leafless branches reminded Alina of the linden blossoms of summer. The park had been abandoned by all but a boy throwing sticks across a frozen pond for his dog to chase. Each time, the puppy skidded on the ice on its big clumsy paws and the boy hooted with amusement. Alina laughed with him and was still smiling when she reached her building.

The unheated hallway was no warmer than outdoors. She pressed a switch and a dim overhead bulb flickered on. A faint hum signaled the start of her minute of light. By the third landing it failed, and only the pale illumination seeping under doorways guided her up the last flight. Outside her door, she set her shopping bags on the floor and, relieved of their weight, stretched her neck.

She was bending to the right when Tolek opened the door and instantly tilted his head to peck her lips. "I'll help you," he said and picked up the bags.

"They're heavy," she warned him.

"I noticed."

Alina hung her coat and cap on hooks inside the door and plucked free the limp hairs stuck to her forehead. She was a thin, nervous woman, and her movements were quick. She followed her husband into the kitchen. The room, painted a faded green, was cramped with their two-burner stove, a small table, and Alina's prized full-size (albeit ancient) refrigerator that clanked whenever the compressor started up.

The last of the day's feeble light barely brightened the window. Tolek heaved the bags onto the counter as Alina told him, "It's all potatoes and onions. There was nothing else fresh today, and the girl didn't know when any more would be coming. I bought as much as I could carry."

Tolek dumped the potatoes into a bin. "I want you to be careful, and carrying heavy bags isn't being careful. You could have slipped on the ice."

"I was careful and I didn't slip. You're home early. Did the power go out again?"

"They made it official today."

"*Today*? Without any notice?"

"Today without any notice."

"That's not possible.

"We knew it was coming."

"Knowing it was coming doesn't change things. What are we going to live on?"

"We have savings."

"Savings?" For a moment Alina was too anxious to say more. All her worries were creeping up on her. She shook as she unloaded a bag of onions into a basket and snatched up the papery brown skins that landed on the counter. "What savings, Tolek? Do you know how much food costs these days?"

"What's it matter what food costs, if there's nothing to buy?"

"We still have to eat." Alina sagged into a chair. "I don't know how we'll manage when prices keep going up."

Tolek rubbed a spot clear on the window. Everything outside was blurred by the slow drifting snow. His shoulders seemed too wide for the narrow kitchen; almost as wide as a bear's, and like a bear he was afflicted with a natural awkwardness. "I'll go to the embassy tomorrow and ask about our visas," he said.

"I teach *English*, Tolek. They don't need English teachers in America."

"So, you teach them Polish! Think how many Americans don't speak Polish!"

"You will look for a job here, won't you?"

"Not before a kiss." He pulled Alina out of the chair to embrace her. "Don't worry so much."

She stood stiffly in his arms; but smelling him, his peculiar dusty scent, she gave way to his comforting embrace, imagining that his arms, thick as tree limbs, shielded her from the worries and fears that threatened to roust them from their small kitchen. Alina could have cried, had she let herself. She could have cried for the food they couldn't buy, the jobs that didn't exist, the mourning doves which had yet to return for spring. Times had been worse and she hadn't cried then, not even when Tolek was arrested. She loved him, and trusted him, and opened her mouth to his. She wanted to take him by his hands and draw him to their bed; his big-knuckled hands that for fifteen years had held her and loved her, protected her when she was frightened. They kissed hard and long, and when he started to pull away, she pulled him back, using his mouth to stop a buried cry.

When their kiss finally broke, Tolek said, "I should lose my job more often."

Alina slipped from his arms. "I'll start supper." She ran water into a pot, lit a burner, and checked the potatoes for rot. "I suppose they have potatoes in America."

"Meat, too," he said cheerfully.

"Who can afford meat? Here, make yourself useful and peel these." She carried some potatoes to the table and handed him a knife.

The front door opened. "Is that you, Tadzu?" she called.

"Yes, Mama." The boy dropped his book bag by the door and stepped into the kitchen. "Hello Mama. Hello Tata."

"Don't track in," Alina reminded him.

"I wiped my feet," he said, exasperated by her familiar nagging. He pulled off his cap, freeing the black curls he had inherited from Tolek; his watery blue eyes came from his mother. He watched his father finish peeling a potato with a single cut.

"Why are you home early, Tata?"

Tolek held up his long ribbon of potato skin. "Now your father is part of the unemployed majority, unless someone is hiring a potato peeler!"

"Hush, Tolek. You'll worry him."

"How did you do on your test today?"

"I missed three questions."

"Did you ask for the answers afterwards?"

"Yes, Tata. I stayed after school and Pan Czarniecki explained my errors."

Tolek turned another potato in his big fist. "Explain them to me."

The boy straightened and held his hands at his side. He recited the equations he had answered incorrectly, which were easy enough, and then explained his mistakes. When he concluded, Tolek said, "Didn't I teach you that when you do something on one side of the equation, you must do the opposite on the other?"

"I forgot, Tata, I'm sorry. May I practice piano, please?"

"You have time to start your homework before supper," his father replied.

"I only have to read a story, and I finished that on the bus."

"Are you sure that's all your homework?" Alina asked.

"Of course I'm sure. Now can I play the piano?"

Tolek said, "You can practice before supper, but afterward, I want you to reread the introduction to equations. You need to know the basics before you can move ahead."

"Yes, Tata. May I have some juice, please?"

"Of course," Alina replied.

"Thank you, Mama." The boy took a glass from the cupboard and opened the refrigerator. "What's this?"

Alina looked over his shoulder. "What's what?"

Tadzu pulled out a bundle wrapped in newspaper spotted by grease. "This."

She opened it enough to see inside. "Sausage? You bought meat?"

"It's my severance pay. Two kilos." Tolek sneered, "For twenty fucking years of work, those *cholerniks* give me two kilos of sausage and a handshake!"

"Watch your language, Tolek." Alina set the bundle of sausage on the counter. "What were you practicing yesterday?" she asked Tadzu.

"A Chopin prelude. I'm only learning it."

"It was nice, wasn't it, Tolek? Why don't you go and play that?"

"But you study after supper," Tolek reminded him.

"Yes, Tata."

The boy went into the living room.

Alina folded open the newspaper. "We can get six meals from this," she said and sliced off some links. She measured oil into a frying pan, lit a second burner, and started peeling garlic. In the living room, Tadzu warmed up by repeating the opening chords of the Chopin piece before settling into playing it. "He has talent," she remarked.

"He needs to learn practical skills," Tolek replied, and was ready to dump the potato skins into the trash when she stopped him.

"Give me those. I can make a broth with them." She quartered the potatoes he had peeled and dropped them in the boiling water. "Lilka telephoned this morning. She's worried about Aleks."

"She's always worried about Aleks."

"He's started working for Jacek again."

"At least he has a job."

"He's a bad influence on the boy."

"Jacek's his father. You can't change that."

"He's not been coming home some nights and Lilka is worried."

"He probably has a girlfriend. Lilka should worry if he didn't at his age."

"She says he's secretive."

"After you and I met, I didn't always come home, and I was only a year older than he is."

"A year at his age means a lot of growing up still to do."

"Were we so much more grown up? Remember the risks we took?"

"I remember," Alina replied, recalling all their deceptions, but as quickly as her memories of happier times flooded back, so did her worries. "Oh, Tolek, what are we going to do now? How will we manage?"

"I said I'd look for a job until we get visas."

She had pushed him enough; she didn't want an argument, and he was ready for one. He rarely was, but his day had been a special strain. He knew, better than anyone, the job prospects for a second-rate scientist let go by a government-sponsored and lackluster institute: none. He'd be lucky to sell newspapers.

"I'll fry the sausage with onions. Would you like that?"

"It's all we have, isn't it?" Tolek slammed his fist into the table. "After forty years we finally got rid of those sonofabitch communists, and look at us, eating potatoes and onions like we're goddamn peasants, and happy when they throw us a scrap of meat!"

"It takes time for things to change. We have to be patient."

"Be patient, and live on what? I didn't go to jail for some *cholernik* to hand me two kilos of sausage and tell me he's sorry but I'm out of a job." Tolek grabbed the vodka bottle off the counter. "I'm going to listen to Tadzu."

From the living room, Alina heard him say sharply, "Play some Mozart, will you? It's more cheerful."

She started peeling onions, listening to a Mozart sonata that Tadzu had memorized the prior spring. She remembered how the mourning doves had cooed on the window's ledge as she listened to him practice. She peered out the window into the gelid twilight. When the weather warmed enough to call it spring, she would open the window and strew breadcrumbs on the ledge, hoping the doves would return.

She imagined them, gray and plump, pecking at the crumbs, occasionally splaying their tail feathers in a gluttony-induced courtship dance.

Alina started to slice an onion. Her eyes stung, and she wiped away tears with the backs of her hands. Again she looked out the window, imagining the cooing of the doves. Of course she hadn't heard them. Only silent snow steadily layered the ledge.

She cut into a second onion and wiped away more tears. Just as she hoped the doves would return, she worried they would not. All her hopes, it seemed, were only her worries reversed. She sliced another onion and another, letting the tears run down her cheeks.

Listening to Mozart, she cried.

Listening for the doves, she cried.

Listening to her own hopes, she cried.

CHAPTER TWO

GENERAL DRAVKO MLADIC PRESSED HIS substantial weight against the stubborn window. If left to him, he would leave it open through the bitter winter, but his wife Ulia feared sickness from cold. In her soul she was a peasant, and for superstitious reasons badgered him to leave the windows closed until the almond trees blossomed. She couldn't explain why; it was just something she knew should be done. That afternoon, leaving work, he had passed through Belgrade's cheerless neighborhoods and glimpsed the first white flowers in the wooded outskirts where the privileged cadre lived. When he arrived home and announced his intention to open the window in his study, Ulia, clattering pots on the stove, crossed herself.

The window groaned and sprung open, surprising the pigeons nesting on the ledge. Dravko shooed them away and with a rolled up newspaper sent their nest tumbling into the hedge below. He flared his nostrils and sucked in the fresh forest air to dispel the odor of the blood sausage cooking in the kitchen. The smell, too reminiscent of headquarters, nauseated him.

His phone rang and he picked up the receiver. "Mladic," he said.

"*Drrrravko*," he heard, instantly recognizing Sergej Ustinov's voice. Only the physicist could make his name sound like a French perfume.

"Hello, Dr. Ustinov. It's a surprise—" A burst of static made it impossible for Dravko to say more. He couldn't determine if it was real or made by the physicist blowing into the receiver.

It stopped long enough for Sergej to say, "We have a bad connection. I'm going to Moscow. The lines are better from there. I'll try on Monday."

The line went dead.

The signal had been received.

The physicist had always said he would cross on a Monday.

"Why Monday?" Dravko had asked him.

"Because the guards are drunk on Mondays, drinking off their hangovers from the weekend. Everybody knows on Mondays you can cross for vodka. Ha!"

Dravko opened his window wider. An early moon floated over the birch trees. He liked this time of evening, before the neighbors turned on lights that flickered between the chalky branches and spoiled his sense of being alone. He needed this time, when destiny left him alone long enough for his soul to catch its breath.

He had met Dr. Ustinov a year earlier in another birch grove while attending a secret conference of arms merchants from the former Soviet bloc countries. Their patron was in its death throes—a death few would mourn—and all agreed that it was collapsing under the weight of bureaucrats pilfering the communal pie until mere crumbs remained. Bribery had become so widespread that it figured in setting government salaries: corruption (communism's spin on capitalist savvy) had been the hallmark of success. But General Mladic had welcomed the Soviet Union's demise for another reason: it was an opportunity for Greater Serbia to reassert herself, unfettered by Russian overlords and eventually cleansed of non-Serbs.

During a break between the conference's tedious speakers, Dravko escaped into the forest that surrounded the mountainside spa and came upon a man urinating. When he finished his business, the man turned back around, and Dravko recognized him as the tall spindly man with unruly hair he'd seen shuffling through the spa's corridors—stoop-shouldered as if carrying the weight of the world's worries. The man smiled, revealing a mouth full of teeth reinforced by gold scaffolding. "Have you noticed how your bladder becomes more insistent with age?"

"Luckily not yet."

"You will. Ha!" He extended his hand.

Obviously the man had not washed his hand, and Dravko grasped it reluctantly. Worse than unwashed, it was limp, and he let it go. "I am Dravko Mladic."

"Yes, yes, I know, head of the State Security Service for what remains of Yugoslavia. Of course I did not anticipate that we should rendezvous in the woods."

"I apologize, but should I know you?"

"Of course not. I am Sergej Ustinov."

"Dr. Ustinov, next on the agenda?"

"It's the first time I have seen my name in print."

"Everyone has heard rumors of your project, but no one has ever seen you."

"I am rarely permitted to leave Kosmonovo, and if you believe the maps, my town does not exist. We are only a forest, and every map that purports to pinpoint Kosmonovo always puts it in the wrong spot. Somewhat like your elusive Serbia, which has disappeared from the map. Ha!"

"*There* you have touched on a sore point."

"Purposefully."

"Purposefully?"

"I intended to meet you. Not while peeing in the woods, of course. Ha!"

"Yes. Ha."

"I should imagine that you are preoccupied with your situation at home. War seems certain."

"Our war has already started, but like your Kosmonovo, it is hidden."

"It's because of my project that I intended to meet you."

"Why is that?" Dravko asked.

"Because I can put Serbia back on the map."

"Yes?"

"Yes. But we must discuss it later. I have a presentation and I don't want to be late. It's my first public appearance in twenty years."

"Are you nervous?"

The physicist shook his head. "No. I feel liberated. Shall we walk back together?"

They set off along the muddy path. Sergey held a branch aside for Dravko to pass. "Are you enjoying the conference?" he asked. "Of course they never import enough women. Ha!"

The conference pavilion loomed over the trees in an uninspired joining of concrete slabs. They entered the lecture hall and the moderator waved in their direction. "The brilliant Dr. Sergej Ustinov." The physicist hurried down the aisle, trying to tame his asteroidal hair.

He gripped the lectern and waited for the assembled men and women (there were many stern Soviet women among them) to quiet down. "I don't exist," he began, "and if you say otherwise, or repeat what I am going to tell you, possibly you will cease to exist, too." He enjoyed their uncertain laughter and used the moment to push his loose teeth into alignment. "What I am going to tell you is true, unlike the truth you read each morning," he continued, referring to the Russian newspaper whose name meant *Truth*, which everyone knew was laced with falsehoods.

"The first effort to build a portable atomic bomb was the Davy Crockett, tested by the Americans in 1958. It weighed thirty-five kilos and looked something like this." Sergej raised his long arms in the shape of a fat egg. "It was not something that could be moved undetected or be hidden in an airport locker. Since then, we have been in a race with the Americans to build a truly portable bomb. Gentlemen, I can report today, we have won the race."

Applause, and then more applause, and soon everyone was on their feet, cheering in a way they hadn't cheered for too long; as they had for the Soviet Man until he became myth. Sergej waited for them to sit back down before he continued. "We have designed a new beryllium reflector, which has enabled us to reduce the critical mass of fuel and thus miniaturize all other components. A conventional nuclear bomb requires twenty-five kilograms of U-235 uranium. My design requires only ten kilos. That brings the total physics package to under twenty kilos. A suitcase bomb, gentlemen, that a fit man can carry without obvious effort. One in each hand if he is muscular. It is the perfect ultimate weapon."

Indeed it *was* the perfect weapon! thought Dravko. Having one in his possession would secure his destiny. The film that often played in his mind's eye started to run. A film in which each scene was a step on the path to his glory: reigning over a free Serbia. Around him, the men in the conference hall repeatedly broke into applause, and

Dravko heard them to be his own cheering crowds. Raised on a platform, surrounded by an honor guard of handsome soldiers, anointed by fate: that was the destiny he previewed each time the film played in his mind.

Dr. Ustinov launched into the bomb's specifications and tactical advantages, keeping the audience spellbound despite the lengthening hour when their thoughts usually turned to vodka and overbooked hookers. "Overnight, any country or terrorist group can become a nuclear power," he boasted. "No more inconvenient ballistics or expensive guidance systems. Just set the timer and boom. Goodbye Washington! Goodbye London! Goodbye Anyplace!"

Dr. Ustinov retreated from the podium to an explosive ovation.

Dravko pressed his way to the front of the lecture hall. "A remarkable achievement," he congratulated the physicist, "and intriguing. If we could continue our earlier conversation, I have questions."

A smile spread across Sergej's face. "Of course you do."

They weren't to be asked at that moment; the physicist was swept off by conference organizers, but not before they arranged a rendezvous for the next day. That night a fierce ice storm pelted the pavilion, rat-a-tatting on the roof and exacerbating Dravko's habitual sleeplessness. He tossed on dreams of greatness and turned on fears of failure, and only toward morning had he managed to fall asleep. When he awoke, the world had turned white. Ice covered everything. Too late for breakfast, he made his way down the pavilion's treacherous steps and entered the forest. The sun shimmered in the trees and cast off rainbows, and the ice-encased leaves—autumnal reds and yellows—sounded like wind chimes in the light breeze.

He found Sergej in the forest where they had met the day before with his head tipped back, looking at the top branches of a tree. "Do you know birds?" he asked as Dravko approached.

Dravko searched out the bird and said, "It's a common wren, I should think."

"Nothing is common that can fly. To be able to escape borders—to fly away—that's my dream. And I shall, because you have big dreams too."

"But not too big if I have the right . . . resources."

"Yes, yes, the right resources. And if I had wings I could fly. Ha!"

"If I had a suitcase bomb, the threat alone has deterrent value. NATO would never risk losing Paris or London."

"Unfortunately there is only one bomb, and it's not for sale. Shall we continue to the source?"

"The source?" asked Dravko, confused.

"Of the spa's hot spring." As Sergej stepped past Dravko to lead the way, he whispered, "They have listening devices in the woods close to the conference hall."

They followed a creek upstream and occasionally crossed it. Vapor clouds trailed off the thermal water. Twice Dravko slipped and soaked his feet. Past a concrete dam where wide-mouthed pipes carried the sulfurous water to the conference center's spa, the path became steeper and the stream ran faster, its gurgling the only sound in the snowy forest. Sergej easily navigated the icy scree on his long legs, and without warning he yelped gleefully as he bounded over a boulder. Dravko heaved himself after him and dropped to the other side.

"The source!" the physicist cried out.

A natural dam had created a pool where the subterranean geyser bubbled up. Sergej yanked off his shoes, and his clothes fell around him until he was naked. Scrawny and pale, he tiptoed into the pool, where he bent his long legs and squatted until his genitals floated like a wad of dead leaves on its surface. Once accustomed to its prickly heat, he sank to his shoulders. "Undress quickly," he instructed Dravko, "and you won't notice the cold."

Hesitantly Dravko removed his shoes. At headquarters, nakedness was feared, a state of vulnerability. He slung his coat over a branch, plucked at the buttons on his shirt—stretched tight from an unremitting diet of sausage—and clumsily removed his pants. Dravko fretted over his own masculinity: the men in prison, shrunken by fear, were unreliable barometers for how he measured up. Loosely shielding himself with his hands, he slipped sideways into the thermal water.

The physicist laughed. "I would have thought you a proud man, Dravko. I suppose everything cannot be learned from the files." He sank still lower, until the water lapped against his chin. "Ahhh . . . this is beautiful . . . beautiful . . . and we can be sure that there are no listening devices, and if there are, the sound of the water will mask our voices."

"You are so afraid?"

"It is *they* who are afraid." Sergej tapped his temple. "Afraid of losing this. My brain is a national treasure. Ha!"

"Of course I know your reputation."

"The price of my reputation, can you imagine what it has been? It is not just my bombs, no, Dravko, it is my genius. Like an animal I have been caged and mated. The eugenicists, Dravko, *they* are mad scientists, it's their secrets they don't want told. There are so many things you can't know. How they picked Natalya to be my wife because she, too, was brilliant. How we tried to love each other, and had children, a boy who is autistic and a girl born dead. For the state it was a bad experiment and they sterilized Natalya, not wanting to waste my seed. That's right, Dravko, I have been harvested like wheat. A quota to meet each week in a dingy lab. I've made love to the same women in the same magazines so many times they feel as worn-out as my wife. Can you imagine what it has meant?"

"But . . . but why?" sputtered Dravko.

"But why?" Sergej repeated solemnly. "Because they had substituted the common man for God, and the common man—the Soviet Man—wasn't good enough. Isn't that the irony? So they have used my body for their experiments. I will never know how many children I have fathered. I know I have met some. I can spot a special resemblance. Of course, *your* perfect man already exists; he need only be a Serb. It is your country that does not exist, not as you dream it to be. Greater Serbia restored to its ancient borders! You see, Dravko, I know your dreams, I have studied you. You would do anything to give birth to your Serbia. Am I right? Am I right?"

"You are," Dravko admitted.

"Ha! Of course I am! For men like you, what is it to steal from a man what can only be his? There are many forms of torture. My body, protected by the state, has been stolen from me. You break bodies, burn or discard them, but the principle is the same: the individual can be sacrificed. I wonder, Dravko, would you believe the same if you could have children?"

"We've tried, but Ulia . . . well, she can't conceive."

Sergej slapped the water. "Ha! I told you, I know everything about you. I know about your tests. I even know your sperm count! You can father no one, and while I have fathered many, we are both childless. Let us hope that your daughter, Serbia, should she be born, at least has the ability to speak."

"Dravko!" Ulia, standing in the doorway to his study, interrupted his thoughts. "I have been calling you for ten minutes." She rubbed her red nose with the back of her hand. Her coarse shawl reeked of sausage.

"I've been working, Dumpling," he replied.

"While standing at the window? Sometimes I worry about you, always daydreaming." Ulia pulled the shawl tighter around her broad shoulders. "It's freezing in here. With heating oil so expensive, what are you trying to do, ruin us? Shut that window and come for dinner."

"In a minute."

He heard her heavy steps on the stairs.

"Don't you ever dream?" he shouted after her.

"Isn't it enough that we are alive?" she called back. "And not for long if we catch pneumonia!"

"Is it enough that we are alive?" he recalled Sergej asking in the thermal pool. "Not for us, Dravko. It's not death that we fear but being erased by history if we leave nothing behind. For most men having children is enough, but not for you, Dravko, not for men of destiny."

"And for you? Is it enough to have been harvested? To know you have children even if you don't know them?"

"Of course not. I wanted to have children like most men. For years I dreamed of making love to a woman who carried away my seed gratefully, not a frowning clinician who measures my production in a test tube. And I dream to be free. To be free to take a walk, or board an airplane, and yes, to find my own women. Free to do what most men take for granted. Our dreams distinguish us, General Mladic. Mine are modest while yours are grand. Let's talk about making them come true."

So they had. The physicist proposed a plan as elaborate as his design for the suitcase bomb itself. In its construction, every part was essential to the whole and no detail had been overlooked. He explained how the first three couriers would each deliver enough uranium fuel for one bomb. Dr. Ustinov himself would follow with the portable detonator, also filled with uranium. "The detonator can be reproduced as easily as making a photocopy. You shall have an arsenal. An arsenal! Ha!"

"How will you get out of Russia?"

"The border between Russia and Poland is forest for nearly eight hundred kilometers. Every day, hundreds of smugglers cross for a small bribe, their only hardship a pair of muddy boots."

"You will go to Poland? That's nowhere near Belgrade."

Sergej stretched out in the pool, fluttering his hands to stay afloat, steam rising from his body. "It is true what I hear, you Serbs lack imagination. You are preparing for war, yes? And buying lots of Polish weapons."

"How do you know that?"

"I am frequently consulted on weapons. I overhear things. So sometimes when you go to Warsaw, you will return with an extra package in your diplomatic pouch."

Dravko crouched to the side to avoid the physicist's gnarly toes bobbing up to him. "If it is so easy, why haven't you already left?"

"I am finished with communists, even old Polish communists who now call themselves capitalists. They change their hats but have the same heads. You and I will make a trade. I give you Serbia for America. But not for beads! Ha! You must make me an American passport, and of course, I need dollars. Lots of dollars. One million American dollars."

They had remained in the thermal pool, rehashing the physicist's plan until their fingers were waterlogged and every detail committed to memory. Sergej had even second-guessed Dravko's misgivings as if fashioning failsafe mechanisms for his suitcase bomb. "*Drrravko,* who will be able to stop you? No one will even challenge you. Then, all who are not Serbs, they will be yours to do with as you want."

Dravko felt himself stir as only interrogations could stir him, and he became aroused, remembering bodies in his tortuous hands. So distracted was he by his recollections that when Sergej abruptly stood, saying, "It's time we go, the days are growing short," Dravko jumped up as well, momentarily forgetting the swagging heaviness below his paunch.

Seeing him, the physicist had exclaimed, "Look at you! Are you not the father of Serbia?"

"Dravko!" Ulia cried from the kitchen. "Your sausage will be cold!"

"I'm coming!"

Dravko went to the closet where he had concealed the three canisters delivered by the couriers. The seal on the third had been broken and he opened it, rolling a uranium pellet in his palm, marveling that something so inert could be the genesis of a dream so grand.

"Dravko! I'm not waiting for you!"

"I'm coming now, Dumpling!"

He replaced the pellet and hurried downstairs, suddenly hungry.

CHAPTER THREE

A DOORMAN DRESSED IN BLUE livery held the door open to a bitter wind that stung Jay's cheeks. He gripped his briefcase, heavy with Detective Kulski's files, and ventured onto the slippery sidewalk.

Shopkeepers struggled to lift shutters that had frozen tight during the night. Streetcars, squealing to stops, disgorged riders frowning at the new day. On the corner, an old man, his bristly moustache yellowed by tobacco, turned roasting chestnuts with his callused fingers. Jay bought some and ate them while wandering through the open market that filled the enormous parking lot surrounding the Palace of Culture.

The long-feared Russian invasion of Poland had occurred, not by soldiers but by an army of vendors who sold Soviet military paraphernalia: caps with hammer-and-sickle insignias, battalion watches and medals, and whiskey flasks emblazoned with Lenin's silhouette. They stood behind flimsy tables bundled against the cold as people as poor as themselves bargained for goods they would resell in more upscale neighborhoods—if they were lucky, to Westerners who had made Soviet-wear chic.

Situated on otherwise elegant Aleje Ujazdowskie, the American embassy looked like an ice cube tray on steroids. The guard noticed a bulge in Jay's coat pocket and was satisfied to let him pass for a couple of still-warm chestnuts; the receptionist, also happy with her bribe, buzzed him in.

His caffeine addiction steered him straight to the coffee machine. As he sipped, he looked over a bulletin board with advertisements for baby cribs, retirement seminars, and depression therapy. A young woman rounded the corner and bumped into him, sloshing coffee on his fingers.

"I'm so sorry!" she cried, her hands fluttering to her mouth like birds.

"That's okay." He set down his cup to reach for a paper towel. "The coffee's not very hot anyway." It was true. Just like the day before, the coffee was tepid, weak, and almost not worth drinking.

"Here, let me." Grabbing for the towel, she sent his cup into the sink. She gasped and her hands flew to her straw-colored hair, which was escaping its bun. Her mouth revealed, improbably, a full set of metal braces.

Jay declined when she offered him a new cup, so she took it for herself. She added three sugar packets, followed by a dose of powdered non-dairy creamer. She raised her shoulders in a reflexive apology. "I'm lactose intolerant."

Jay extended his hand. "I'm Jay Porter."

She laughed. "Libby Barnstable," she said, wiping her palm on her dress before taking his hand. "You must be the FBI guy. And, if you're wondering, I am his daughter."

"I know. I was briefed before I left Washington."

"About me?" She looked worried.

"About the embassy. It's standard procedure."

"Oh." Libby reached into one of her many pockets to pull out a wrinkled tissue and sneezed into it. "Allergies," she said, again lifting her shoulders as if hoping she could drop right into her oversized dress and disappear.

At twenty-four, Libby Barnstable was thought to be the youngest Consul General in the State Department's history, a distinction she had achieved through loving nepotism. She came from high Pentagon brass and happened to be in Warsaw when her predecessor was fired; in fact, her father had probably wielded the hatchet from afar to square the job for her. The standing joke was that she had all the qualifications she needed except experience, temperament, constitution, and initiative.

Jay gave her an ingratiating smile. "You wouldn't happen to know where my office is, would you?"

"I saw them moving some boxes to make room for you. Follow

me." Libby led him through intersecting hallways filled with humming copiers and warbling faxes. "Are you enjoying Warsaw?"

"What's not to enjoy? Snow, grit, and ice—it has them all."

"It's tough to get used to, I know. It's not for everybody."

"I didn't say I didn't like it," he finally replied. "I said it had—"

"Snow, grit, and ice." Libby smiled, displaying her braces fully for the first time. Jay wondered where, in a country with an orthodontically disadvantaged population, Libby had found an orthodontist, or if her father flew her home periodically. She swung open a door. "Voilà. Your new office."

Jay stepped into what was little more than a long cubbyhole. Shiny squares on the otherwise dusty floor indicated where boxes had been removed to make a path to the desk. "It's cozy," he remarked and crossed to the grimy window. It nearly filled the wall. Outside, large flakes of snow drifted down.

He turned back, saw the phone on the desk, picked up the receiver.

"Dial eight for an outside line," Libby told him.

He did; it worked, and he hung up.

"The men's room is at the end of the hall to the left. My office is there, too."

"Then I imagine I'll be seeing you." Jay fished out the bag of chestnuts from his coat pocket and handed over what remained of them. "I owe you. Thanks."

As soon as she left, he spread Kulski's files on the desk. The detective had been thorough, translating into decent English the pathologist's estimates for the victims' ages, heights, and times of death. A detailed inventory of clothing had been included. All tags had been removed, as had the victims' wedding bands, evidenced by a paler circle of flesh. Someone didn't want these men traced. Kulski had added a note to the third victim's file:

18 February 1992 – During autopsy by Dr. Z. Nagorski, Geiger Machine makes determination of radiation present.

His telephone rang.

It was Kulski. He wanted to meet.

Ten minutes later Jay was in an embassy car rumbling across the Poniatowski Bridge with its metal pillars flashing past. Craning to look over the rail, he saw the river's black tail disappear in the distance. "This is the Praga side," his driver, the same man who taken him to the airport, informed him as they pulled off the bridge. "You want to be careful on this side."

"Why is that?"

"Praga has many elements."

"Elements?"

"You want a gun? A girl? Pills to make you crazy? Whatever you want, you can find here," the driver elaborated.

"Oh, *those* elements," Jay said, getting out of the car in front of a building familiar for its Soviet-era indistinctiveness. He told the driver not to wait and went inside.

A receptionist directed him up a flight of stairs to Kulski's office. There, too, the hallways were lined with padded doors, outside of which the town's scoundrels and petitioners sat docilely on benches waiting to be summoned. Violence didn't spill into these premises like it did in America's police stations.

The detective's secretary stood to greet him. Nothing about her bleached hair or snug leotard suggested she worked in a police station. "You are the FBI?" she asked, clearly impressed.

"I am, or at least a part of it."

"I will tell Detective Kulski that you are here." She put her hand up to knock when his door swung open.

"Good morning, Agent Porter." He reached for Jay's hand. "Thanks for coming on short notice."

"Not a problem. I'm glad you have some time."

"Time," Kulski sighed, "there is never enough of it. Will you try another Polish coffee?"

"I'll give it another chance."

"Eva, *dwie kawy proszę*," the detective said, and with a clap on Jay's back steered him into his office.

A bulletin board filled one wall. On it, the detective had pinned a large map with the Vistula River running diagonally through its center.

On the Praga side, he'd drawn three red dots, with lines attaching them to photos of the victims as well as artist sketches without their mutilated cheeks. Dates and times of death had been noted with a marker pen. It was gruesome art that Jay knew too well. Crime boards came with the job.

Kulski limped around his desk and dropped into the chair. Behind him on a credenza were pictures of his family: his wife, a stout woman with a ruddy, pleasant face; two young daughters, chubby-cheeked and blonde; and the whole family in hiking clothes with a mountain peak looming in the background. Next to a collection of sports trophies, Kulski had framed a snapshot of his younger self in a soccer jersey.

"Looks like a nice family," Jay commented.

"Thank you."

"And sporty."

The detective smiled. "Yes, we enjoy hiking."

"You can manage with your leg?"

"Hiking I can do but not soccer. Elzbieta, she's my older girl, has a better—" Kulski interrupted himself to ask, "Is it correct, 'foot-work'?"

"Exactly right."

"She has a better footwork than me. She is only ten, and already wants to go to the Olympics!"

"You sound like a proud father."

"I am. You have two sons, is that right?"

"Did I mention them?"

"I was informed."

Jay felt at a disadvantage. He knew nothing about Detective Kulski other than his name and the fact that he was heading the investigation into the murdered couriers. When the communists were finally routed, it happened too swiftly, and too broadly, for the West to have intelligence on someone so far down the new hierarchy as a chief detective in a police precinct. But apparently the Polish intelligence apparatus was still as efficient as its reputation and had learned something about the FBI expert coming to help them. Did Kulski know about the other murder cases Jay had investigated? His couple of years in Army intelligence? Or that his two sons were being held captive by his now ex-wife following an ugly divorce? Those were the kinds of things he'd like to have known about the detective.

Eva tapped on the door and entered, set a tray with their coffees onto Kulski's desk, and slipped back out.

"The trick to our coffee is always use sugar, and never stir it," he advised Jay. By example, he dropped two cubes into his cup and looked at it expectantly. "You wait until you think the sugar is dissolved."

"I don't usually take sugar."

"Then you will never like our national coffee."

Jay compromised and took one cube. The detective opened his bottom desk drawer to prop his foot on it.

"What happened to your leg?" Jay asked.

"I was arrested three times. The last time, three goons with steel-toed boots took their turns breaking it. It was a week before a doctor came. It couldn't be set properly."

"Jesus."

"He wasn't there, though I prayed to Him—to anybody—until I was too feverish to pray."

"Why'd they break your leg?"

"They said because they were tired of arresting me. They wanted me to stop doing what I was doing."

"What were you doing?"

"Handing out flyers for demonstrations."

"They broke your leg for that?"

"When it happened, I confess, I was not so philosophical. Now I can say, it was a small price for freedom." The detective tested his coffee. "You can drink it now."

Jay took a sip, grimaced, and suggested, "You're busy, so let's get started."

They ran through what was already known: three couriers, faces slashed, a single bullet to the heart. Cleaned up, dressed again, and left on the riverbank. Were they actually displayed? The bodies hadn't been dumped, so both men agreed there was some element of display. "Do you agree with Pani Husarska that they're Russians?" Jay asked.

"I am not one hundred percent sure, but I think yes."

"If not Russians, where would you guess?"

"I will only guess not Polish. Our national police receive information about missing people from every district. We have no match with the victims."

"What if they are not reported missing?"

"We are small for a big country. Someone will always recognize someone from a picture in the newspaper."

He was probably right, Jay thought. Two or three major newspapers covered the country. Kulski had provided him with copies of his missing-persons ads, relying on artist sketches of the victims, not identifying them as murder victims but simply unaccounted for. The sketches were remarkably good, but of course, only one side of the victims' faces had been ruined.

"Okay, the odds are that they're Russian," Jay conceded. "They are all missing a wedding ring. Why haven't their wives reported them missing?"

"Maybe the wives have boyfriends and haven't noticed."

"Wouldn't your wife notice if you disappeared?"

Kulski smiled. "I hope she doesn't have a boyfriend! But there is something else. All their hands were soft."

"Soft?"

"They were not workers."

"You mean laborers."

"I suppose they worked in an office," the detective elaborated.

"Tell me about the murder weapon."

"The TT?"

A 7.62 mm pistol designed by Fedor Tokarev in the 1930s for the Russian army and able to rip through a bulletproof vest if discharged at close range. Standard issue for nearly forty years to soldiers and reservists. Freely available in the flourishing post-Soviet black market. All that according to the FBI's briefing files, to which Kulski added: "It is a favorite gun of the mafia because it is so powerful. We think all the wounds are made by a TT, but without the bullets, we cannot be sure."

"And they all passed through their bodies?"

"That's right."

"Tell me about BPZ," Jay said. "Why is Husarska involved in the case?"

"Because the mafia could be involved."

"*Could* be involved. Is there any proof that it is?"

"Only the suspicion."

"And that's enough for BPZ to get involved?"

"We don't expect much help from the national authorities."

"You mean it's political?"

"If it is a big case, it is a big victory."

"And if it's not, who cares?"

"Exactly," Kulski agreed.

Jay glanced back at the three red dots on the detective's case board on the wall. "I'd like to see where the bodies were found." They both glanced out the window at the darkening sky.

"Today is not a good day. It will snow soon," Kulski decided. They arranged to meet in the morning.

Jay stood to leave. "There's not much to go on, is there?"

"We only wait for the fourth courier. Maybe we will be lucky and have a witness."

"We might be lucky, but not the fourth courier," Jay said and left the detective's office.

Back on the street, Jay aimed for the river. He had a good sense of direction and felt confident that he would end up close to the waterway's bend where the couriers' bodies had been found—*if* they were couriers, he had to remind himself. He passed through working-class neighborhoods that had a sense of depleted familiarity. Unlike its sister city Warsaw across the river, which had been rebuilt after World War II to recreate its center in precise architectural detail (except for upgraded plumbing), Praga had risen from the war in long relentless blocks of monochromatic concrete. Even the sky was pavement gray.

As Detective Kulski had predicted, it started to snow heavily, and Jay gladly let a taxi rescue him. Soon they were dodging traffic in Praga's bustling commercial center. A church's onion dome loomed over the bent women and broken men who plied those streets. Here a man sold oranges displayed on his car hood; there a woman used a stick to rummage in a refuse bin; and everywhere the poor scuffed their shoes in the gritty snow, bargaining for toss-offs.

Back at the embassy, Jay grabbed a cup of coffee, which he dumped in the men's room before reaching his temporary office. He checked his watch. It was too early to call his assistant, Ann Rewls, back home. He couldn't fault Detective Kulski for not making much progress in the case; there wasn't much to go on, and he hoped Ann had found something in the DOE's inventory reports. Killing time, he flipped through the case files, hoping something might jump out that he hadn't noticed before.

He checked his watch again. Still another hour to go. He was debating whether to go in search of an alternative coffee machine when his telephone rang. He picked up the receiver. By habit, he answered, "Porter here."

Ann said, "Hello, Jay."

"How did you know I was waiting to call you?"

"I'm surprised you didn't. Impatience is your best virtue."

"I'm not sure that's a compliment."

"It's not."

"Did you find anything in the DOE reports?"

"Nothing that merits an alert."

"You mean something else."

"What I mean, Jay, is that if you have enough pennies, you have a million dollars."

"How many pennies do we have?"

"Does ten kilograms add up to a million dollars?"

"Close to it."

"And that's only in fourteen months," she reminded him.

"You're going to tell me about the research reactors, aren't you?"

"You're a mind reader."

"I was raised on this stuff. I'm surprised I don't glow in the dark."

"Maybe you do." She sighed. "Noise Machine is snoring in the bedroom and a baby is kicking my bladder. I hope you're having more fun than I am."

"Are you that pregnant?"

"There aren't degrees of being pregnant, Jay. Only stages."

That's what his wife—*ex*-wife, Jay sometimes had to remind himself—had said about both of her pregnancies. She had to get through the stages to get to the baby. He flashed on his sons, newly born, before he said, "Tell me what you learned about the research reactors."

"There are hundreds of them all over the Soviet Union—*former* Soviet Union—and periodically they need to reprocess their fuel, which can be done at only three reactors inside Russia. For two of them, I have reports for two years, and I've gone through them comparing how much uranium was sent in by each research reactor and how much was returned."

"If the measurement is precise enough, there will always be some natural attrition," Jay told her. "Fuel-in never equals fuel-out."

"Would measurements to four decimal points in milligrams be precise enough for you?"

"Probably."

"Good, because I stayed up all night adding them up. Nobody thought to total the columns."

"The Russians don't like to make their cheating conspicuous."

"Well, their strategy worked. When you glance at the numbers for individual reactors, nothing seems to be missing. In fact, for two of the reprocessing reactors, I don't think anything is missing. In percentage terms, their numbers are comparable, and in most instances what's not returned is in milligrams. Then there's the third reactor."

"Which one?"

"Kosmonovo."

Jay let out a soft whistle. "Kosmonovo? The DOE has inventory reports from there? I'm impressed. Until three years ago, the Russians didn't even acknowledge it existed."

"Apparently it does, and every month for fourteen months, it's come up short on the reprocessing roster. Fifty grams here, a hundred there, but spread out over hundreds of batches of uranium, no one noticed."

"And who's to say it only started fourteen months ago? Someone could have been stockpiling material a lot longer."

"Enough pennies for a million dollars?" Ann asked.

"More than a million dollars. That's good work."

"Good, because I'm going back to bed."

"Thanks for spending the night working on this."

"I didn't exactly volunteer."

"Thanks anyway."

Jay called Detective Kulski. "It's Agent Porter. I think that I can confirm that you're right about where the couriers are coming from, and that they are couriers."

"Tell me the details in the morning," Kulski suggested. "I can't be sure that I have a secure line."

Now that Jay had a likely place of origin to associate with the couriers, he was curious to see their pictures again. He retrieved the files from his briefcase and laid out the grisly portraits. All had blunt foreheads, thin noses, and mops of sandy hair. They could have been brothers. Or maybe Director Husarska was right: all Russians looked alike.

Kurt Crawford knocked on the half-open door and walked in. He grimaced when he saw Jay's photos of the victims' lacerated cheeks. "Facial cuts hurt," he said, touching his own scarred checks. "Beirut 1983."

"The barracks?"

"Twenty-fourth Amphibious Unit out of Camp Lejeune. I was shaving when the mirror exploded. Fortunately most of the mirror hit my chest, not my face. A few stitches and nothing hit my eyes. I was on my feet the next day looking for my buddies' body parts. It added new meaning to 'all accounted for.' You ever been in the service?"

"My dad was one of the original conscientious objectors."

"Somehow that doesn't explain the FBI."

"I wasn't allowed to play with guns as a kid. Now I can."

"Except in Poland," Kurt complained. "It pisses me off that we're not allowed to carry a weapon. I don't like the disadvantage."

"You're an unlikely agent for Poland," Jay said, "with or without a gun."

"I spent two years as an embassy guard in Moscow. When Langley was looking for a Russian-speaking spook, I fit the bill."

"They speak Polish here."

"After English, Russian is the *lingua franca* for the bad guys in the weapons world."

"You're that good at languages?"

"I can say ten thousand megatons and ten million dollars, and that was good enough to get me the assignment. Are you any closer to sorting out who these guys are?"

Jay briefed him on what his assistant had uncovered in the DOE reports. When he mentioned Kosmonovo, Kurt said, "That's a serious place."

"You know about Kosmonovo?"

"Top secret weapons research. The Russians only confirmed it existed a couple of years ago when they were taking glasnost seriously. I'll check with Langley if there's any buzz about the place."

"Thanks."

"I came here to bring you this." Kurt gave Jay a handset.

"A walkie-talkie?"

"Do you know how to use one?"

"Roger that. My brother and I had a set when we were kids. We warned each other when danger was approaching—like parents or teachers—when we weren't just using them to goof around."

"This isn't for goofing around. It's our emergency security system. Home base—that's the embassy—is Graceland. You press this button and you're automatically connected to the duty officer. Press here to broadcast. Otherwise you're receiving. Your code name is Cher."

"*Cher?*"

"All the subscribers are rock stars."

"But Cher? Is that a Langley joke?"

"Don't worry, your secret is good with me, but if someone ever says anything, just say that 'Sonny' was taken."

"Roger that."

Kurt handed him a form. "You need to fill this out, too."

"What is it?"

"Basic information in case you get lost, wounded, or go missing in action. You're divorced, right?"

"Didn't Langley brief you?"

"You might need this, too." Kurt handed him another form. "These are the rules for fraternizing with the locals. Unlike in the past, fortunately we don't have to report everyone we talk to, but you do have to file a report if you sleep with someone. Women, or men if that's your thing."

"That's a little personal, isn't it?"

"Ambassador Lerner insists on it. He sent a guy home last year missing a vital body part. His dick."

"Shit. I wasn't briefed on that."

"DC is good at withholding the juicy stuff."

Kurt started to leave. He turned at the door to say, "Between you, me, and the US government, I only report men. Is that a problem working together?"

"Sounds like we've got all the bases covered."

When Kurt left, Jay unfolded the napkin with Lilka's blurry telephone number. Hoping he'd be lucky enough to have to report her, he dialed it.

"Hello?" she answered.

CHAPTER FOUR

J AY WANDERED BETWEEN THE GROUPS of spectators, peering over shoulders and around hats to see a juggler, or Peruvian flutists playing music too tropical for the nippy air, or a man with a lopsided grin lurching around with a divining stick—all braving the cold for coins dropped in a can or on the corner of a shawl. Snowflakes hung suspended in the air, defying gravity. He kept an eye out for Lilka. She was late and Jay worried that he was being stood up. Finally he recognized her silhouetted by lights on the pink Krolewski Castle, and hurried across the square to meet her.

"Lilka."

She turned to him.

"Ja-ay."

Once again, she made his name sound new.

She offered her cheek for him to kiss, but Jay surprised her by taking her hand and brushing his lips to the back of it. It was something else his Polish tutor had taught him.

Lilka laughed. "How do you know that Polish men do that?"

"I had a good teacher."

"Maybe you are a little Polish, too?"

"I'm probably more Neanderthal than Polish." She laughed again.

"Where are we going for dinner?" he asked.

"*Restauracja Kurczak.*"

"*Kurczak*? Chicken Restaurant?"

"You don't like chicken?"

"No, I like chicken. I like almost everything. Which way?"

"We go by that street." Lilka pointed across the square. Wearing short heels, she had trouble navigating the slippery cobblestones, and he offered his arm. She gladly took it, and as they walked, she pointed out different buildings, all pastel-colored and awash with the warm light of lanterns swinging from hooked posts. The street artists had set out lanterns, too, that illuminated the faces of spectators pinched red by the cold. They paused to watch a mime, shiny with grease paint, act out a sad story before he hooked his fingers in his frowning mouth and pulled it into a smile. Jay dropped coins in his beret before he scurried away, crablike.

Lilka shivered.

"Are you cold?" he asked.

"Only a little."

"Let's go eat."

He steered them toward a carriage, its draft horse snorting as they approached.

"We can walk," Lilka protested. "It is not so far."

"It's too cold. *Restauracja Kurcza*," he told the driver and helped her into the buggy.

The driver clucked, and with a jolt, the horse started across the uneven stones, throwing them together on the seat. They laughed and braced themselves upright, though Jay didn't try very hard; he was happy for an excuse to fall against Lilka. Through the side flaps they glimpsed the passing shops; their weak lights displayed dusty collections of icons, chunky jewelry, overblown crystal: the old wares. The driver soon tugged at the reins. The horse stopped and they climbed out.

The restaurant's heavy door groaned on iron hinges, and just inside, a squat woman with twists of gray hair on her chin took their coats.

A waiter appeared and Lilka told him, "We have reservations."

"Of course, Pani," he said, and led them into a dining room filled with tables draped with white cloths; candles behind glass cones flickered on the silver settings. Except for them, the restaurant was empty. "You may sit where you want."

"What table do you want?" she asked Jay.

"You pick."

"Here, I think, not so close to the door."

The waiter pulled out the seat for her and handed them menus.

Jay glanced at it and was surprised by its extensive selection. It was a struggle, but he could make out basic category headings such as meat or vegetables. He zeroed in on something called *nadziewana kapusta* and asked what it was. "Not that I want to eat something that sounds like *kapoot*," he added.

"Stuffed cabbage," Lilka answered.

The waiter piped up and said, "*Nie ma.*"

"*Nie ma?*"

"There is none."

"Oh. Okay. Next question. What is *cielence kotlety?*"

Lilka asked, "What is your name for baby cow?"

"Veal. No, I don't eat veal. I believe in meat but I don't believe in torture."

Not understanding what he said, the waiter volunteered, "*Nie ma.*"

Jay closed his menu. "So what do you have?"

"*Tylko kurczaka.*"

"They only have chicken," Lilka translated.

"Then why did he give us menus?"

"It is his job to give us menus."

Jay smiled and handed his back. "*Kurcza,*" he ordered.

"And you, Pani?"

"Also I will have the chicken."

"And *wino biały,*" Jay thought to add.

"*Nie ma wino.*"

"There's no wine?" Jay was ready to leave.

"We have only *szampan.*"

He asked Lilka, "Is champagne okay with you?"

"I like champagne."

"Sure, we'll have champagne."

The waiter walked off.

They sat, two complete strangers in an empty restaurant without the diversion of watching other people. Jay finally asked, "Are you a flight attendant, too? Besides working in the lounge, I mean."

"You mean in an *airplane?*"

Jay nodded encouragingly.

"I am too afraid to fly."

"You work at an airport and you're afraid to fly?"

"Like LOT, I never leave the ground."

It took Jay a moment to get her joke made at the expense of the national airlines. He chuckled. Of course she had told it before. He realized she must have a patter for the men waiting for flights in the Executive Lounge: set lines, jokes, and witticisms for almost any occasion, all used to keep the men at arm's length without discouraging tips. He'd been in enough business class lounges to know the scene. "Is that who you work for? LOT?" he asked.

"No. I work for the airport. Are you a businessman?"

"I'm sort of a policeman."

"A policeman?"

"You sound surprised."

"Your nose is not broken."

Jay laughed. "It could happen, but I'm a different kind of policeman."

"What kind of policeman? FBI?"

Her question startled him. "You know about the FBI?"

"It is always on the television."

"Would you like that, if I worked for the FBI?"

"It must be very exciting."

"I didn't say that I did. I said *if* I worked for the FBI."

"It's okay. I believe you."

Jay laughed again. He didn't know what she believed or understood and didn't care. He was glad to be with her.

The waiter interrupted them by setting an ice bucket on the table. He lifted the bottle to show the label to Jay. It was in Russian. "Is Russian champagne okay?" he asked Lilka.

"Of course," she said. "There is no Polish champagne."

He flashed the waiter a smile. "It's fine."

The man popped the cork and poured the champagne. Before walking off, he folded back a napkin on a small plate to reveal a small blue tin. "You want Russian caviar? Black?"

Lilka caught Jay's eye and shook her head. "Maybe it is black from shoe polish."

"Thanks, but I'll pass," Jay told the waiter in English.

He left and they clinked glasses.

"*Na zdrovia.*"

"Not bad," Jay remarked. "Maybe a little sweet."

"You are an expert?"

"All I know is that it's supposed to be bubbly." He pulled the bottle out of the bucket to look again at the label. "Do you read Russian?" he asked.

"Of course. Everybody reads Russian."

"Someone else told me, everybody speaks English."

"Not everybody, but soon many more will speak English. We are capitalists now."

"She said that, too."

"We say it about many things."

"Like what?"

"We said it at first about the bread lines. Now we say it about the price of bread."

"I take it there are shorter lines now."

"Now there are no more lines."

"Higher prices can cause that."

"It's been only two years, and there have been so many changes, good and bad changes."

"Like what?"

Lilka smiled when she answered. "There was no executive class."

"So now there is and you have a job. That's a good change, isn't it?"

"Yes, of course it's good, but I worry for my son. He is not ready for capitalism. I see it every day in the lounge. The telephones, the computers, everybody has nice clothes."

"How old is he?"

"Eighteen."

"He still has time to get ready for capitalism. So you were married?"

The shake of her head was tentative.

"Sort of yes, sort of no?" Jay ventured.

"If I understand you, yes."

"Me too. Sort of yes, sort of no. Once upon a time, I had a wife who had a bad temper, and one day I came home and she had kidnapped our sons."

"You had sons?"

"That's right—*had*—before she took them and convinced a judge it was too dangerous for them to spend time at my house. She has full custody until a final hearing next month."

"I'm sorry I don't understand everything," she said.

"I don't either," Jay sadly acknowledged.

They talked easily through dinner, pausing only to find words in a language they barely shared. He explained how a stalker—a defendant in one of his cases—had threatened his family, and it had so panicked his wife that she eventually moved out and took the boys with her. His visitation rights were almost none, and gave no allowance for makeup visits if he was away on a case. Lilka described being forced to live with an abusive ex-husband whom she feared, displaying a bruise on her wrist as a sailor might a tattoo that bespoke a sentiment no longer felt.

As the hour became a wee hour, the waiter hovered more insistently, especially after they drained a second bottle of champagne and weren't likely to buy a third. When Jay finally asked for the check, he brought it on the same small plate with the tin of caviar. "Only five American dollars," he said.

Jay examined the tin. "You're right, it says ingredients: caviar and shoe polish. I've always loved shoe polish." He handed the man five dollars and they left.

Outside, the streets had been all but abandoned. They passed through puddles of orange light cast by the overhead lanterns, unaware of the cold, only aware of each other. At her car, they kissed. Jay wanted it to go on longer, but she pulled keys from her purse. "I drive you to the hotel."

"If you do, will you come in?"

He sensed that she wouldn't, and he was right. "Not tonight," she said, leaving it open for another night. "I drive you to your hotel."

"I'll walk."

"*Nie*," she protested. "It is too far."

"It gives me time to think about you."

Lilka kissed him again.

He murmured between her lips, "Would a nightcap tempt you to come inside?"

"Yes."

"Do you want to be tempted?"

"Not tonight."

Jay pulled away. "Then I won't tempt you."

He wanted it to be another night because she did, and she was right. When they finally made love, it would be better the better they knew each other. Their evening had felt that promising. "I'll telephone you tomorrow," he said.

"Promise?"

"I promise."

Lilka got in her car and pulled away and braked to turn a corner. One of her taillights was out. He would tell her that tomorrow, he thought, pulling his cap tighter. He rewound his scarf. It was a dark night and he was alone on the street, but for the first time in a long time, he didn't feel alone.

CHAPTER FIVE

J AY WAITED IN THE LOBBY of the police station for Detective Kulski. A minute later, he came down the stairs. They shook hands and went out into the brisk morning. Thin clouds foiled the sun's efforts to break through and Jay turned up his collar against the clipping wind. Both men were dressed in sneakers and casual clothes.

Kulski led them to a beat-up miniature Fiat that looked like a stray amid a dozen or so police cruisers. Jay folded himself into the passenger seat. His knees pressed the dashboard and he looked for a way to push the seat back, but Kulski told him there wasn't one. "You have probably never conducted an investigation in such a miserable car," he added.

"It depends on the case."

"Nothing should depend on this car. The communists designed it for people not permitted to travel." Kulski pulled out the choke and turned the key. The engine coughed and died. After a couple more tries, he pounded the dashboard with his fist. "And like a communist, you must hit it to make it work!" The pounding worked and the engine sputtered to life. Careful not to flood it, he gently revved the motor to warm it up. "I don't usually use my own car, but I prefer it when I visit a crime scene. I don't want to announce that I am a policeman."

They drove down streets with dirty melting snow in the gutters. Concrete high-rises, claustrophobic in their massive sameness, pressed close to the pavement, leaving little space for gardens or trees. All were made of prefab concrete panels that had already fissured, even in the new buildings. The factories wedged between them belched black smoke from chimneys more reminiscent of the Industrial Revolution than the approaching end of the high-tech twentieth century.

Jay reported on what he'd learned from Ann Rewls about the missing uranium without mentioning the secret town's name.

"Is ten kilos enough for a bomb?" Kulski wanted to know.

"Any amount can be destructive. It's more critical how you deliver it. It's one thing to scatter it on sidewalks to contaminate an area, and another thing to actually explode it. And who knows how much might actually be stockpiled? Or how many couriers were missed? Or taking different routes? There are many things we don't know, except that a significant amount of uranium is missing."

They agreed it was ominous, and that Kulski would inform Pani Husarska about it. Jay wanted to know why the detective worried he might not have a secure line. "Because here in Poland people changed faster than technology," Kulski explained. "If the communists were listening to you, maybe the devices are still there, only someone different is listening. Nobody knows."

Kulski pulled up to a corner where a life-size crucifix stood upright in a patch of faded plastic flowers. It made for rather grim yard art. The detective pointed to the building behind it. "I live there," he said.

"There?"

"You sound surprised."

"Only because I don't really know how anybody lives in Poland."

"I think how we live, because we must live this way, would surprise most Americans. We only have two rooms."

"Most Americans would find two rooms with two kids a tight squeeze."

"Until last year, Magda's parents also lived with us."

"A very tight squeeze."

"We waited seven years for our two rooms, so we are glad to have them."

The detective turned off the main road. Eventually the apartment blocks gave way to more fashionable buildings that had survived the Soviet era's obsession with conformity. He pulled up catty-corner to a four-story pinkish building which, while peeling, at least had been painted sometime in the last half century. Bushes flanked its entrance; overhead, narrow balconies wrapped around its corners. "That is where Pani Husarska lives," Kulski told him.

"It's nice," Jay said. "So who chooses where you live?"

"Before the transition, this building was only for *nomenklatura*."

"So the Party. And now?"

"I think you say in English, she is the life of the party. We have the same expression. Basia has many friends and knows many secrets."

Kulski drove off, and soon they slipped past the Warsaw Zoo to merge with traffic on a busy road following the river. In a short kilometer, they made a fast left in front of honking traffic and bounced along an asphalted track that ended at a whitewashed building. Needing repair, it bore a sign that simply identified it as Nightclub.

"We walk from here," Kulski told him.

A dirt road continued to the edge of bigger bushes turned brown by winter. Deeply grooved by tires, it had frozen and was rough walking. Jay followed the detective through underbrush tamped down enough to make a path that took them to the edge of the river. A short cement jetty led to a sandbar overgrown with scrubby brush. The jetty was narrow, and the black water swirled dizzyingly at their feet as they crossed it.

"The first body was found here," the detective said.

"Who found the bodies?"

"Fishermen."

"Even in winter?"

"Poor people must eat, and there are still fish, yes?"

Jay looked back where they had walked and couldn't see the car through the thicket. "It would take a strong man to carry a body out here."

"Maybe the murderer had help."

"Is there anything to suggest that?"

"No. It is only my thought." Kulski pointed to a shoal at a distance upriver. "The second body was found there, and the third, there." He pointed an equal distance downriver.

Each site was in prominent view. Each had a rise to it. Display cases for the dead: the killer wanted his work to be admired.

"What's the chance that other bodies were never found? Maybe there were other couriers. A fourth, or a fifth or sixth?"

"We never lose a body. The river has many shallow places where the weeds catch them."

"Even when the river is high like this?"

The detective shrugged inconclusively. "Possibly."

"Possibly what? Possibly the weeds catch them, or possibly a body or two might slip past?"

The detective smiled. "Never a body that we found. Now I will show you where was the second victim."

They crossed back over the jetty and followed a path upriver. Trash peppered the ground, as did the leavings of fishermen who had squatted for relief in the cover of the dead greenery. Twice they turned back from paths that ended at love nests—discarded condoms witness to what had flattened the weeds. Eventually the path turned soggy and sucked at their shoes. Around a bend in the river, they came upon two skiffs pulled onto the shore and in such disrepair that neither appeared seaworthy. Short wooden steps led up the sandy bank to a yard littered with auto parts. Next to a toolshed, a white van was jacked up at its front end, and beyond that was a derelict shack.

"Is this the mechanic's place you mention in the files?" Jay asked.

"Yes."

"I didn't realize it was so close to where the bodies were found. What's his name?"

"Billy."

"He says he didn't hear or see anything. Is that part of the Polish tradition of not cooperating with the police, or do you believe him?"

At that moment, the shack's door swung open and two dogs charged out, growling and running hard for them. Jay grabbed an oar off a skiff and held it with both hands over his head. When the bigger and blacker dog came flying off the bank, he caught it in the chest and sent it sprawling. The smaller gray dog retreated to a safe distance, but the black dog was instantly lunging at them again. Jay was fending it off when a man rolled out from under the white van and stood up. He had a bushy black beard and a broad chest—strong from heavy lifting—that gave him a brutish appearance. "Aleks!" he shouted, and a young man—pimply, gangly, and tall—stepped outside the shack and yelled, "*Chodź!*" The dogs ran back to him, dodging the bearded man, who kicked at them.

Another man stepped into view around the boy. Had Jay ever imagined the face of someone risen from the dead, this was it. His jaundiced features appeared pinched from a rotting apple. Instinctively, Jay stepped back, and his movement roused the dogs. They sidled venomously at the boy's feet, panting growls, the hair on their backs stiffening on end.

The detective displayed his badge. "*Policja*," he called.

"I remember you," hideous Billy replied.

The exchange that followed was too fast for Jay to sort out what they were saying. At some point he realized that they had switched into Russian. Billy's tone, never friendly, grew increasingly abrupt, and the dogs, sensing the tension, growled at the boy's feet. The bearded man retreated back under his truck.

Finally Kulski said, "Let's go back." They retraced their footsteps along the mucky path. Halfway back to the car, the dogs caught up with them. They threw stones to fend them off. Nevertheless the animals grew bolder, egging each other on, daring the other to attack first. Kulski, realizing that waiting any longer might be waiting too long, pulled out a concealed gun and fired once in the air. The animals fell back, but as soon as the men started to move, the gray dog nipped at their heels until they left the territory he had marked as his, which ended at the clearing where their car was parked. The dogs watched from the line of bushes as the men crossed the open field. The closer they got to the car, the quicker they moved, and the dogs, sensing their vulnerability, raced for them again. They had to kick them back before managing to shut themselves protectively in the car, and even then, the animals lunged at the windows and dragged their claws down its sides.

When Kulski started the engine, the dogs ran off. The two men sat there, not moving, giving themselves a moment to recover from the explosion of violence.

Jay finally broke the silence by saying, "You never mentioned the dogs in the files."

"I never saw them before."

"And the bearded guy and the kid? You don't mention them either."

"It's the first time I saw them, too."

"The dogs are obviously the kid's. So the bearded guy isn't a mechanic?"

"Billy rents the toolshed for people to make their own repairs."

"That many people want to repair their own cars?"

"We learned to be very self-sufficient under the communists. If you think about it, it's a good business model. Off-the-books, no labor, just money in the pocket."

"Billy didn't seem too happy about what you were saying to him."

"I told him he might need a license if he wanted to keep watchdogs on the property."

"Does he?"

"As you also say in English, I like to keep him on his toes."

"Why did you switch into Russian when you were talking to him?"

"He speaks it better than Polish. For me, it is the same."

"So he's from Russia?"

"Ukraine."

"Is he legal?"

The detective shrugged. "His papers are legal, but he has too much for a Ukrainian to be operating legally. He repairs cars, and he also has a business—a bar—at the train station. How can a Ukrainian have two businesses in Poland?"

"Is he a suspect in the murders?"

The detective pursed his lips thoughtfully. "He lives at the shack, near where the bodies were found, and he is not a good character. For those reasons he is a suspect. But I don't agree with my own thought on that. I think there is another possibility. All the bodies were found on small islands with sidewalks to them."

"You mean sandbars with concrete jetties? What's your point?"

"They are the only three such islands, perhaps the whole river, I don't know."

"And those would be the best places to display the victims, which would mean, the shack's proximity is only coincidental. Is that what you're saying?"

"It's my thought," the detective replied.

"I wonder what the killer will do now that he's run out of islands. Unless he's finished."

"I suppose we should hope he is not finished," Kulski said, "because if he *is* finished, perhaps it means someone has a bomb."

He backed up to turn around and retreated up the rough track past the nightclub, gunning his engine when he turned onto the riverside road.

"I didn't know Polish policemen carried weapons," Jay remarked. "I was told that I couldn't for that reason."

"You didn't bring a gun?"

"What's the correct answer to that question?"

"Not to answer it."

Jay nodded. "How can you carry a gun when nobody else can?"

"Almost all my cases are violent."

"What happened to Billy's face?"

The detective winced. "Would you ask him?"

"No, but I would want to. Do you believe he never saw a car on the nights of the murders drive up close to the river? The road isn't exactly good, and not everybody wants to risk their oil pan even if they're hoping for a fuck. Wouldn't he be curious who did risk it?"

"He's right, people come every night, even in winter. I used to bring Magda here. Living in two rooms with two children and her parents, where could we make love? Especially love like we really wanted to make?" Kulski grinned and shifted into gear. "So did everyone else who was here on those nights. She won't come here now."

"Why not?"

"Her parents moved out. We don't need to now." Kulski veered up the ramp to the Dambrovski Bridge. "Are you going to the hotel or embassy?"

"Hotel."

A few minutes later, Kulski pulled into its circular drive.

"Can I buy you a drink?" Jay asked.

"I promised Magda I'd try to be home early."

"Anything special?"

"Nothing more than fatherhood, and my wife has modern ideas about it."

"You don't seem to mind."

"I don't. Not for one minute."

CHAPTER SIX

ELTING SNOW DRIPPED FROM HOLES in the rusty gutter running above the train station's entrance. Dr. Sergej Ustinov tried dodging the water and only managed to splatter mud on his cuffs. Lugging two suitcases, he pushed through the double doors, which swung back to smack him from behind and propel him into the low-slung hall. He had always felt insulted by the station's ungrateful design: its spare construction might be suitable for the gold rush towns of Vladivostok or Magadan, but not the country's premier nuclear facility. Kosmonovo deserved better.

He followed a trail of muddy footprints to the ticket counter. As cold indoors as out, he could see his breath. From behind a glass partition, a clerk, preoccupied with yesterday's newspaper, glanced up. A heater burned perilously close to her long coat.

"A ticket to Moscow, please," Sergej said. "First class, no smoking."

She dropped a hand into the gully under the partition. "Your pass."

He slipped it to her.

She studied it. "You are authorized to go to Reutov, not Moscow."

"It's a suburb of Moscow. I'll pay the difference in fare."

"Your pass says Reutov."

"I was hoping to go into the center to buy a gift for my wife. It's her sixtieth birthday next month. She's depressed about getting old, and I want to find something nice to cheer her up."

"Looking at you, I'd guess a nice young boyfriend might do the job."

"Ha! My wife already complains that I still act like a young man!"

"I don't think she'd be complaining if you did." Again the woman dropped her hand in the gully. "Identity card."

He passed it to her. She glanced between him and his picture.

"It's me!" Sergej sang, pulling at his disheveled hair.

The clerk pushed his documents back under the glass. "I can issue a ticket to Moscow Central. It's the same fare. The regulations allow it." She bent over her desk to write out his ticket, pressing hard through multiple carbon copies. Sergej, always hoping for a glimpse of cleavage, leaned closer to the partition, but his breath fogged the cold glass. He was ready to pay with exact change—he had researched every detail of his journey—and carried his suitcases to the platform. They were identical, dark tan with buckled straps, and each weighing twenty-two kilos. He had been precise in matching the weight of his personal possessions in one with the bomb's physics package installed in the other. Just add uranium, which was waiting for him in Warsaw, to make it atomic.

Sergej knew he didn't have to hurry even after the train hissed to a stop alongside the platform. The stopovers in Kosmonovo were lengthy, giving the stevedores time to load reprocessed fuel for delivery throughout the former Soviet Union. He stopped at a kiosk, bought hard mints, and took his time unwrapping one while peeking over the shoulder of a man thumbing through a sex magazine devoted to women in black leather.

A whistle blew to signal the train's readiness to leave. Sergej struggled aboard the first-class carriage and bumped his way down the corridor, peering into compartments at the seat numbers above the facing banquettes. He found his and heaved his suitcases onto the overhead rack before crumpling into the seat and inadvertently farting in the confined space.

The door slammed open hard enough to rebound halfway on its track before a woman stuck out a sturdy shoe to stop it. Rather sturdy herself, she wrestled with a duffel bag as she came into the compartment. Sniffing, she wrinkled her nose accusingly at him. He instantly leapt up to help with her luggage, which turned out to be two duffels, not one, and both clumsily laden. Their clunky contents moved around as he struggled to tuck them securely on her overhead rack.

The woman checked her seat number and plopped next to the window opposite him. When he sat back down, his pointy knees bumped her dimpled ones. They both turned in the same direction at the same time, first one way then the other, each time touching knees again, which made them laugh. People were always surprised when they saw his mouth full of gold teeth. Some were repulsed, but most were curious or freakily attracted. The woman admired them with a cannibalistic look, as if she envisioned his fillings strung like sharks' teeth around her neck.

"Is it all eighteen-karat?" she asked.

"Twenty in front." He showed his teeth.

"Oh yes, now I see."

"It's my savings account."

"For so many teeth, of course, so expensive."

"For me they were free."

"Free?"

"Because of my job."

"People have jobs in Russia? I thought they only worked."

"Ha!"

The woman turned her attention to making herself comfortable by testing the armrest and wiggling her bottom deeper into the plush seat. Her slick dress, in a creamy satin material, rode up her thighs and scrunched at her midriff. She squirmed and yanked its hem to smooth it out, which managed to accentuate her generous bulge.

A mother, coaxing along two mewling infants, peered into their compartment. Sergej prayed she would move on and she did, visibly disappointed when she checked her ticket and continued down the corridor. The whistle blew a final time and the platform began to slip past the window. The next stop was hours away. Until then, Sergej and the woman would have the compartment to themselves. He slipped over to sit by the door.

She asked him, "Where are you going?"

"Moscow."

"Me too, but first I visit relatives. In Gorky."

She spoke accented Russian. Sergej asked where she was from.

"My grandfather was Russian fisherman," she told him. "He fished between Russia and Alaska, and when the communists came, he said, no more Russia. He finished with Russia."

"Is this your first trip here?"

"Of course! Until this year, it was not possible to come here unless—" Her eyes narrowed. "Are you a communist?"

Dr. Ustinov guffawed loudly and let that stand as his answer.

"Good, because communists make me nervous. We can see them from Alaska." She scooted still lower in her seat, until she was half-reclining, her face pressed to the cushioned corner and her legs jutting at him. "My name is Emma," she said.

"Huh?" he replied, distracted by her columns of marbled flesh.

"Emma. My name."

"Dr. Sergej Ustinov." He always included his title at introductions. He couldn't remember not having it, nor a life unrestricted by it.

"A doctor, how lucky! My foot hurts so much. At it will you look?"

"I am a physicist, not a physician." He enunciated both words even though they sounded nothing alike in Russian.

He had no idea what Emma thought she had heard when she replied, "Oh, a foot massage, how wonderful!" She started to unlace a shoe.

"I said I'm a *physicist*."

"Yes, I know, it is almost the same word in English: physical." The shoe came off, and Emma wiggled her toes at him. "You have such long fingers. I predict you to be especially good."

Sergej tried to ignore her and stared into the corridor. The late winter's feeble sunset, draining through their compartment, reflected on the long sideways window. They were passing through a birch forest, and Emma's silhouetted toes sprouted like mushrooms in its blurry mulch.

She slipped even lower in her seat, until she *was* reclining, and dropped a foot on his thigh. "Please. It hurts, and my relatives, they will make me hike all the time. They have no car!"

Of course he couldn't exactly ignore her foot resting on his leg, nor entirely block her squirming toes from view. Her nails were painted cherry red, which he realized did make her feet attractive, certainly more attractive than the coarse yellow nails his wife hadn't painted since their first anniversary. Oh, why not massage her foot? he decided. It might be fun, and he couldn't remember the last time he'd touched someone's foot other than his own. Tentatively he wrapped his fingers around her arch and squeezed. "Is that where it hurts?" he asked.

"Oh yes . . . but harder . . ."

He gripped her foot tighter and massaged it with his thumbs. He found he rather enjoyed it; there was an unfamiliar sensuality to it, and as a bonus, from this angle he could peek up her skirt to where her heavy legs disappeared in a dark shadow. Gradually his fingers migrated to her toes, which they worked vigorously, rooting down between them, and bending them to crack them. For the first time he understood why some people sucked toes for sexual pleasure, and if his back had been more limber, he might have dared to bite hers.

Emma sighed. "I can tell you are professional. Yes . . . oh yes . . ."

Suddenly the situation, and certainly his fantasies, seemed ludicrous to Sergej. He released her foot and said rather coldly, "I hope it feels better."

Emma, who had also been enjoying the massage perhaps a tad too enthusiastically, was puzzled by his sudden dismissal. She pulled herself upright in the seat. "It does feel better. Thank you," she said, putting her shoe back on. "Are you hungry?"

"Hungry?"

"Of course you are, after all that work!"

She stood to unzip a duffel, wagging her wide bottom close to Dr. Ustinov's face. The shiny cloth stretched before him like a movie screen and reflected passing images. He leaned closer and grinned to see a reflection of his teeth. In that moment a cascade of tin cans fell from Emma's bag, and she jumped back, bumping his nose.

"*Uch!*" he cried.

"Soup!" She held up a can to display its red-and-white label. "I bring all my relatives soup."

"Soup?" To Sergej, it seemed more an offering than a gift to bring soup to a country that survived on it.

She pulled a paper sack and loaf of bread from her bag, repacked the cans of soup, and sat back down. She offered him the sack.

It was oily and he was suspicious. "What is it?"

"Dried fish."

Sergej detested dried fish. He had eaten too much of it as a boy, the only source of protein his family could afford. It reeked of poverty and his mother's nagging reminder: *Never say no, say thank you.* Reluctantly he peered into the sack and picked out the smallest piece he could find.

Emma tore bite-size pieces off her loaf of bread, pressed morsels of fish into the soft dough, and popped them into her mouth. Soon the compartment reeked. Sergej nibbled at the piece he'd taken and declined her offer for more. When she finished, she licked her lips and loudly closed the bag. Again she stood to rummage in her duffel and sat back down with what appeared to be a limp balloon. "Sleep, sleep," she said and blew into it. A pillow expanded to reveal Oregon: The Beaver State stenciled above crossed rifles.

Sergej wondered if she hunted.

Emma wedged the pillow into the banquette's corner, took off her shoes, and tried to find a comfortable position in the upright seat. The pillow squeaked annoyingly. She blinked at the overhead light, hinting that she wanted him to dim it, but Sergej was too engrossed in watching the roll of her legs. He jumped when she unexpectedly tapped him with her unshod toes and pointed to the switch over the door. He dimmed the light until only a purplish glow illuminated the compartment and drew the curtains to block the light from the corridor.

Sergej leaned against the cushioned headrest. It smelled like someone else's face. He was drowsy but not sleepy, and by the way Emma fidgeted, he knew she feigned sleep as well. He squinted, blurring his vision to bend the gray light, and tried to imagine her in a different way: slimmer, or slinkier, or not what she was. But he couldn't. She was too solid to remake.

Night closed in. Spotlights mounted on posts at irregular intervals hunted the compartment's corners to reveal their faces. Sometimes their eyes met, or so Sergej thought; he could never be sure. His eyes, finally growing heavy from the train's comforting rhythm, sagged until he could hardly keep them open, and a moment later he was free-falling into Emma's abundant breasts. He jerked awake and realized he was aroused. He discreetly pressed a hand to his lap to conceal his state.

A light swept the compartment and he saw Emma was watching him. She puckered her lips and sent a kiss in the direction of his crotch, or so he fancied, but the hypnotic rails blurred the edges of wakefulness until he was uncertain where his dreams began when Emma twisted in the seat, her broad knees rising to his face, and he fell between her weltered thighs—until his head rolled off the banquette and hit the glass door. His eyes popped open and again she was staring at him. Was she provocatively flicking her tongue or simply licking her lips? He grew more aroused, and again dropped a hand to conceal himself. Emma slipped her foot under his hand and touched him. Now Sergej knew he *was* awake. A moment later, her knees, round as moons, orbited his face as she dropped the latch on the door. Yanking at his belt buckle, she pulled him free and mounted him, flashing a breast as they grappled in their unaccustomed positions. The passing chunks of light took snapshots of them. Immediately they succumbed to the rhythm of the chugging rails as their fingers mashed the other's flesh in their hurried coupling.

"Tickets!" the conductor cried from the end of the car.

Emma pressed Sergej into the angle she needed.

"Tickets!"

He shifted under her.

"Tickets!"

"*Don't stop!*"

"Tickets!"

"I *can't* stop . . ."

"*Don't . . .*"

"Tickets!"

The next compartment's door slid open.

"Tickets, please."

Emma's eyes pleaded for a moment more, and it was all he needed, too.

"Tickets!"

The conductor knocked on their door. "Tickets!"

Emma wrestled her skirt over her hips while he repaired his trousers.

The conductor rattled the handle harder. "Tickets!"

She pressed her face to the plastic pillow.

Sergej unlatched the door.

A rectangle of light fell into the compartment.

Emma snorted, awakening to it. "Are we already in Moscow?"

CHAPTER SEVEN

L ILKA PULLED TO A STOP behind the other cars waiting for demon-
strators to pass. Several hundred of them, mostly elderly men,
were shuffling through the intersection. Some carried banners painted
with hammer-and-sickle symbols, others with the wobbly signature
of Solidarity. Even Jay, new to Poland, recognized that their act of
political solidarity was unusual. "What do they want?" he asked.

"I don't know the word in English," Lilka answered.

"Try Polish."

"*Emerytury.*"

"Fur hats?" he asked facetiously.

"No! More money."

"Everybody wants more money."

"But these are old people. Many have problems now." Lilka told
how her father, after years in the diplomatic corps, had a monthly
pension that was less than what Jay's breakfast had cost that morning.

Drivers, impatient with the delay, blew their horns, but the bedrag-
gled protesters paid them no heed. Instead, a rare young woman
among them started to sing the national anthem, and soon they all
took it up, the old men an especially gravelly chorus for her soaring
high notes, all praising one country despite different visions of what
it should be. Finally the last demonstrator passed, and the cars behind
them flashed their lights as if Lilka could hurry up the cars ahead of
her.

Soon they left the city and entered low-lying country where rusty
fences demarcated small garden plots. The Polish *dzialka* had survived because their unwelcomed overlords, the Russians, also had a
tradition of *dachas*. For the Party elite, that translated into cozy country homes with sizable gardens; for everyone else, it meant scrappy
patches for growing vegetables that weren't available in the stores. In
the Everyman Society, every man had a right to fresh tomatoes.

Lilka turned onto a track that lost its asphalt in a hundred meters. She pulled over and parked, and they continued on foot, winding through gardens bruised by winter. A few plots had shacks with smoke billowing from their chimneys. Lilka stopped at one where a man, his back to them, was snipping rose hips and collecting them in a handkerchief spread open on a tree stump. "That's my Tata," she told him.

Her father, wiry with a full head of silver hair, turned a stiff neck and smiled at his daughter. How many false smiles had she interpreted, how many men had she dreaded, and here was a man who, with his loving smile, made men good again. She opened the gate. "Tata, this is my friend Jay," she said in English.

Mr. Wolnik set aside his clippers to shake Jay's hand. "Welcome."

"*Dzenkuje*," Jay thanked him.

"You are American?"

"Is my accent that bad?"

"It was my job to know accents."

"Why are you outside, Tata? It is too cold."

"There's too much hot air inside. You know how your mother likes to talk, and now Tolek can only talk about America. He thinks it will be so different, and easy. Is it?" he asked Jay.

"Easy? No, I would not call America easy."

"Of course it is *different*," the old man allowed, "but everywhere has problems. Sometimes the same problems. It's impossible to convince Tolek."

"He has a dream, Tata."

"You think we didn't have dreams, too? It's not practical to dream when so much is uncertain. My wife is waiting, we should go inside." The old man loosely tied his handkerchief around the rose hips and led them onto the porch. It swayed under their weight.

Inside, the air was pungent with cooking cabbage that had steamed up the windows. A burly man in the corner was fiddling with a kerosene heater, and no sooner had Lilka introduced him as Tolek, her brother-in-law, than her mother emerged from the kitchen, wiping her hands on an apron. She burst into a stream of Polish and kissed Lilka with loud smacking sounds. When Lilka introduced Jay, her mother, all atwitter, pulled him against her generous bosom and kissed his cheeks. "*Amerykanin!*" she cried. "*Witamy!*"

"My mother-in-law is very excited to meet an American," Tolek remarked.

"I noticed."

"I'm Alina," Jay heard, and turned to see Lilka's sister in the kitchen door. Blue-eyed like her mother, she had a shy smile.

"I'm Jay."

"It's very nice to meet you."

"Did Tadzu come too?" Lilka asked.

"He stayed home to practice piano. He has a recital at school this week. We are very proud of him," she told Jay, but a discreet glance at Tolek suggested she wasn't sure about her husband.

Martyna, as Lilka's mother insisted he call her, organized her two daughters into carrying platters of food from the tiny kitchen. They crowded around a wobbly table with their knees touching. Everyone fell silent when the older woman crossed herself, closed her eyes, and said grace; rather, she started to say grace, which went on for so long that Mr. Wolnik gave up, poured vodka into his thimble-sized glass, and knocked it back in lieu of his "amen." His wife scowled at him, but even that was good-natured, like everything about her, and a moment later she was exhorting them in English, "Eat! Eat!"

Jay did, on a cold spring day feasting from a winter's table of sauerkraut, sausage, and pickles, eating more than he thought possible, and not realizing more was to come: white borscht and veal, and a cake so sweet it made his teeth hurt. With each new dish, he conjured his best skills at pantomime to indicate that the food tasted wonderful, and Martyna chirped with pleasure, clapping and insisting that he drink more vodka. Through Lilka, she asked to know all the places he had traveled, and seemed to know something about each one, though she had been to none of them. Had he seen this church, or that icon, or visited the pilgrimage sites of saints and martyrs that she could describe in detail? Soon the first bottle of vodka was empty, and Mr. Wolnik fetched another from the cupboard.

Everyone but Martyna spoke decent English, which they used for his benefit, only occasionally lapsing into Polish, and in those respites he had a chance to observe them. In the daughters he saw traces of their mother's faded beauty, and in Tolek's glances at Alina, his fretful love for her. From time to time, Mr. Wolnik cast a stern eye at his wife to check her boisterousness, which he never succeeded in doing. Martyna was a woman whose dreams had shrunk, but she could make enough of the dreams she still had.

Jay said to Tolek, "Lilka says you hope to move to America."

"Yes," Tolek said solemnly. "We hope to go soon."

"You're an English teacher, is that right, Alina?"

"I think that a native speaker would find me deficient."

"Not this native speaker. Would you teach English in America?"

"Me to teach English in America? That is a funny idea."

"Trust me, we need teachers of all kinds."

"See, I told you," Tolek said.

"Tolek and Alina go to America," Martyna attempted in her broken English. "I cry very much."

"What will you do in America?" he asked Tolek.

"Anything."

"He is a scientist," Lilka spoke up.

"A scientist?"

"I *was* a scientist. They closed the lab a couple of days ago."

"He's a nuclear scientist," Alina elaborated.

"Nuclear? Really? Doing what?"

"Mostly analyzing data from other studies. I'm on the Chernobyl team, or at least I was, studying the radiation's effect on children."

"That sounds like important work."

"Apparently, not important enough."

"You must know Dr. Nagorski?"

"Of course. We have met frequently. How do you know him?"

Jay realized he should have anticipated that question and stumbled for an answer. "I've read articles that mention him," he replied.

"Lilka says you work at the American embassy," Alina said.

"I'm only here for a short time to help on a project."

"Maybe you could help with our visas?"

"Alina!" Lilka said, shocked.

"Does it hurt to ask for help?"

Jay wondered if he had misunderstood something. "I thought you didn't want to go to America?"

"Tolek is determined to go. He won't look for another job here. Will you?" she asked her husband accusingly.

"To do what? Shine shoes?"

"America's streets aren't paved with gold," Jay told him.

"At least they're not paved with ex-communists."

"You only talk good about America and never about your own country," the old man complained. "Things are changing here in Poland, too!"

"Should I talk about your eleven-dollars-a-month pension?"

"They raised it to thirteen."

"And you say I ask for too much?"

"You do."

"Is it too much to want more than two kilos of sausage and a half day's notice when they eliminate my job? My 'important' job?"

An argument ensued in Polish, little of which Jay understood other than no one but Lilka thought Alina had breached a line in asking for his help. Certainly Jay did not. He'd walked enough of Warsaw's gray streets and grim underground passages, glancing at the faces of passersby—each a map of a wounded country—and wondered if what he considered his rebelliousness, bred in America's suburban comfort, could have survived what they had endured. Or would he have resigned himself to the half-empty glass of their existence? Tolek, apparently, had not.

"Lukasz, more vodka!" Martyna commanded.

Dutifully he splashed another round in their thimble-sized glasses, then lifted his and toasted, "To the Russian Navy!"

"*Do dna!*" everybody but Jay shouted—*To the bottom!*—and knocked back their shots. They laughed at the popular joke, which Lilka translated for him, and for good measure drank a second round to sinking the Russian navy. Inevitably the conversation turned to the state of political affairs, which cheered no one. His bladder, too, was unhappy, and he looked around for the bathroom. He didn't see one and asked where it was.

"We go together," the old man said.

They went outside and around to the back of the shack. Jay was surprised it was already deep twilight. They were at the top of a small rise that looked along a shallow valley checkered with garden plots. In the air were lazy threads of smoke from cooking fires. "We piss here," Lukasz said. They stood beside each other, unzipped, and aimed for the garden. Their splatter was about the only thing they could hear until the argument started up again inside and Tolek's fist hit the table with a growl.

"Everybody fights now," Lukasz grumbled, zipping up. "In the past, we knew what was possible. We didn't need more."

Jay, made philosophical by the vodka, asked, "What about freedom? Free speech? The right to travel?"

"You cannot imagine the end of the war. The Germans were very thorough. Freedom. What good is freedom in this place at such a time? More than ninety percent of Warsaw was destroyed. We needed food, houses, protection—but not too much of any of them. If they thought we had enough of something, they took some of it away. They always wanted us to work harder. Their five-year plan was to have another five-year plan. It was enough to keep alive. I suppose it is different in America."

"It's different in America because we have freedom."

"Everything is different in America!" Tolek proclaimed, coming around the corner, three shot glasses in one hand and a bottle in the other. "Hopefully the women make more sense in America."

"Then I want a visa, too," Lukasz joked.

Tolek splashed vodka into their glasses. "I should apologize that my wife asked for your help."

"I'm not really part of the embassy," Jay replied.

"Lilka explained."

They tossed back those shots and Tolek poured more.

"*Can* you help with their visas?" Lukasz asked.

"Tata! What are you asking?"

"He can quote your presidents. All of them."

"Not all of them, Tata."

"Most of them. Go on, quote Kennedy."

"Now you want me to go to America?"

"Go on. He will appreciate it."

Tolek sighed, unhappy at being put on the spot, and felt foolish as he said, "'We observe today not a victory of party, but a celebration of freedom—symbolizing an end, as well as a beginning . . .'" By the end, he never felt foolish at quoting such honorable words. "It is Kennedy's inaugural address. I know the whole thing."

"He's smart," Lukasz said. "He could be the next American president. He already knows their speeches."

Tolek looked puzzled. "You've changed your mind, Tata?"

"I think this is your home, but you go and find out."

For the first time the old man had sanctioned their departure for America. Tolek was deeply moved. His voice cracked when he said, "Thank you, Tata."

"I'll ask at the embassy about your visas," Jay offered. "Maybe I can help speed things up."

Lukasz held out his glass. "That demands one more vodka!"

Tolek finished off the bottle, spilling almost as much on their fingers as he managed to get into their glasses. "To America!" he toasted.

The three men raised their glasses in a moment of blurred camaraderie. "To America!"

Down the hatch the last shot went. They were licking their fingers when Alina came around the corner, her teary eyes swollen. She slipped a hand under Tolek's arm. "We should go. Mama is tired."

Lilka and her mother showed up next. Lilka frowned at the empty vodka bottle while handing Tolek a key. "Please don't forget about the toilet."

"You see, I can be a plumber in America!"

Everyone said goodbye with kisses and handshakes. "*Moi kohani!*" Martyna repeatedly exclaimed to Jay. *Sweetheart!*

Tolek and Alina started down the lane. She held out her hand and he gave her the car key. They walked off, embracing, her head against his broad shoulder. They would go home and make love, it seemed certain.

The path seemed longer and less navigable than Jay remembered, and he stopped frequently to admire the gardens in a ploy to sober up. When they reached Lilka's car, she said, "You like Polish vodka too much."

"Too much tonight is right," he agreed.

They started back along the rutted road. Despite the chilly night, Jay rolled down his window for air. "I like your family," he said and tried to touch the loose hairs on her neck.

She slapped his hand away.

They rode in silence the rest of the way to his hotel. She pulled into the circular driveway and stopped for him to get out.

That was not how he had envisioned the end of their evening. "I'm sorry," he said. "But I *did* like your family. Can we have dinner tomorrow?"

"No."

"No is not the right answer. Try perhaps."

"No perhaps. No!"

"No? Really no?"

"Perhaps," she relented.

"I'll take that for a yes."

He got out and she drove off.

He staggered to the elevator, and from the elevator to his room. He made a quick pass through the bathroom before he undressed and slipped between the fresh starched sheets. He realized it was his own fault that he was alone between them. He thought about Lilka, imagining her next to him, remembering the tufts of hair on her neck. He imagined kissing her there. He thought of the many places he wanted to kiss her, and imagining his hand to be hers, he touched himself before rolling over and falling into a dreamless sleep.

CHAPTER EIGHT

WHEN JAY WOKE UP, HE wasn't sure where he was. His suitcase lay open on a spare bed in the unfamiliar room. Light peeked around the edges of blackout curtains. He pulled them open to a view of Warsaw's skyline. A nauseous memory flooded back of too much vodka the day before. Hangovers had a way of accentuating remorse, and he groaned aloud, already practicing his apology to Lilka.

He was aiming for the bathroom when his telephone rang. He reached for it.

"Porter here."

"Are you on a secure line?"

"No. It's a hotel line."

"Do you think anyone is listening?"

"You reread *1984*, didn't you? If it's urgent, say it fast, and maybe whoever is listening won't catch it."

"Don't mock your father."

"What time is it there?"

"I think two."

"In the morning?"

"Your mother and I just walked in the door getting back from DC."

"What's wrong with the boys?"

"Your mother and I are worried."

"You're always worried. Tell me why this time."

"You lose children by twelve or thirteen. After that, if they're lucky, they manage to rehabilitate themselves."

"Sorry, Dad. That was too fast for me. Is this about my missing Marty's twelfth birthday?"

"This is about a condom in her wastebasket."

"Why were you looking in Cynthia's wastebaskets?"

"It was open. Everybody could see it."

"At least she's practicing birth control."

"I'm not going to tell your mother that you're joking about this."

"What else?"

"Where do you want to start? Unhappy kids or Cynthia?"

"Kids."

"Brett's getting taller. Big enough to win fights, so he picks them."

"And Martin?"

"Backup on Brett. He's been getting detentions."

"Brett or Marty?"

"Brett! Aren't you listening? I'm worried he'll get suspended."

"He's only ten years old."

"It doesn't matter." ·

"Cynthia never told me."

"And she told the boys not to tell you."

"Why?"

"She doesn't want you to have any ammunition against her before the final custody hearing. And where is Martin?" his father asked rhetorically. "Even if he's in the room, he's not there. He has become totally withdrawn. His Little League team is playing in the regional championships at the end of next week. It would mean a lot to him if you went to the game."

"That depends on the situation here."

"He's threatening not to play."

"What?"

"If you're not here. I overheard him tell Brett."

"Why?"

"Kids often blame themselves when their parents split up. It's a way to punish himself."

"Dad, please. I feel guilty enough as it is."

"James, you weren't the problem in your marriage."

"We didn't have a problem in our marriage. Cynthia had a problem with my job."

"She definitely has problems now. I took pictures to prove it."

"Pictures of what?"

"A condom. Marijuana paraphernalia everywhere. Plus the place was a pigsty."

"Cynthia never was very neat."

"Try squalor. You know, I'm not a fuddy-duddy about sex or marijuana or anything people want to do that's between them, but I don't think these things should be done in front of children. I'll get the photos printed and send them to you."

"What am I supposed to do with them?"

"Show them to the judge, of course. You need to fight for at least joint custody."

"Was it legal taking photos inside her house?"

"You work for the FBI. You tell me." His father hung up.

Jay, worried about his sons, was grateful that his dad was pitching in when he couldn't be there himself. Given the demands of a nuclear scientist during the Cold War, his father had missed many of Jay's school events and birthdays. Jay had been determined not to miss his own sons' special events. But there he was in Poland, missing his older son's birthday, essentially still fighting Cold War battles. He could better appreciate the work pressures that had been on his father, though it didn't make his own absence any easier.

CHAPTER NINE

GENERAL DRAVKO MLADIC IMPATIENTLY TOED the yellow line while the passport officer argued with a woman who had slung a baby under her arm like the potato sacks she was probably used to carrying. The baby shrieked pitifully and the general turned away, wearied by the desperation of its little claws scratching at its mother's coat. He pulled his passport from his pocket and was bored enough to study his own identity. Born: 17/01/1943. Birthplace: Beograd. His photo showed a much younger man, but then, passport photos bore false witness to anyone's age.

"Next!" the officer cried.

General Mladic stepped forward to hand her his passport.

She didn't look at it, instead examining his suitcase. "Your baggage must be inspected first," she said.

He pointed to the gold-embossed word on the cover of his passport, which she held in fingers with nails chewed down to the quick. "Diplomat," Dravko read aloud for her benefit. "My baggage is never inspected."

She frowned and stamped his passport. "Next!"

He hauled the cumbersome suitcase into the departure hall. Dr. Ustinov's instructions had been precise: bring his million dollars in a dark tan suitcase with buckled straps of specified dimensions from a particular Moscow factory. The plan was to exchange their bags—his money for a bomb—and if anyone later studied the airport's surveillance videos, the physicist wanted the general to appear to arrive and depart with the same suitcase.

Acquiring the matching suitcase had been a challenge. Central planning had never translated into central dispatch. It was almost easier to organize shipments of weapons from Poland than to place an order for a suitcase with a Moscow factory. But he was confident that the suitcase exactly matched Sergej's, even in weight, for again the physicist had been precise: twenty-two kilograms. In accumulating the million-dollar payoff, Dravko had begun to think of sums by their weights: so many bills translated into so many grams. Like a bargaining housewife, he had had to juggle denominations to fit his allowance.

A mesmerized crowd stared up at the departure board suspended from the ceiling. Periodically it updated itself with the sound of shuffling cards as the cockeyed letters and numbers reset themselves. Each time it did, the women gripped their scarves tighter, the men scratched more furiously under their caps, and all prayed that the scrolling messages would bring good news, but for most, good news—along with their flights—had been DELAYED or CANCELED. Dravko elbowed his way through the crowd until he drew close enough to read his flight's status: ON TIME.

Overhead signs directed him to the gate through overheated corridors filled with sweaty travelers uncomfortably draped over plastic seats. While some slept, others stood weary sentry, protecting meager belongings stuffed into duffels and backpacks. They were the intellectuals and merchants, always the first to flee. Dravko thought they looked like tramps and gave them wide berth. Sometimes children touched him, begging, and he spun around, scaring them away.

A haphazard queue had formed at the gate. Ticket holders without reserved seats jostled for places in line. They were willing to go anywhere, and clutched wads of dinars in fists too small to hold enough of the worthless money to buy their way out. Some offered to pay in dollars or marks, and the clerks wrote down their names, their hard currency making them the favored among castoffs.

"Only passengers with tickets!" the two harried agents took turns shouting. One blonde, the other brunette, they had matching bangs and eyeliner.

"Wait over there," they told everyone else.

The passengers who had anted up hefty bribes for tickets shuffled forward, using their suitcases and children as fortifications against line jumpers. No one doubted that the plane was overbooked. With each person who checked in, the remaining passengers fretted that their life savings couldn't save their lives after all.

"I'll sit on the can!" one man shouted.

"Please, let the children stand in the aisle! Save them!"

"We need another airplane!"

"That's right, another airplane!"

The complaint spread and people grew unruly. What remained of the queue collapsed. General Mladic tried to maneuver his way to the check-in desk—his seat was definitely protected—but his suitcase proved too cumbersome. A security guard recognized him and came to his aid. "General Mladic, sir, let me help you with that."

The guard forced a passage for them to approach the counter where the brunette took Dravko's ticket. She wore too much makeup, trying to downplay her fleshy nose. "I need to see your passport."

He handed it to her.

She glanced between the picture and him. "You looked like Marcello Mastroianni when you were younger."

"And now?" he asked.

The clerk turned red and stammered, "I don't know."

Dravko started down the gangway.

"Hey Colonel Big Shot!" a young man called after him. "I'll carry your suitcase if you save me a seat!"

"Hush! Don't you know who that is?"

"That's Dravko Mladic!"

Dravko, smiling to himself, stepped into the airplane. The stewardess showed him to his seat. She took his cap, but he declined to surrender his coat, preferring to keep it on so people could see his medals. She helped him lift his suitcase into the overhead bin.

It fit exactly, just as Dr. Ustinov had planned.

CHAPTER TEN

JACEK RUMMAGED IN THE SMALL refrigerator, pushing aside juice cartons and jars of pickles. "Where the fuck's the mayonnaise?"

Lilka entered the kitchen pinning up her hair. "I sorted things out in there. Your stuff is on the second shelf."

"Where's my mayonnaise?"

"Did you buy some?"

"There it is." He took a jar from a lower shelf.

"That's mine."

"Fuck off."

Lilka took a box of cereal from the cupboard. It felt empty and she shook it, then noticed the soggy cornflakes in a bowl on the table. "This was mine, too."

"I have a long day today. I have to eat something." He slathered mayonnaise on slices of bread that he'd lined up on the counter. "I'll buy more cereal, for fucking Christ's sake."

"That's not the point. We have an agreement."

"What's a bowl of cereal? A state offense?"

"Only my breakfast. Where's Aleks?"

Jacek displayed a can of tuna. "I bought this."

He grabbed an opener off the counter and started working around the tin.

"I asked, where is Aleks?"

"I'd'a told you if I knew."

"You're not telling me something about him."

"I can't tell you what I don't know."

"Where is he staying at night? You must know that."

"I haven't seen him."

"Doesn't he still work for you sometimes?"

"Not when he doesn't show up."

The opener jammed on the can's rounded corner. Jacek twisted it free and used it to pry open the can instead. Using a fork, he spilled tuna flakes over the mayonnaised bread. "He's eighteen and got a girlfriend."

"I know. She has those mean dogs."

"He likes them."

"Why does he have to take care of them?"

"He's trained them good."

"I think she's got Aleks trained. She's not helping him. I don't like her."

"He likes her. He's also got a dick and is growing up. You think he wants to sleep here?"

"Growing up is one thing. Getting a girl pregnant is another."

Jacek tossed the empty can into the trash. "You think I don't understand what you're insinuating?"

"We should want it different for him. Both of us should."

"You and me'd be okay if you didn't have such highfalutin ideas."

"Aren't parents supposed to want it better for their kids? And to be better than we are?"

"He's no different than me or you. He's us, Lilka, *us*, and you didn't raise the average as much as you like to think."

"I don't pretend I'm not part of him. I don't pretend I'm not part of you and me. And I'm not pretending when I hope everything is better for him."

"Yeah, well, don't get your hopes up."

"What's that supposed to mean?"

"Nothing. And don't drink my coffee. I got a long haul today."

"I'm taking half a cup. We'll call it even on the cereal."

"We'll call it even! Jesus, it's like a fucking bank around here. Everything has to be negotiated."

"We have an agreement."

"You and your fucking agreement! Here, you want cereal?" Jacek dumped the dregs of his cereal into her bowl. Milk splashed on the table. A few soggy flakes floated to the surface.

Lilka dumped it in the sink. "I'm not hungry."

Jacek laughed at her. "Sure you're not. And what's it matter, you can always eat at the Lounge. So who's your new fuck?"

"What are you talking about?"

"You were gone all day yesterday."

"I was at the *dzialka*."

"Is he another one of your rich businessmen? A Rockefeller? Is that it, he's a Rockefeller and I'm only a Rypinski?"

"It was never about money and you know it."

"If I dropped the whole world in your lap and said, 'Here, it's yours,' you'd say, 'Make it bigger, make it better, make it shinier.' It always has to be first class for you. Working the first-class lounge. Fucking first-class lovers."

"He's not a lover."

"Only because you haven't fucked him yet. What is he, another pilot? You like your pilots, don't you? Or is he a steward who settled for you because he couldn't find another steward's asshole to fuck?"

"You make me sick." Lilka turned to leave the kitchen.

Jacek grabbed her arm and swung her around. "Who is he?"

"He's a policeman."

"What kind of policeman can afford a first-class whore like you?"

"An FBI policeman," she boasted.

"FBI?"

"Like on TV."

"I know the fucking FBI. I watch TV, too. What's he doing here besides fucking you?"

"He's investigating a murder case."

"What murder case?"

"He hasn't said."

"You didn't ask?"

"I sensed it was confidential."

"Don't you think you should ask him?"

"Why do I need to know?"

"Don't bring him here. I don't want a cop sniffing around."

"Why would he sniff around here?"

"Because cops can't help themselves."

"That implies he'd find something. What are you hiding here?"

"It's Aleks who's hiding stuff. I don't know where he's keeping it."

"What stuff?"

"Do you ever look around and see what's going on? Or are you just wearing sunglasses all the time?"

"I don't know what you're talking about."

"Heroin. You don't see the signs? You're a fucking stupid cow sometimes."

"You got Aleks on heroin?"

"Whoa, hold on. Aleks got Aleks on heroin."

"No. Tell me you're not supplying your own son."

"He knew all the dangers. Fuck, he just has to look at me. Isn't that what you would tell him?"

She lunged at him. "He's our son!"

He pushed her away. "Okay, I'm responsible. I'm trying to get off the shit but he knew I can still get it."

"You could have said no."

"I told him it was a bitch to quit."

"Why didn't you tell me?"

"And have you crying all over him? I'll get him cleaned up, and I don't need a goddamn cop sniffing around the apartment. And don't say anything to Aleks, either, because he might really run away if he knows you know."

Jacek poured coffee into his thermos. "I'm saving you a cup," he said, and slipped it back on the warmer. He put his sandwiches, two liters of water, and a six-pack of beer into a Styrofoam cooler and walked out.

Lilka listened as he left the apartment and heard the reassuring sound of the latch as the door closed. His footsteps quickly faded away. He often forgot things and came back a minute later, sometimes dealing her one last punch for making him forget whatever it was, but not that morning. She knew he was far enough down the stairs that he'd only climb back up if he'd forgotten the key to his van. She went to the kitchen window, where she could see the exit from the parking lot. She felt numb, responsible because she hadn't paid attention to what was happening to Aleks. As Jacek's white van drove off, she crumpled over the sink, sobbing, gagging every time she thought the word *heroin*. It had destroyed her husband, destroyed their marriage, and now it had its hooks in their son.

CHAPTER ELEVEN

THE BUS SHUDDERED TO A stop.
The end of the line.

A dead end in the woods where the road deteriorated into a rough track.

Dr. Ustinov stepped down into the mud, clutching his twin suitcases. The driver followed him off the bus and faced the dark woods to piss. Judging from the absence of waiting passengers, he had a lonely return journey ahead of him that night.

Sergej started walking up the road. A dense fog made it hard to see trees only a few feet away. Soon he came to the guard hut with its door slightly ajar. He set down his suitcases, retrieved a flask from his satchel, and swallowed from it, followed by a second shot, needing vodka's encouragement to approach what might be his own end of the line. Sergej was gambling that the government hadn't unleashed its teletypists to make a wholesale broadcast of his disappearance. Defections were a national shame that connoted a massive failure of Russian intelligence.

Behind him, he heard the bus drive away. He slipped the flask into his side pocket and stepped to where he could see inside the guard hut without being seen. Two soldiers, bundled in blankets, were playing cards at a small table. Underneath it, their knees touched, and their mud-splattered boots filled the space. With every breath, they exhaled a foggy cloud; a glowing heater in the corner barely dented the frigid cold.

The fairer soldier, with ginger curls sticking out from under a stocking cap, threw a card down and declared the game over.

"How do you do it, Boris?" asked the darker, handsomer soldier with a trim beard. "How do you always win?"

"You let me."

"I let you? How do I *let* you?"

"Because, Nikita, you play cards so badly, you invite defeat. You never have a strategy."

"Maybe I wanted the game to be over," Nikita said, inching a hand suggestively up Boris's thigh. "Maybe that's my strategy."

When his hand made it high enough, Boris grabbed it and pressed it to his crotch.

Nikita laughed. "You're already hard!"

"Maybe that's *my* strategy!"

Dr. Ustinov moved to where he could be seen in the door's narrow band of light and cleared his throat.

Both soldiers instantly sat upright.

Nikita asked, "What do you want?"

"To cross the border, of course."

"The border's closed."

"It's never supposed to be closed here. Has something happened?"

"Yeah, something has happened," Boris grumbled. "It's too fucking cold to stand outside and check your bags. That is, if someone is stupid enough to be out in this weather."

"I guess that would be me."

"What's to guess?" Boris gathered the cards to shuffle them. "You'll have to come back in the morning."

"But the bus has already gone. You can't expect me to spend all night waiting outside. You said yourself, it's too cold." Sergej made a point of looking at the shack's floor. "Can I can sleep in here? I'm skinny so I don't need much space. Ha! And with three of us, the place will be warmer."

The two soldiers exchanged a look: they had expectations for the evening that didn't include an old geezer sleeping on their floor.

"We're warm enough, grandpa. We don't need your gas." Nikita pushed back his chair and joined Sergej outside. "Put your suitcases on that long table and show me what you have."

Sergej lifted his suitcases onto a high table with a pitched roof sheltering it and handed the soldier his documents. "My ID and invoices. I sell lipsticks." He grins adding, "I try to make the girls pretty."

"With those teeth, grandpa, you could be forging wedding rings!

You haven't crossed here before, have you? I'd recognize that ugly mug."

"It's my first time. I have a new customer in Białystok."

"Come to think of it, I remember someone who looked the same as you. He was tall like you, too, and crossed a month, maybe six weeks ago. Where are you from?" Nikita asked while flipping back through Sergej's passport.

"Kosmonovo."

"Yeah, so was this guy, I think. We thought he said he was a kosmonaut. They must grow 'em ugly in Kosmonaut City, or do you all have the same father?" He laughed at his own joke and handed back the documents.

"I feel sorry for you boys," Sergej remarked, tucking his papers away. "I know how cold and bored you can get."

"Sure you do, grandpa."

"I was a border guard once," he lied.

"Is that what made you so ugly?"

"I was never too ugly for someone on a cold night. Men have to find a way to keep warm."

"I'd be careful what you're implying, grandpa. You might talk yourself into spending the night out in the cold."

"Well, if the first way doesn't work, here's a second way that's sometimes more reliable." Sergej offered Nikita one of his flasks of vodka.

The soldier twisted it open and greedily took a couple of swallows.

"You must be thirsty."

"We've had nothing but water for three days."

"When I was wearing army boots, I always made sure that I had vodka."

"In your day, grandpa, they still paid soldiers and you could afford to buy it. The army's been runnin' on empty for a while." Nikita swigged from the flask again and tried to hand it back.

"Keep it," Sergej told him.

"Are you trying to bribe me?"

"With only a flask? Ha! I have a full bottle to bribe you!"

A horn sounded close by up the road.

"I can't miss my bus!" Sergej fretted.

"Don't worry. It's a fifteen-minute warning. So where's that bottle?"

Sergej looked between the two suitcases. "My wife bought me matching suitcases and all they do is confuse me!"

"It's your bus to catch."

"I think it's in this one." Sergej sprung open the suitcase's latches and shiny tubes of lipstick exploded out its sides, bouncing off the bench and rolling in every direction. Futilely Nikita grabbed for them, trying to help Sergej stem their escape, but the brassy cylinders slipped through their fingers and bounced at their feet.

"Oh! Oh!" Sergej cried. "Oh this is terrible! They are for my new customer!"

Boris came to the hut's doorway. "What's happening, Nikita?"

The bus driver blew his horn again.

"Please help me! I can't miss my bus!" Sergej opened his suitcase to fish out empty plastic bags that he'd brought for just that moment. He pressed them on the soldiers. Not all the lipsticks had escaped, and at the bottom of the suitcase, floating in a sea of shiny tubes, was the promised bottle of vodka. The soldiers eyed it hungrily.

The teletype machine clattered to life.

Boris looked around at it. "There's something coming across the ticker."

The machine stopped.

Nikita started scooping lipsticks into his bag. "Come on, Boris, give a hand!"

"Piss off! Just take the bottle and let him catch his fucking bus."

"Ah come on, he was a border guard like us. Now he's trying to make an honest living."

Reluctantly Boris picked up a few scattered tubes. "Who makes an honest living selling lipstick?"

"I do," Sergej answered, grabbing their plastic bags and tossing them into his suitcase. "I can't miss my bus!"

Again the teletype machine started clacking away and abruptly stopped.

Nikita said, "Sounds like trouble on the line again."

Sergej handed him the vodka. "To Mother Russia! May she rest in peace."

The teletype started again.

"Someone is trying to reach us." Boris went back inside.

"What's in your other suitcase?" Nikita asked.

"More lipsticks."

"I've seen enough of those tonight. Go on, grandpa, go make the Polish girls pretty. I'll lift the barrier."

Dr. Ustinov ducked under it and handed Nikita a lipstick. "Why not have some fun tonight and paint your balls with this? Won't your friend be surprised!"

The handsome soldier burst into laughter. "You kinky old man!"

"Ha!"

Sergej disappeared in the fog.

"Crazy Ruski!" Nikita called after him and slipped the lipstick into a pocket.

Boris was back in the doorway. "Did he go?"

"He's gone. What came across the ticker?"

"Something about missing kosmonauts!"

Nikita paled. "You mean someone is missing from Kosmonovo?"

"I thought you called it Kosmonaut City?"

"The old guy was from there. Just now."

Boris snorted. "I don't think you have to worry about his being a missing kosmonaut. They're probably required to have teeth."

"Maybe he's wanted for a lipstick heist!" Nikita joked. "How did he have so many of them when half the time my mother can't find one in the stores?"

"What's it matter? Come inside. It's fucking cold out here."

Dr. Ustinov had paused to listen to their exchange. So word was out about his disappearance, but the two border guards weren't going to try to drag him back. He set down the suitcases and removed the safety mechanism on the second exploding lipstick mechanism. He was ready for a second performance with the Polish guards. The lipsticks had been a gamble, but one he had considered and reconsidered endless times over the five years or so he had collected them. He needed a ploy that was unexpected but harmless, that would deter the guards from opening the second suitcase if they thought the same silliness might happen again. If the soldiers insisted on examining the other suitcase, his options would have been to surrender or to set off the bomb and be done with it, though Sergej never seriously considered that either would come to pass. He had always been a trickster. As a boy, he earned rubles playing sleight-of-hand games along the rat-infested quays of Odessa's harbor, and his inventive gadgetry won him the attention—and benevolence—of a science teacher who recognized his genius and secured him a place in the local academy. Sergej never doubted his ability to trick a couple of soldiers with a dozen lipsticks.

He picked up the suitcases and continued through no man's land until he came to a second brick hut with its door ajar. It looked so similar to the first hut that for a moment Sergej feared that he had become disoriented in the fog and mistakenly returned to the Russians. Then he heard Polish and, relieved, stepped up to the door. He tapped on the door and said, "Hello."

Two soldiers glanced up from their chess game. A third stopped doing push-ups and asked for his papers. He spent an inordinate amount of time scrutinizing his bogus commercial papers. Sergej realized it was time for another bottle of vodka to appear. He pulled a flask from a deep jacket pocket, and as soon as the soldier saw it, he exchanged his papers for it.

"You can just scoot around the barrier," he told Sergej.

"Can you raise it?"

"What?"

"It's not how I've imagined it."

The soldier snorted. "I should've guessed. Another first-timer out of Mother Russia, are you?"

"That's right."

"Hey guys, it's another loony who wants me to raise the barrier," he said to the chess players.

"To freedom!" they both shouted.

The soldier joined Sergej outside. The barrier was a simple metal crossbar resting on two posts, with a spring mechanism on one end and fastened by a rope on the other. It would have been easy enough to walk around, and was in fact only symbolic, which was precisely why Dr. Ustinov wanted it lifted. He wanted to walk to freedom with his head held high. It was a moment he had dreamed about, and only he had made it possible.

He stepped up to the crossbar as the soldier slowly let the rope slip through his hands. "The bus is up the road," he told Sergej. "You've got five minutes. You'll make it."

Finally the bar was high enough.

Sergej took his first step into freedom.

With his second one, he landed in a rut and twisted his ankle. He yelped in pain.

"Are you all right, grandpa?" the soldier asked.

He wasn't all right, but Sergej was determined to make it. He gripped the suitcases and took the next painful steps. Every time he landed on his left foot, he winced in pain. Soon he saw the red tail-lights of the bus, then the dark hulk of the bus itself tilting slightly on the edge of the road. Sergej didn't relax his urgent walk and hobbled toward the bus as fast as he could.

The bus horn sounded.

The driver started its engine.

"I'm coming!" Sergej shouted.

He heard the hiss of the brakes being released.

"I'm coming!"

The driver shifted into gear.

"I'm coming! I'm coming!" he begged.

But the driver didn't hear him. He pulled onto the asphalt and started down the road.

"I'm coming. I'm coming." Sergej, distraught, fell into a heap in the middle of the road. "I'm coming."

Suddenly spotlights illuminated the road and the driver saw Sergej in his rearview mirror. Sergej lifted his head, realized the bus had stopped, and struggled to his feet. He hobbled to it.

The driver opened the door. "Welcome to the free world," he greeted him.

CHAPTER TWELVE

GENERAL DRAVKO MLADIC AVOIDED STAYING at Warsaw's flashy new hotels, preferring the comfortable guesthouse run by the same hotelier who had once catered to the Party elite's assorted whimsies. He ran a discreet establishment and knew when to be absent. The rooms still retained their brothel-like decor, though the wallpaper's red flock was noticeably worn and the tassels on the loveseat frayed. Standing at the wet bar, Dravko tossed back a shot of scotch and caught a glimpse of himself in the mirror overhead. He thought he still cut a dashing figure.

He pulled back a curtain to look outside. Snow swirled in the street-lights as pedestrians, bundled against the cold, hurried along the side-walk. How small their lives must be in that shabby neighborhood, the brooding husband or wife they went home to, the television and children, the mediocrity of it all. General Mladic could not conceive of passing through life with so little claim to it.

He crossed the room to close the closet door on the steamer suit-case that Sergej had instructed him to buy. Multiple mirrors of vary-ing sizes (some were only shards) hung everywhere—walls, corners, ceiling—creating infinite images of him, or parts of him, depending on their angle. In the bathroom, too, handy mirrors let him admire himself as he took a piss. Once handsome in a strapping way, Dravko's paunch had surrendered to the combination of gravity's pull and his wife's relentless sausages, but he did not yet see himself as other than desirable. He would soon be king of his new Serbia. He stood straighter, admiring His Highness from many perspectives, when the doorbell rang. He zipped up and opened the door to Basia Husarska.

As she stepped inside, her knees knocked open her full-length fur coat to reveal a miniskirt cut short. "Someone is parked up the street pretending to be asleep," she said.

"Someone who just saw a whore come into the lodge." Dravko closed the door behind her. "They only care if it's a person of interest, and a whore is never interesting unless she's yours for the night."

"Who watches you here?"

"I'm a person of interest wherever I go. I wouldn't be surprised to learn there's still a camera over the bed."

"There's not. I had it removed." Basia flung her fur onto the loveseat. "But just in case, I'll act like your whore."

He smiled. "Of course you will. Champagne?"

She joined him at the bar. "And caviar? You have made a love nest, Dravko."

"'Black, from the Caspian,'" he said, imitating her husky voice. "Those were your first words to me."

"And my first caviar."

"You sounded like you'd been raised on it."

"How long has it been since the Academy? Sixteen years? You were handsome, Dravko. I remember you on the target range. So self-assured, and you never missed."

The cork popped. He filled their glasses and raised his to say, "To Piła."

They clinked glasses and sipped.

"Unfortunately, you've gotten fat," she said.

"I was always too skinny."

"No you weren't." Basia smeared a cracker with caviar. "Have I changed so much?" She stuck the cracker in his mouth. "Don't answer that."

All those years they had known each other, fucked each other, in cautious terms almost said they loved each other, neither wanting to change personal circumstances enough to make living together a possibility. They were both too ambitious to abandon what they might still achieve. After the police academy, Dravko returned to Yugoslavia, and it proved easy for them to arrange a rendezvous two or three times a year, at conferences or trainings or occasional secret vacations, until they became less secret, but by then it didn't matter. They had both become too lethal to blackmail. Nor would Dravko's wife have cared. Ulia would have been more curious that Basia had somehow managed to arouse him; for Basia's part, her Party bosses encouraged her relationship with Serbia's most popular nationalist.

"You're sounding nostalgic tonight," Dravko said.

"Maybe it's the reminder that it's been sixteen years."

"We've been friends a long time."

"Why does that sound like goodbye?"

"It's not. And you *haven't* changed very much," he added.

"You're such a liar."

"It's my professional training."

"Even that's a lie. You never needed training."

"But it's true, you aren't fat."

"Then why haven't you kissed me?"

They did, and he watched them kiss in the mirrors. *His* whimsy was to watch himself make love, or more specifically, watch him make love to himself. He could almost always find mirrors angled in such a way that, in a third mirror, they created a reflective montage in which he appeared to be kissing himself, or blowing himself, or fucking his own ass. When he kissed himself, he saw himself kissing a man, and that specter fueled his arousal. He pushed his tongue deeper into Basia's mouth.

She wasn't ready for sex and rolled out of his arms to light a cigarette. She dominated the mirrors, tall in black boots, hundreds of Basias exhaling a long stream of smoke. "I need to know more about the couriers," she said. "Your smuggling operation has turned into an international murder investigation. Even the American FBI is involved."

"I'm finished here after tonight. It won't matter."

"It matters to me. I need to know what I've been doing so I can protect myself. I've organized the pick-ups, Dravko, and each courier has been murdered."

"Not on my orders."

"You never told me about the uranium until it was accidentally discovered. What are you doing? Building an atomic bomb?"

"Three. The fuel has already been delivered. Tonight's courier is bringing a prototype delivery mechanism with designs to replicate it."

"Then what?" Basia asked.

"What else but Serbia? They called me Mad Max at the Academy, do you remember?"

"I remember."

"Am I so mad now that my mad dreams are coming true?"

"The world won't let you resurrect the old Serbia. Not on the scale that you dream. That's why you're mad, Dravko."

"The world will have no choice."

"You *are* mad."

"It's destiny."

"Can you tell the difference?" Basia stubbed out her cigarette and wagged her empty glass at him. "You are forgetting me."

He refilled their champagne flutes. "To a seventeenth year!" he toasted.

"No, I won't drink to that," Basia replied. "I want a seventeenth year but more than the status quo. You've promised me more. When you talk about your future Serbia, I imagine myself seated next to you, in a chariot or on thrones next to each other. Am I there, Dravko? Am I the one next to you when you imagine yourself the happiest? Because I will be there if you want."

As soon as she mentioned a chariot, or twin thrones, Dravko saw himself seated in them, but not with Basia beside him. She could not be the Mother of Serbia. Ulia, his barren wife, wore the headscarves of tradition, and it was from tradition's lore that Serbia would be born again, not from Basia's irredeemable loins. Ulia would ride beside him in that imaginary chariot. "I never promised you that," he answered.

"I've taken the risks for that," she reminded him. "You wouldn't have your couriers without me. But like you, Dravko, I am finished here. At some point, my tapes won't protect me anymore."

"Your blackmail still works?"

"Why not? The last ones are only three years old," Basia reminded him, "and sometimes I still watch the early ones of us. I believed it when you said you loved me. You did say it, Dravko. I have it on tape."

"There was a time when I was mad about you, but this is foolish talk. Or is it a threat?"

"The boys, Dravko? When did they start?"

"Of course you would know."

"Why else do you get such pleasure from torturing men? And it is only men. You don't care enough for women to torture them. Your torture is narcissistic. You torture yourself."

"You are a psychologist now?"

"You are obsessed with men. I have never seen you look at a woman on the street unless she is looking at your medals."

"I admit, sometimes I want men more than you."

Basia lit another cigarette. "It's true, Dravko, you never promised me a throne. But you promised me an island. I'm redeeming it now."

"Now you're the one who is mad."

"Not a whole island, Dravko. Only an apartment that's not a communist dump and with a sea view. Mad Max owes me that. Some promises you have to keep." Basia sat on the loveseat and patted the spot next to her. "Come. Sit next to me, Dravko."

He drained his champagne and joined her.

"I've made it easy for you tonight," she said and unfastened the top button on her thin sweater. She undid a second button to reveal her shoulders.

He brought his lips to her neck while watching himself in the mirrors.

"Are you already planning your escapes from your acceptable wife?" she asked.

He murmured, "I won't be able to stay away from you."

He tickled her ear with his tongue, and in a mirror saw himself tickling his own ear.

She pulled off her sweater and reached to embrace him.

He stopped looking in the mirrors long enough to glimpse a bruise in the bend of her arm. "What's this?"

"It's nothing. I had a blood test." She tried to pull him into a kiss.

His lips landed on her neck instead. "Are you healthy?"

"I'm healthy. Don't worry, I won't infect you."

Basia drifted a hand across the front of his pants. Coaxingly she toyed with his zipper and pulled him out. He felt the first stirrings of arousal at seeing himself reflected from so many angles in the mirrors. "Let's make your little soldier healthy, too," she said in her sexy voice, and wiggled down the bed, opening his prolific buttons as she did, biting his nipples and nuzzling his soft belly hair before burying her nose in a wirier patch. With her every move, Dravko shifted ever so slightly to find the melded triptychs in the mirrors that showed him biting his own nipple and nuzzling his belly. When he went down on himself, he instantly exploded in Basia's mouth.

While he was recovering, she turned aside and spat him out.

There was no afterplay or cuddling. After seventeen years they had grown too accustomed to each other. They were useful to each other. Their sex had hardened as their lives had.

"You like this part the best," she said.

"What part?"

"When the sex is over."

"I enjoy the sex with you."

"You enjoy sex with yourself. And worry how you'll do."

"Don't all men?"

"Most men assume they're very good or the best."

Basia buttoned her sweater.

"Can you imagine what I am feeling?" he asked.

"I can never imagine what a man is feeling."

"For so many years, I have known what will happen, and how it will be. It's like a film I've rewound and played so many times. I see it that clearly and it always ends the same. I can not change my future."

"I confess, Dravko, I *have* dreamed of being your queen. I know, foolishly."

"Next to me on a chariot?" He smiled at the caricature of himself.

"Oh Dravko, if you only knew my dreams."

"I think I do."

"I dream of days in the sun, having servants—"

"*Slaves.*"

"—rub oil on me. And the boys—"

"*Men.*"

"—massage me. And you, Dravko?"

"We have the same dreams."

He helped Basia into her fur.

"A gentleman to the end."

"It's not the end."

"Of certain dreams, it is. We go too far back to have another begin-ning, but it's only the beginning for you." Basia finished the last bit of champagne. "How does your film end, Dravko? Am I in it to the last scene? Because if I'm not, rewind it and watch it again. I'm there until it says *The End*. I've already memorized my lines."

She left his room.

CHAPTER THIRTEEN

DR. USTINOV FELT A LITTLE woozy after three days of sipping vodka and no sleep other than catnaps. He shared his last flask with the bus driver, who had turned talkative under its influence. How hard life had become, he complained, a dog-eat-dog world where only one thing mattered: money. Now he worked double shifts just to feed his family, and yes, he agreed seven children was excessive, but there they were. He was a man, wasn't he? And his wife, God bless her, had never denied him his conjugal rights. Who were they to deny the Pope his? Birth control was a sacrilege or worse, and what man could synchronize his desire to the few days in a month when it was safe? He couldn't. Not when desire rose every morning as sure as the sun. Ach! It was a hard life, bread cost double what it had only a month ago, and he had eight hungry stomachs to fill, not counting his own. Was there any more vodka in the flask?

The driver tooted his horn after dropping him at Białystok's train station, and Sergej waved goodbye. He felt a momentary pang of sadness, as if bidding farewell to a friend, and entered the train station lugging his twin steamer suitcases. He had not expected the sallow faces or gritty floors or scratchy speakers announcing arrivals and departures. Freedom had always sounded cheerful to him, clean and bright, not this sullenness he recognized from Kosmonovo.

Inside the station, he sought out the left luggage counter. The attendant, dangling a cigarette from his mouth, squinted from the smoke. "Short-term or long?"

Sergej's limited Polish wasn't adequate for the question. "Do you speak Russian?"

The man squashed his cigarette on the floor. "We all learned Russian. They fed it to us like we were geese: by ramming it down our throats. How long you want to check them for?"

"It could be a while."

The man shrugged. "That's more money for me. I'll warn you, rates go up almost every day, and I don't take rubles. You checking both bags?"

Sergej pushed a suitcase forward. "Only one."

The attendant handed him a ticket. "You'll need that to claim it."

Sergej reached into his pocket. He had the money ready, and slipped the man a hundred-dollar bill. "Like I said, it could be a long time. Make sure it doesn't get lost."

The attendant quickly put the money out of sight. "Don't worry about that. And give me back that ticket." The man scribbled on it. "I marked it 'paid in advance.'"

Glad to be rid of one suitcase, Sergej wandered over to the kiosks selling newspapers and snack foods. Attracted to the sex magazines, he reached for one when the vendor stopped him. "You buy it, then you can touch her all you want. You old Russkis. It's like you've never seen dirty pictures before. What, you don't have naked women in Russia?"

"It's a cold country," Sergej said, trying to make a joke of it. "Do you sell vodka?"

The man pointed to a shelf. "That's not bottled water. Fifth, half, or full?"

"Three fifths."

"It's the same price if you buy one liter."

"It's not all for me."

The man wrapped the bottles in newspaper, leaving their necks exposed. "You have a long trip tonight?"

"To Warsaw."

"You just missed the evening train. Russkis!"

Sergej traded money for the bottles and slipped them into his coat pockets. "Do you sell stamps?"

"Do I look like a post office?"

"I want to send a letter to my wife. I'm traveling for the first time away from home. I want to let her know that I arrived."

The man handed back his change. "They got stamps in Warsaw."

Sergej went outside and found a sheltered bench where he'd be easily seen. He sat and massaged his sprained ankle. A bitter wind blew on his neck through a gap in the boards and he pulled his scarf tighter. He took a moment to let it sink in where he was, where he had arrived, and how all his meticulous planning had paid off. Ultimately he had crossed for vodka, which he knew he would, but Sergej Ustinov a border guard? He chuckled at his own guile. For years he hadn't been permitted near a border! All had gone like clockwork, the information he had gleaned at conferences or in Moscow's libraries, surprisingly precise on locations, distances, and timetables. There had been unplanned moments, of course, Emma among them, and he felt his loins stir at her memory. For so long, his love life had exhausted itself between the covers of girlie magazines, forced to donate his sperm—his genius sperm—to upgrade the Soviet Man's eugenic pool. They left him literally too drained to have much enthusiasm for his wife; so much so that eventually they stopped making love altogether. Sergej began to think a woman's naked flesh felt like the magazine pages he touched while making his weekly donation to troubling science.

Natalya was probably in the kitchen when the authorities arrived, the coffee cup in her hand trembling slightly from old age, not fear, but almost dropping it when they knocked—loud, sharp, invasive—on the door. To protect her, he had told her nothing, so she had nothing to tell them and her tears would be real. What had she felt when she realized he was gone? Of course he'd always been honest about how caged he felt, a national treasure rarely let out, almost always to weapons bazaars described as science conferences in the Soviet sphere, and never to the West, where he would likely be kidnapped if he didn't defect first. On rare occasions he bared his anguish to Natalya, dismayed that his sperm was used to bring a sheaf of babies into a world that he was designing weapons to destroy, a world that further anguished him by being off limits. Without his saying so, she sensed he was justifying suicide, and begged him not to do it, preferring he find a way to defect, even if it meant abandoning her, rather than knowing he killed himself because he had stayed.

He rummaged in his satchel for a pen, paper, and envelope. He had always known this moment would come. What to tell Natalya?

He had thought of her on his journey, though not in Kosmonovo until the train had left the station, and not in Emma's abundant arms. When his escape was complete, he had imagined her in their woeful kitchen. Words—he didn't know where they came from—now bombarded him: *love*, and *life mates*, and *thankfulness*. He had predicted this moment to be happy, deliriously happy, and instead he felt emptied, as drained as when he left the clinic, his seed carried away in a test tube. He had wanted to chase after the clinician to reclaim himself, but now he didn't know what to chase after, he felt that empty. Sergej bent over the paper and started to write.

A white van came up the road and slowed. The driver peered at him through the windshield. Sergej, preoccupied with his letter, didn't notice him. Jacek circled back and pulled over as Sergej was sealing his envelope. "Are you the guy I'm taking to Warsaw?"

"If you know General Mladic, I am," Sergej replied.

Jacek jumped out of the van to open the rear compartment. "We don't use names," he told the physicist, grabbing his suitcase.

"Don't knock the latches!" Sergej cautioned.

"Why, is it going to explode?"

"It's possible. Ha!"

Jacek cautiously swung the bag into the back.

Sergej told him, "I want to mail a letter."

"We have post offices in Warsaw. Get in, we got a long drive."

Sergej slipped into the front seat. "You speak Russian?"

"What, am I speaking French?" Jacek spat out the window. "If you Russkis had your way, Russian is *all* we'd be talking." He shifted into gear and pulled away. Soon they were out of town and he sped up.

Sergej said, "You drive fast."

"You got a problem with it?"

He didn't, and pulled a flask from his pocket, "You want a slug of this?"

"Does the Pope pray?"

Sergej unscrewed the top, and Jacek took the bottle and drank from it. When he tried to hand it back, Sergej refused it, saying, "I have my own." They rode a distance in silence, tipping from their bottles, until the physicist finally asked, "Did you pick up my sons? Three of them. The last crossed six weeks ago."

"Yeah, I picked them up. I thought I was going crazy thinking they all looked like the same fucking scarecrow, and you're the fucking scarecrow!"

"I'm tall," Sergej admitted.

Jacek snorted. "You're more than tall."

A two-way radio suddenly had a burst of static. Through the noise they heard a woman ask, "Are you there?"

Jacek picked up the handset. "Yeah, I'm here. We're about an hour out."

"There's been a change in plans. Bring him to Centralna," she said, referring to Warsaw's central train station.

"What the fuck do I care?" He hung up.

Sergej asked, "Is there a problem?"

"You ask a lot of questions."

"I don't like it when plans change."

"They only changed for me, not you."

Suddenly Jacek pulled off the road.

Alarmed, Sergej asked, "What are you doing?"

Jacek opened the van's door. "Taking care of nature. I gotta piss."

Sergej joined him on the side of the road. They both looked up at the thin stringy clouds crossing the moon as they splattered the bushes. "I can't do this at home," he told Jacek. "People are always watching."

"No wonder you Russkis are full of shit!"

Jacek laughed at his lame joke all the way back to the van.

Sergej said, "You don't know what it's like, always having someone watching you. It can make you crazy. Ha!"

"It did you, that's for sure."

Soon a dirty orange glow appeared on the horizon. Warsaw. Sergej watched it approaching with awe. How many times had he studied his map of Russia, tracing its borders as a prisoner paces his jail cell, until he had worn the borders away? To be in Warsaw meant he had escaped and was on his way to America.

"So you really got a bomb back there?" Jacek asked.

"It's my passport to a new life!" Sergej replied, giddy with anticipation.

"Or a heavenly one if it explodes. So where are you planning this new life?"

"New York! Ha!"

"It takes money to go to New York."

"One million dollars! Ha!"

Jacek glanced at the physicist, curious if he was sincere. "A million dollars? What the fuck is it, an atomic bomb?"

"Ha!"

Jacek drained his vodka and tossed the bottle out the window.

• • •

LILKA CAME AROUND THE CORNER illuminated by spotlights on the theater's ivory columns. She had a self-conscious walk, like a child wearing high heels and worried about embarrassing herself. Jay kissed her and told her she was beautiful.

She started to weep.

"Is something wrong?"

She sniffed. "I am sorry. I am so stupid."

"You can tell me."

"It's only, Jacek is so mean and you are so nice."

New boyfriends were always at a loss how far to go in reviling an ex-husband, and Jay's task was complicated by the fact that he didn't know anything about hers. Not to mention that they still lived together in some torturous arrangement. "Did something happen?" he asked.

"Let me tell you later when I'm not going to cry."

"Okay."

They joined the opera-goers streaming through the wide doors. Chandeliers sprinkled them with light. While the theater had retained its original neoclassical façade, inside contemporary design had invaded, bringing lots of glass and mirrors.

"We have time for a glass of wine," Jay suggested.

They found the bar and he ordered, "*Wino biały*."

"Your Polish is improving."

"You wait. I'll graduate to 'red wine' next."

"I prefer white."

They clinked glasses. Around them, the crowd chattered in a buzz of anticipation. Here and there, an ostentatious gown or gaudy jewelry shouted nouveaux riches, but for the most part the crowd was a common lot, dressed up in their best and having a good time. Lapel pins had become the fashion for men, displaying tiny flags or the logos of goodwill groups. Solidarity's wavy signature, once a lonely standard-bearer for the resistance, now competed for lapel space with the emblems of aid organizations which handed out souvenir pins like gimme caps.

"I realize that I never really asked if you like opera," Jay said.

"Oh yes, very much, and *Madame Butterfly* is my favorite. It's a sad story, especially for their son, but still, it is my favorite. Sometimes I come alone."

"Your husband didn't like it?"

"So much changed in Jacek. Jay—" she said, and stopped herself.

"What is it?"

"I am scared for my son."

"Why? What's happened?"

"Jacek makes me afraid to tell you because you are a policeman."

"I'm not a policeman in Poland."

"Aleks is using heroin. Jacek told me this morning. He gives it to him, I am sure. His own son!" Lilka's eyes welled up with tears. "I don't know what to do."

Jay touched her arm. "There's got to be help available. Do you go to church?"

"My mother does."

"Ask her priest if the church has a program to help. Or knows of one. I'll ask at the embassy, too."

The lights flashed and a bell sounded. "Are you okay to go in?"

Dabbing her eyes with a tissue, Lilka nodded that she was.

• • •

JACEK DROVE THEM THROUGH A congestion of high-rises that were dreary even at night. The yellow streetlights cast sinister shadows. Closer to the center, it was livelier but no cheerier. Staring up at the Stalinist-era Palace of Culture, Sergej's heart sank. "It looks like Moscow," he muttered in disbelief.

"Same flies, too," Jacek said.

They pulled into the central station's parking lot. Dr. Ustinov retrieved his suitcase and followed Jacek into the building. Trains moving through its bowels rumbled beneath their feet. Everything smelled vaguely of soot and piss. Sober, bundled-up people and drunks with lolling tongues scraped past him, lost in private worlds as grim as the world Sergej thought he had escaped. Freedom, he was learning, had many faces, and hopelessness was among them.

Jacek left him in a corner of the vast station. "You don't move," he said firmly. "I'll be back in ten minutes."

Sergej set down his suitcase. "Where is General Mladic?"

"Just don't move."

"What about my letter?"

Jacek was already walking off to disappear down an escalator.

Dr. Ustinov looked around him, gawking. He had seen very little in his life, which had largely been confined to laboratories in secret concrete towns that epitomized monotony. Occasionally he had traveled to Moscow but had been confined to conference hotels. At that moment, what truly startled him was how many people were traveling, especially how many people had suitcases they pulled on wheels. In Mother Russia, where traveling was so restricted as to be forbidden, it would be tantamount to a public confession of sedition to announce you were such a savvy traveler. Of course, not everyone in that vast station was a traveler. Closer to earth—indeed, sleeping on it—the new economy's detritus competed for space on flattened cardboard boxes.

Sergej's stomach growled, reminding him that he'd eaten a tuna sandwich Jacek grudgingly offered, and before that, almost zilch for three days. He glanced around to see what he might find to eat. A row of kiosks held the only promise of food and he carried his suitcase over to them. He settled on cream pastries and scarfed them down, leaving a film of frosted sugar on his lips. "Do you know who sells stamps?" he asked the vendor.

The man pointed to a newsstand. "He does."

When he asked at the newsstand, the vendor, rummaging in a drawer, said, "To Moscow, huh? I wish we could send all you Russkis back to Moscow for a postage stamp. I only have stamps for post-cards."

"But it's a letter."

"I can see it's a letter. You can ask tomorrow at the post office."

"No, no," Sergej protested. "Just give me enough stamps."

"How many you want? The price goes up every day."

"Five?" Sergej had no idea. He'd overlooked researching the price of postage.

"Make it six if you want guaranteed delivery," the man said. "Three thousand zlotys. There's a mailbox by the escalator. Just there."

Sergej followed the man's finger to a post box with a collection schedule that had disappeared under graffiti. He decided to trust the sturdy iron box and deposited his letter. When he turned back to face the crowded station, Sergej couldn't remember where Jacek had told him to stay. He set down his suitcase to watch for his return. People streamed past him, stooped over with suitcases and worries, and to a person they failed to look up, which is where Dr. Ustinov was looking. He had glimpsed a bird, and he craned his neck to watch it flit about the skeletal ceiling.

• • •

JACEK NAVIGATED THE UNDERGROUND MAZE of corridors choked with stale air. Only a few vendors remained open. From the end of one deserted tunnel, he heard Basia's laughter and followed it to the half-open door where rotating beer signs lit up Billy's Bar. Basia sat on the middle stool of a threesome with smoke drizzling up her chin from a loosely held cigarette. She laughed at something said by the man seated next to her. He had slicked-back hair and a rumpled suit and watched Basia's legs, not her face, calculating when he dared to press his knee to hers. Basia puckered her rust-colored lips and sent a smoke ring past him.

Billy's woman pushed a broom in Jacek's direction without looking at him. Like Billy, she was a castoff: too ugly for the world, with circles as dark as bruises under her eyes. "She said she's waiting for you," the woman muttered.

"What's she been up to?" he asked.

"She can tell you."

The stranger, emboldened by Basia's laughter, dropped his hand to her knee.

Jacek slipped up to the bar and sat next to her.

"That's a sweet story," Basia said to the stranger, and pursed her lips as if ready to kiss him. She turned and kissed Jacek instead.

He succumbed to her dishonest mouth.

"Hey! I bought you that drink," the stranger protested.

Basia shot him a smile. "Thanks."

She got off the stool, careful not to let her fur touch the phlegmy floor, and followed Jacek into the passage. "Where's the Russian?" Basia asked.

Jacek turned on her angrily. "Our deal is, you stay clear of my business."

"I didn't come here on police business," she replied, "if that's why you're worried."

"Police business, that'd be something new for you. You've been buying shit here, haven't you?"

"When I don't get it from you."

He grabbed her arm and pushed her up against a steel shutter; it reverberated in the empty corridor. "I don't remember ever refusing you," Jacek said, "not when you ask nicely." Then he pressed his mouth hard to hers.

When he let her go, she wiped her mouth of his and said, "Mladic wants me to handle the exchange tonight. Alone."

"The fuck you will."

"He knows this one. Where is he?"

"By the magazines. He's been talking about a bomb in his suitcase—an *atomic* bomb— and a million dollars. Something a lot bigger's going on than he's told you, and he hasn't been paying us enough if it's as big as what I'm thinking."

"Leave the thinking to me."

They came to the bottom of the escalator and Jacek held her back. "I think we should take this guy's suitcase and see what Mladic is willing to pay for it."

"I'm not double-crossing Mladic. People who do end up eating their own guts. Now let's find the Russian before he disappears."

Jacek followed her up the escalator.

• • •

DR. USTINOV WATCHED BASIA SLOWLY emerge from underground on the halting escalator. Her fur coat hung open to reveal long legs sheathed by black stockings. She looked as glossy and sexy as if she'd stepped off the page of one of his girlie magazines. He recognized Jacek behind her, and realized they were together. Dravko had sent that black-clad angel of seduction for him! Sergej raised a hand and feebly waved.

Her knees bobbed in the slit of her coat as she approached him. Jacek had disappeared; Sergei hadn't noticed where. "Are you the mad Russian scientist I am here to meet?" she asked.

"I hope so," he said.

"Come with me."

She didn't seem especially friendly, and Sergej asked, "Where's General Mladic?"

"That's where we are going."

Outside the station, Basia dodged cars while drivers leered at her through windshields that distorted their hungry smiles. Sergej, hauling his suitcase, struggled to keep up. When they reached her car, Basia popped the trunk. "Put your suitcase in there."

He stumbled lifting it, and she reached to help, knocking it on the bumper. Sergej flinched, and nervously she asked, "How sensitive is this?"

He pressed his wobbly teeth into an anxious grin. "There's a trick to the latches."

She closed the trunk. "Get in."

Even unlit, the dashboard instruments appeared luminescent, and Dr. Ustinov touched them as if examining crystal formations.

He'd designed satellites with less gadgetry. "Who *are* you?" he asked, impressed that she had such a car. "Dravko never mentioned you."

"I'm a present. Perhaps I should have worn a bow."

She pulled into the street and rolled down both their windows to blow out his putrescent breath. "Dravko said you would like me."

"Like you? Ha!" Sergej fantasized running his fingers up her stockinged thigh, or kissing her neck where shadows bled like bruises on her creamy skin. He was about to touch her when she asked:

"Do you want to spend some time with me? Before we meet Dravko? I know a spot for us."

"A spot for us! Ha!"

She made a sudden left turn and accelerated into traffic. Sergej was thrown back in the seat. Suddenly freedom was fun—he'd couldn't recall ever being in a car so fast—and he laughed and slapped his knees. Soon she veered onto a cobbled ramp and cut her lights to follow the service road a short distance along the river's embankment. The only houseboat along that stretch appeared abandoned, and the steady snow had kept away anyone else.

Basia pulled to a stop. "Welcome to Lovers' Lane," she said.

Lovers! Sergej couldn't contain himself and lunged for her. "You're so beautiful!"

"Wait. The car's too small." Basia got out, flung aside her cigarette, and reached back for her purse. "I always carry something for protection."

She started for the river before Sergej could unwind himself from the seat and scramble after her. "I'm healthy," he cried gleefully, "the clinic made sure of that!" He slipped on the steep part of the embankment, and when he'd picked himself up, Basia had stopped to turn to him and open her arms, spreading her fur coat like a welcoming cocoon.

Sergej slipped his arms into her warmth.

She said, "Don't kiss me."

His legs trembled from excitement. With one hand anchored to her waist, he used the other to rummage at his fly.

"I've got a little cap for that," said Basia, and fumbled in her purse.

"You're right, we don't need to start a family yet! I already have my three sons. They made the first deliveries."

"Dravko only told me about the last one."

"The lab technician," Sergej remembered proudly, then cocked his head. "I never told Dravko about my sons. How did you——"

Her bullet punctured his heart.

He sagged against her, and in a moment so brief that he would have calculated it in nanoseconds, he knew the answer. "Ha!" he said.

Basia stepped back to let him fall on the ground.

From nearby, a man cleared his throat. She saw the burning end of his cigarette before she saw him. "What took you so long?" she asked.

"I was probably here before you left the station. Where else were you going to take him?"

Jacek rolled the dead physicist onto his back, popped open his switchblade, and slit his cheek, folding it back to reveal his teeth. "It's a shame to leave so much gold behind," he remarked. He wiped his knife clean on Sergej's clothes and twisted off his wedding ring.

Basia's lighter flared in her face. "He tried to kiss me." She shuddered at the thought and pulled hard on the tobacco.

"What are you going to tell Mladic when this guy's suitcase shows up but he doesn't?"

Basia inhaled deeply from the cigarette trembling in her fingers and tossed it away. "Let's hold onto the suitcase. I'll convince him to stay until I come up with a plan."

"Don't blame his no-show on me. I don't want to eat my own guts, either."

"I'm just holding him to his promises."

Jacek snorted. "What, is he reneging on the island? You got blood on your coat."

A car turned off the main road and started down the ramp. Bouncing on the cobblestones, its headlights strafed them. Jacek pulled Basia into an embrace and moved her over to block the driver's view of the body. The car paused on the ramp. It was slick and too narrow to turn around, and the driver came all the way down to the embankment. Basia, still high, encouraged Jacek's tongue, and their mouths pressed together so steadfastly that no one would dare interrupt them. The driver didn't. He retreated up the ramp with his tires spinning.

Basia had enough and pushed Jacek away.

"We could be a good team," he said. "You the 'inside man' except you're a woman, and I got the van. It wouldn't take too many deals to set ourselves up on an island."

"I'm finished with everything here."

"And you're trusting Dravko?"

"He wants what this one was bringing."

"Is it what this guy said it was?"

"An atomic bomb," she confirmed. "A small one."

"Fuck."

"That's why Mladic is willing to pay so much."

"You have an atomic bomb *in your car?*"

"It's not going to go off just like that. Let's get away from here."

They retraced their steps up the short embankment, their earlier footprints already blurred by the wet snow. When they reached her car, Jacek said, "There's been another change in plans." He reached into the driver's door to pop her trunk. "I'm taking the suitcase."

"You don't trust me?" Basia asked.

"Why would I start tonight?"

"Careful!" she warned when Jacek banged the suitcase lifting it out. "Don't knock the latches."

• • •

GENERAL MLADIC WASN'T A PUBLIC man. He enjoyed power but not the glitter of bars, women, and other temptations that his power awarded him. They made him anxious: he had to perform. However, establishing an alibi on the nights the couriers crossed was part of Dr. Ustinov's careful plan, and there was no better place to be seen in Warsaw than the Marriott's bar.

"Another one?" asked the barman.

Dravko slid his glass toward him. "Sure."

The barman—or barboy, really, he had such boyish features—poured

two fingers of scotch, dropped one ice cube into it, and passed it
back. "I've seen you in here before, haven't I?"

So the barman had remembered him.

"I remember you, too," Dravko said.

"Who can forget your medals?"

Dravko tried to see himself in the mirror behind the rows of liquor
bottles. His chest of medals was no less colorful.

"You must be a real hero," the young man remarked.

"Because of these?"

"They look heavy to carry around."

"I'm used to them."

"So you're in good shape, too. You look like you are. Don't go
away."

He stepped away to serve another customer.

Dravko watched him until the TV diverted his attention. He recognized Sarajevo, and even if he didn't understand all of the broadcast-
er's English, the footage of people running to avoid a sniper's bullet
was message enough: the siege was underway, and he felt a swelling
sense of pride.

The barman came back. "How are you fixed with that drink?"

"I'm okay."

"I could top it off."

"I have to be somewhere."

"Me too, and I wish it weren't here. Are you staying at the hotel?"

"No."

"Too bad. I get off in a couple of hours, and I bet each one of
these babies"—the barman reached across the bar to touch his medals—"has a story to tell. Maybe I'll see you later at the Arena, and you
can tell me one or two."

"The Arena?"

"Any cabbie knows the baths. I'm there most nights after work,
unless I get lucky with a hotel guest. Too bad you're not one. I'd
like to keep you topped up all night." The barman winked before he
stepped away to serve other customers.

Dravko sensed he was blushing. He had never been so blatantly propositioned, certainly not by a man. He found himself staring at him, and only glanced away when he realized he was becoming obvious. He looked at the television instead. The Sarajevo sniper story had been updated with footage of a woman throwing herself on an infant to protect it. When they didn't show if the infant had been hit, Dravko, disappointed, knocked back his scotch and left the bar.

• • •

BASIA STEPPED INTO HIS ROOM.

Dravko shut the door behind her. His steamer suitcase sat by the door, ready to go.

"You can put that away," she said. "Your man didn't show, so we're not going to the shack." Basia had traded her blood-splattered fur for a shiny black jacket. She stubbed out a cigarette and looked at Dravko as if *he* owed an explanation. "He never made it to the pick-up in Białystok. Jacek circled the station for two hours."

"He was supposed to leave after thirty minutes so not to draw attention to himself," Dravko replied critically.

"He thought he was doing you a favor."

"Where's your fur coat?"

"I spilled a drink on it. So I need another one. It appears that the scotch is already open."

"I'll get it," he said quickly, but she was already there.

"What is this?" Basia held up a magazine with bare-chested men on its glossy cover.

He snatched it from her and tossed it aside.

"You are hiding it from me?"

"It's a diversion. Such magazines are not available at home."

Basia settled on the loveseat, reaching for the magazine. She flipped through the pictures of men engaged in various acts of primitive masculinity. "We thought we had not so many decadent desires as in the West, isn't that so, Dravko? Is it liberating for you to know how common these things are? I imagine not. How unsettling it must be for you, to control so many things and yet be unable to control your own passions. What will you do when you have achieved your destiny? When you rule Serbia. Will you live with your demons—the world be damned!—or will you continue to fight them?"

"They will have no place in Serbia," he said flatly.

"No queers and no Muslims. How certain you are of your perfect world. What happens, Dravko, if you don't fit in the world of your own making?"

He tossed back his scotch, and in the overhead mirror glimpsed Basia's booted calves hanging off the loveseat. For many years she had been diversion enough. How quickly he had grown tired of his wife who, once married, thickened at the waist, grew stouter in the legs, and became too reminiscent of his mother to even contemplate carnal pleasure. He abandoned their bed without explanation, relegated his marriage to the rank of civic duty and sought pleasure elsewhere. Basia's tricks exposed him to a troubling sensuality and freed him to conjure fantasies he could not even name, had he dared. They beckoned him with bodies resembling his own, and soon enough, he found himself searching the faces of men for evidence of shared desire. Would that he could vanquish his lust! Uproot it from his soul and cast it away! Dravko brooded over his shame. Even the tortured confessions he prodded from his victims failed to mollify his sense of unique sin.

Basia held up the magazine to show him a boy. "You were once so handsome."

Indeed, Dravko recognized a semblance of his youth in the stocky, smooth-skinned lad with a pouting rosebud mouth. "Do you remember me like that?"

"*You* remember you like that. How is it possible for a man to love himself and hate himself so equally?" she asked.

"What exactly did Jacek say?"

"Mystery Man Number Four didn't show, that's what he said. He'll go back tomorrow."

"Sergej always said he'd only cross on a Monday."

Basia put the magazine next to her on the loveseat, open to the pouting lad. "Things don't run on time in Russia. Apparently not even the days of the week. What do you want Jacek to do?"

"Go back tomorrow, I suppose, on your theory that he's only delayed."

"And if he doesn't show tomorrow?"

"He'll cross next Monday."

Basia took hold of his belt and pulled him to her. "Perhaps I can convince you to stay a week, Dravko. We've been friends for too long to abandon each other. You will be king, Ulia your queen, and I will have my island. My villa. When you want, you will come for me, and we will all live happily ever after."

She drew him closer and fondled him through his trousers.

She opened his buckle.

Unzipped his pants.

Pulled him out.

He saw himself reflected in the mirrors and thickened.

He watched her kiss him.

She said: Your barman *is* beautiful.

She said: It could be a fun week, Dravko.

She said: Your war can wait a week.

In the mirrors it was the boy's rosebud lips that slipped over his cock. ·

• • •

AN USHER HAD GUIDED THEM down the center aisle and given them programs. Lilka was thrilled by their good seats. They watched as people filled the red velvet rows that rose to the black vaulted ceiling. The lights dimmed. To applause, the conductor took his stand and lifted his baton. The last whispers evaporated. He struck the air, unleashing runaway strings. The curtain opened to reveal a romantic cottage in Japan. Jay didn't have to search for her hand; she had it ready for him. In song, Butterfly prayed for her captain to return, but prayers answered are not always blessings, and when he did return it was to take their son; certainly, she must understand, a better life waited for him over the horizon. Lilka pulled more tissues from her purse long before their ill-fated love entirely played out. In the opera's final moments, her chest heaved with stifled sobs. Jay, too, was moved. He had forgotten that the opera was as much a custody battle as a tragic love story.

The audience clamored their approval. The hall lights rose, and around them, more than a few sniffles were extinguished. A final wail of appreciation rose from the crowd, and the cast came forward and bowed a last time. Their tears brought forth a great communal sob. Then a collective sigh escaped, the sadness gave way, and the audience, now chattering, gathered itself to leave.

Leaving the theater, Lilka said, "It was perfect. Thank you. But sad, yes? The American thinks Cio-cio-san is only a toy, but she loves him very much. Their cultures are so different, they can't understand each other."

"Do you understand me when I say I want to invite you home?"

"Your home in America?"

"My home at my hotel. I have caviar. 'Only five American dollars.'"

She smiled. "I remember."

"And I'll order French champagne."

"It sounds romantic."

"Good. Where did you park?"

"At your hotel. I thought it was practical."

"Practical?"

"In case you invite me home."

Lilka wanted to walk to the hotel. The icy air was refreshing. They crossed the broad square and detoured down smart Nowy Świat, where the first wave of post-communist shops were struggling to survive in a blistering economy. She guided them to a terrace in a wooded area overlooking the river where they leaned over the balustrade to see headlights flicker on the midnight water. Jay wrapped his arms around her and kissed the back of her neck.

"My father taught me all the stars," Lilka said. "We went camping every summer, and it was my favorite game to find them. It's fascinating, isn't it, the sky?"

"The notion of infinity actually frightens me," Jay admitted. "Maybe more than anything else."

"You are a lucky man, then."

"I am tonight."

She turned in his arms and their mouths opened to their own language. How long they stood there they couldn't say, but by the time they next looked, the stars had disappeared. "It's going to rain," Lilka murmured, but they didn't leave their spot until the first icy drops tormented them.

A taxi passed and they ran for it and made it to Jay's hotel and into his room. Again their mouths sought each other. His fingers fumbled with the buttons on her purple dress while she undid his belt. Their clothes fell silently to the floor. They sank onto the bed, legs entwined, exhausting themselves for the first of many times that night until the telephone rang.

It was Kulski. There had been another murder.

The fourth courier.

PART TWO

CHAPTER FOURTEEN

ONCE THE ROPES PREVENTED HIS plunging into the murky, swirling river, Jay struggled to stand back up on the slippery gangplank. When he saw the light go out in the houseboat, he looked back around to where the fourth courier's body had fallen. It was easy to spot by a telltale piece of incident tape twisting in the wind. If whoever was in the houseboat was home the night before, he only had to look out a window to witness the murder.

Rocked by the wind, the boat strained at its moorings as Jay lurched onto the deck. He knocked on a door, and when no one answered, he knocked again before brushing snow off its window to peer inside. It wasn't a lamp that had been turned off, but a lantern, flickering because its battery was dying. Was it evidence of a hasty departure? Who forgot to turn off a battery-powered light? Mail lay scattered on the desk, which Jay wanted to look at, and he was pondering the consequences of not having a search warrant under Polish law when he pressed down on the door handle. It gave way.

"You! Stop!" The shout was in Polish but its meaning unmistakable. He followed the words back to shore, where a policeman tried to wave him off the houseboat. "*Policja!*" he cried.

"Me too *policja*," he shouted back and flashed his FBI badge. "*Amerikanski policja!* Detective Kulski!"

Jay ducked inside and made a quick inventory of the room: an armchair, a desk, a roughly made bed. A man lived there, he guessed by the clothing tossed about, and he was single because of the absence of anything remotely feminine. In the corner stood a spotting scope. The Vistula's errant seagulls were hardly exotic enough to warrant such an elegant spyglass. Jay suspected he was a Peeping Tom with an eye on Lovers' Lane. Maybe Kulski had a Peeping Witness, too, because this Tom had had a view of the last murder—if he'd been looking.

He heard the policeman slip on the gangplank and glanced to make sure he hadn't fallen in the river. He hadn't; the ropes had caught him as well. In two steps, Jay was at the little desk. The mail had been sent to addresses across the United States, and to names as equally varied. A Trent living in Atlantic City had morphed into a Thomas in Las Vegas or a Terry in Tucson. Jay shuffled through the envelopes. Most were bills with nothing more personal than solicitations for cruises and health magazines. Yet someone was forwarding it to the houseboat resident.

The policeman picked himself up. "Hey you!" he shouted.

Jay looked around for the envelope that had been used to forward the mail.

"Hey you!"

He found the manila envelope in the trash—

"Hey you!"

—and stuffed it into his coat pocket just as the policeman arrived at the door.

Jay raised his hands. "English?"

"A little. You go outside!"

"I work with Detective Kulski."

"Detective Kulski told me." The cop pointed to a sheltered spot under the bridge. "I am watching from there."

Good. Kulski already had the houseboat staked out.

The cop followed him up the service ramp and waited until he flagged down a taxi. He slipped into the back seat, glad for the heater's warmth. Jay had been in Warsaw less than a week, yet the streets already had a familiar feel. Perhaps it was their bleak monochromy—gray sidewalks, gray buildings, gray faces, gray sky—that made it seem like he had been there much longer. A red banner, curling in the wind outside a high window, caught his eye, much as a red kerchief once had in Shanghai, curling behind a fast-pedaling girl in a sea of black bikes, black clothes, black hair. Its rebelliousness had been so blatant that Jay had worried for her. Straining to see the red banner unfurl overhead, he glimpsed its revolutionary message in a single rippling word: *Solidarność*. Solidarity.

Outside the embassy, he sorted through the deflated currency and handed the taxi driver a careless wad. The guard, relentlessly following orders, checked his passport again. Jay earnestly needed to pee, but without more chestnuts to bribe the receptionist, she took her time clearing him. He nearly jogged to the men's room.

Kurt arrived just as he did.

"You look more urgent," he said, and opened the door for him.

"Thanks."

Ambassador Lerner was already at the middle urinal. Jay went to his left and Kurt took the right. "Looks like a full house," the diplomat remarked.

"A full bladder, that's for sure," Jay told him.

Kurt said, "I'm just along for the ride."

They all stared at the wall in front of them. Jay was musing whether there was a particular etiquette for urinating while touching elbows with an ambassador when the senior diplomat drawled, "Are you enjoying yourself, Porter?"

"Sir?"

"I know what it's like being on the road with more than time on your hands." He zipped up and clapped Jay's shoulder hard enough to disturb his aim. "There are some pretty women in this country. I hope it's not all work."

Kurt glanced at Jay's splattered shoes and grinned at him.

They all converged on the sink.

"There was another murder last night," Jay told them.

Pulling out a paper towel, Lerner asked, "A fourth courier?"

"The assumption is yes."

The ambassador tossed away his paper towel. "You men grab yourselves some coffee and be in my office in ten minutes."

Embassy coffee was about the last thing Jay wanted but it was the first thing he needed. There hadn't been a cup in sight from the moment he'd been summoned to view the dead body on the riverbank. He filled a cup halfway with the scorched coffee and returned to the ambassador's office. Kurt was on his heels and shut the door behind them.

Ambassador Lerner waited for them to settle in the chairs facing his desk. "I'll be goddamned if there hasn't been another murder." Looking at Kurt, he emphasized, "And Mladic is back in town. Unfortunately our intelligence agencies don't think it's intelligent to share their secrets. We don't call *that* intelligent where I come from. Porter has need-to-know clearance from me."

"General Dravko Mladic heads up Yugoslavia's Security Service," Kurt began. "He comes to Warsaw on a regular basis, a little too often for diplomacy even if his job entails browbeating his fellow Slavs to support his Serbian cause. It's Langley's guess that he's our weapons buyer."

"Why is this need-to-know for me?"

"Mladic has been in town for every murder," the ambassador said.

"So were a million other people."

"Mladic arrived yesterday around five," Kurt replied.

"You think he's the killer?"

"It's doubtful that he's the actual hatchet man, but the pattern is too coincidental. He arrives Monday, the murders happen that night, and he leaves Tuesday."

"Presumably leaving with whatever the couriers brought him in his diplomatic pouch?" Jay asked.

"That's how we think he brings in the cash to pay for weapons, too. With the nuclear angle, it's all the more likely that Mladic is involved. Nuclear blackmail is persuasive if you're trying to grab as much land as possible for a new country. He'd only have to set off one device to claim whatever territory he wanted."

"If he tries, that fight will spread faster than fire in an oil field," the ambassador remarked. "He might as well declare World War III."

"That's why Langley is worried. A conventional war can be contained, but nukes in the hands of a megalomaniac? It could easily become global."

"How do you figure Mladic and the murders?"

"That's your case, but it's obvious they're disposable. Single use," Kurt said. "Does he even know that they're being killed?"

"How couldn't he know?" the ambassador asked.

Kurt shrugged. "In the weapons world, there are scenarios we can't predict until they happen."

"How close are your tabs on him?"

"We know when he's here, when he leaves, and when he has an appointment at PENZIK. He stays at the former lodge where the Party used to put up its *nomenklatura*. Make that a whorehouse complete with red flocked wallpaper. That was one perk the Party men gladly bestowed upon themselves. Some of the guys from the past still like to stay there. A couple of times women have been seen entering or leaving the place when we know he's there, but the place is a swinging door for old whores, and we don't know whose room they're going to. They only stay long enough to fuck, so we assume that's what's happening."

"What about the nights of the murders? Does he have an alibi?"

"He's been at the Marriott's bar the night of every murder. We have spotters there almost every evening. It's flashy and Western, and anyone in town who's vaguely important wants to be seen having a drink there."

"It's where business takes place," Carl elaborated. "Plus, it has the only restaurant that actually has what it offers on the menu."

"Mladic isn't a big-time socializer," Kurt added, "so his showing up at the Marriott is odd."

"Like he wants to be seen," Jay said.

"Or talk it up with a particular barman who happens to work Monday nights."

"Do you make something of that?"

"Reportedly, General Mladic enjoys torturing boys more than he should. My pop psychologist says he's a self-loathing homosexual, and there's a whole profile on the type to back me up."

The ambassador grunted. "Nationalist, pederast, torturer—all in one. A real Serbian success story."

"A success story we don't want him to build on," Kurt said. "He's booked on the evening flight. We need to find a way to keep him here."

"We can't exactly hogtie him," the ambassador muttered.

"Play to his ego," Jay suggested. "Invite him for a diplomatic tête-à-tête with the future president of a new Serbia."

"Maybe you FBI boys got a way to goose the system, but it'll take me days to get State's clearance, especially to meet with a pariah like Mladic." Carl looked exasperated.

"Then just do it," Kurt advised. "If you save the world, no one will care about clearances."

"Once he's gone, he's gone," Jay added.

"Ah hell, I know you're right. Now get the hell out of my office while I figure a way to cover my ass while shooting myself in the foot. That's some gymnastics I'm not used to."

As Jay passed Millie's desk, she stopped him. "Oh Mr. Potter, here are your messages."

"Remember your clue-minder, Millie. I'm Mr. Porter, the man with the lost baggage."

"Your baggage is lost?" she asked.

"Was lost. Past tense." He looked at the first message. "The autopsy is at four," he told Kurt.

"You have all the fun."

"And Lilka's brother-in-law called to confirm an appointment on Thursday. He's applied for a visa and I offered to try to help."

"Is Lilka the hennaed brunette?"

"How do you know she's brunette?"

Kurt could hardly hold back his smile. "The same way we track everybody."

Out of Millie's earshot, Jay said, "I suppose I need to report an infraction of the fraternization rule."

"Technically it's no longer an infraction, only a precaution."

"Trust me, it was an infraction."

Kurt laughed. "Don't share the details, just her name."

"Lilka. Lilka Rypinska."

"Lilka Rypinska. Where does she live?"

Jay admitted he didn't know.

"And you're helping her brother-in-law get a visa to the US?"

"He's a decent guy. Besides, he can quote JFK's entire inauguration speech."

"If she's Rypinska, her husband would be Rypinski, that's how they do male and female names here."

"Ex-husband. His name is Jacek."

"I'll dump her name into the system and see if anything pops up."

They arrived at Jay's office.

"I'll put together a file on Mladic for you," Kurt offered. "He's in an interesting position. Quasi-government, quasi-military with control of a heavily armed security force with fierce loyalty to him."

"Not someone who should get an A-bomb."

"Let's make sure he doesn't."

Back in his office, Jay pulled out the manila envelope he'd snatched from the houseboat. He flattened it on his desk. It was addressed to "Tomasz Tomski c/o Poste Restante." That had to be the houseboat person's real name, because he needed official ID to pick up his letters. Excited by possibly having a witness, he glanced at his watch to decide if he should call Ann Rewls at the office or home. It was far too early for her to be at the office, but he was so out of sync with time—it seemed impossible to have been in Lilka's arms and on a dead man's riverbank before the same noon—that he didn't realize quite how early it was. He dialed her home number.

It rang once.

It was five in the morning her time.

He hung up and stared at the phone guiltily.

It rang.

He picked it up. "How did you know it was me?"

"No one else calls in the middle of the night and hangs up."

"I forgot the time difference."

"What is it, Jay, you want to tell me about your date last night?"

"How did you know about my date last night?"

"I was guessing."

"Are you jealous?"

"Noise Machine has a cold and you're making love to a woman who, knowing your taste, is very beautiful."

"Are you looking for a compliment?"

"From you, only a pat on the head and another couple hours' sleep."

"I'll call back later."

"I'm awake. Besides, I feel guilty waking up Noise Machine to tell him to roll over again."

"Then hopefully this is something you can do in your sleep. See what you can find on this guy: Tomasz Tomski. I'll spell it for you." He did, then explained the circumstances surrounding the envelope.

"Taking evidence from a crime scene doesn't sound exactly legal," Ann reminded him.

"I solve my cases, don't I? I've got more names for you. They're what I can remember from the letters sent in the bigger envelope."

Jay recited what he recalled. When he finished, she commented, "The guy has a thing about Ts, doesn't he?"

"Maybe it makes it easier to remember so many names."

"It would make it harder for me." Ann yawned and said, "If I imagine Ned's snoring as white noise, sometimes I can put myself back to sleep."

"You sound tired."

"I am, and I won't be pretty in the morning."

"You were pretty last week."

"That was pre–morning sickness. You want a description?"

"No."

"Before I put on makeup?"

"Definitely not."

"I should get Ned to take a picture."

"It might ruin your marriage."

"You're right, bad idea," she said, and hung up.

CHAPTER FIFTEEN

THEIR TIRES RUMBLED ON THE girdered Poniatowski Bridge. Dark clouds extinguished the dying sun on the horizon.

The driver had to concentrate on staying between lane markers that had been worn away. "If you sick, you should go to better hospital," he advised Jay.

"My guy is already dead, but thanks."

As they cut through Praga's back streets, the driver pointed out landmarks of the who-slept-here variety, but in his account, it was where Solidarity's leaders had been arrested, held indefinitely, or assassinated. He pulled to a stop and asked how long to wait, and Jay told him to return to the embassy.

The hospital's glass doors reflected the gray dusk. Too often he was in hospitals interrogating the dying or IDing the dead, and knew the antiseptic-smelling foyer all too well. He crossed to the information desk. Someone at the embassy had written morgue in Polish for him on a slip of paper, which he now showed to a woman far too big for her schoolgirl's desk. The note earned him a wave through a set of swinging doors. Then he was lost and showed the note to anyone who looked employed, following their vague directions into the hospital's dungeon-like bowels, where he turned a corner and breathed embalming fluid. He didn't need Detective Kulski pacing in the corridor to tell him that he had found the morgue.

"Dr. Nagorski is waiting," Kulski said.

Jay followed him inside. The room was cold. Bloodied bandages had been discarded on the floor. A fluorescent light, hanging from two short steel chains, illuminated the dead man on a metal trolley. He was shadowless, bone white. A violent red wound, carved and raggedly resewn, bisected him from his Adam's apple to the patch of hair in his groin.

He shook hands with the pathologist. Dr. Nagorski was eighty at the youngest, and impatient in a way that could be mistaken for spry. "Shall we begin?" he asked. "I speak English, Mr. Porter, and will make my summary in English. Unless you prefer Polish?"

Jay knew the Polish words for many body parts, yet they hardly seemed meant for the same species, so crudely were they rendered on the trolley. "English, please," he said.

The doctor picked up calipers and positioned himself at the victim's head. "Caucasian male, it is obvious, late sixties. Two hundred ten centimeters tall and approximately eighty-five kilos." Tall and skinny, Jay translated, and listened as the doctor inventoried routine characteristics: general state of health (fair), distinguishing scars (none), no missing limbs. "I estimate his time of death between midnight and four. With the cold, it is difficult to be more precise. He died from a bullet wound to his heart." The doctor touched the calipers to the chest wound. Made at close range, it was clean, the flesh below it discolored from the heart's last explosive pulse.

Dr. Nagorski grasped the victim's ruined cheek with the calipers. "He was dead before his face was cut. There is little bruising and he swallowed no blood." Before relinquishing the cheek, he added, "The dental work is Russian."

"All the others were cut first?" Jay wanted to verify.

"I only examined the third victim, but yes, I read all the pathology reports. Another difference is the trajectory of the bullet. In this man, it is up, not straight into the heart, and he was shot from seven to ten centimeters, not—"

In Polish he asked Kulski for a word.

"Point blank," the detective told him.

"He was not shot point blank," the pathologist continued. "Also the others had gunpowder on their flesh, but on this man, it is on his clothes."

"What about clothing tags? Or any ID?"

"There was no ID, and like the other victims, all the clothing tags are removed. Jacket, shirt, underwear, and all very cleanly cut away."

The pathologist switched to Polish to say something to Kulski, and the expression on the detective's face changed as if he had hit a mental speed bump. They spoke briefly before Dr. Nagorski resumed his report. "The gun was not a TT this time. The damage to the tissue is much greater. It has the signature of a P-83."

"Police issue," Kulski said tightly. "They are not sold legally, and there's only a small black market for them. Before a gun is issued, we shoot it three times and keep the bullets."

"You have a ballistics fingerprint for every P-83?"

"That way, the guns can be traced."

"Which explains the small market for them. Are you suggesting that maybe a policeman is involved?"

"It has to be considered."

"Too bad we don't have a bullet."

"We do," spoke up Dr. Nagorski, grinning with his own cleverness. He displayed a metal lump in a sandwich bag. "It was stopped by his shoulder."

Kulski took it out of the bag to examine the misshapen slug. He handed it to Jay, who asked, "Is your lab good enough to get the ballistics off this?"

"It may be too damaged."

"Our forensics unit in DC might be able to get something. They invent equipment."

"I will request clearance from Director Husarska."

"Clearance?"

"For releasing evidence."

Dr. Nagorski turned the dead man's hand to display a surgical cut adjacent to the little finger. "Here is another surprise."

"The callus?" Jay asked.

"Not a callus, a sixth finger."

"A *what?*" the other men asked.

"The last victim had the same thing, and like you, I thought it was a callus, so I didn't investigate. In fact, it is a rare genetic condition."

"Are you suggesting that the couriers were related?"

"There is almost no other explanation possible."

"Could radiation exposure cause it?" asked Kulski.

"No," Jay answered. "Deformities caused by radiation are not passed on genetically. How they assert themselves is random."

"Because of his age, and the ages of the other victim I examined, I would guess this man to be his father," Dr. Nagorski elaborated. "Now for the radiation!"

With a gamesman's glee, he unfolded chairs and made the two lawmen sit and lift their feet. He waved a Geiger counter wand around Jay's shoes, prompting an occasional click. "Obviously you are here only a few days. Your shoes sound like Warsaw before Chernobyl." Then he tested the detective's shoes and the counter popped like popcorn. "Unfortunately, this has become background radiation for Warsaw. Now listen." The doctor pulled the victim's shoes from an evidence bag and ran his wand over them. The counter sizzled. "He has walked through a contaminated area many times, yet his body has little trace of it except for his hands." To demonstrate, he ran the counter the length of the dead man and there was hardly a tick until his hands set it off again.

"That's the pattern for someone who works at a nuclear plants," Jay spoke up. "He would have scrubbed when he left a contaminated area, so there is not much on his body. His shoes picked up radiation that inevitably leaks outside. His hands are hot because he was delivering something hot."

"Also, his teeth are very loose, which suggests radiation exposure," continued the pathologist. He pointed the calipers at the man's foot. "He twisted his ankle; you can see the bruising. It occurred before he died, otherwise he would not bruise so much, and I found these." The doctor displayed a bag of mint candy.

Kulski examined it. "It's Russian."

"It's the first proof where he's from," Jay said.

"I have prepared a report for you," the doctor said and handed it to Detective Kulski. "Do you have questions?"

"I will," Jay answered. "May I take some pictures?"

"Of course, but don't ask him to say 'cheese.'"

Jay mused on morgue humor—he had heard a lot of it—as he shot his Polaroids of the man's cut face and mysterious sixth finger. They thanked Dr. Nagorski and left him to his grim tasks.

Outside the hospital, Kulski offered, "I can drive you to the embassy or your hotel."

"I can take a taxi."

"It'll give us a chance to talk."

"In that case, the embassy."

Detective Kulski led them to a proper police cruiser.

"Why the upgrade?" Jay asked.

"I'm not undercover at the hospital."

They got in, and Kulski reached to open the glove compartment. "Before I forget, I have these for you," he said, and handed Jay copies of evidence photographs of the fourth courier's murder's scene. "I will also ask Eva to make a copy of Dr. Nagorski's report for you."

"Thanks."

Kulski pulled onto the road to navigate Praga's congested streets. "It doesn't make sense that the labels are removed," he said, thinking aloud. "Especially so cleanly. The killer would need to move his body and open his clothes, and there was no evidence of that."

"I thought the same thing," Jay replied. "Someone didn't want the couriers traceable, even to an underpants factory. The labels were cut out before they left home, and I think I know where home is. My assistant in DC has uncovered some missing uranium at one of Russia's reactors. I can't tell you where."

"Is it enough uranium for a bomb?"

"A small one, or enough to create havoc in a lot of places. If the fuel is delivered efficiently, even a small amount can make a city uninhabitable."

Their tires hit the bridge and rumbled noisily. Night had swallowed the river. Only headlights on the cars speeding along the riverside drive revealed its course in the void below.

"So last night, below us, there might have been an atomic bomb?" Kulski asked.

"It has to be considered."

They came off the bridge and passed stores displaying cardboard likenesses of products they'd sell if they had them. Kulski deftly steered through a clogged roundabout to shoot past the Forum Hotel; in its shadows, sallow hookers in their sixties competed with twenty-somethings for potential tricks heading inside. Soon they merged with Aleje Ujazdowskie, lined with stately facades of gracious mansions outlined by virgin snow.

"I am afraid for my family," Kulski said. "We have a cottage at the lakes. Perhaps they would be safer there. In an instant, Warsaw could be annihilated."

"I don't know how far away the lakes are, but yes, it would probably be safer, especially if we're dealing with only a dirty bomb. A full-fledged nuclear device, that's a different story."

Then men fell silent, pondering the gravity of the situation. Kulski pulled up to the curb at the embassy.

"I have to believe we will always manage to prevent our annihilation," Jay said. "If we're only postponing it, why bother?" He got out of the cruiser.

"What would you do if your sons were in Warsaw tonight?"

"I'd ask for a key to your cottage," he answered and closed the car door.

CHAPTER SIXTEEN

Back at his desk, Jay spread out his few Polaroids of the autopsy and gave them a quick look before reaching into a drawer for his case files. He opened the one marked #3 first, using a magnifying glass to search the man's hands for a bump constituting a sixth finger. He thought he could make it out, but it might have been the power of suggestion. The photos of the first two victims were inconclusive.

Kurt tapped on his door and walked in. "I promised you this." He handed him a thin file. "We have more on Mladic. He's been watched for a while. These are only my CliffsNotes."

Jay opened the file. Kurt had stapled four photographs inside its cover. The earliest—Mladic at his handsome slimmest—was a formal portrait in his military uniform. His clear blue eyes stared at the camera from under the bill of his cap. The other photographs were more recent, showing a middle-aged man who'd gained weight but not indecently. In one he was out of uniform, sitting at an outdoor café wearing a leisure suit. "Take away his stars," Jay remarked, "and he could be an insurance salesman."

"That picture was taken two years ago on Hvar."

"In Yugoslavia? Funny, Husarska has a poster of it hanging in her office. She says it's her dream to live there. It's an island, right?"

"It's become a big destination for Eastern Europeans now that they can travel." Kurt picked up Jay's headshot of the dead man and handed it to him. "Meet Dr. Sergej Ustinov, chief weapons designer at Kosmonovo. He was expected at a conference in Reutov two days ago and never showed up. Apparently he had designed a suitcase atomic bomb and was expected to display it."

"Is he missing with the bomb?"

"It might be two bombs. Apparently he left Kosmonovo with two suitcases."

"You have surveillance on the ground in Kosmonovo?"

"We try. You up for a workout?"

"I'm up for a stiff drink. Autopsies and missing bombs can do that to you."

"A workout will help relieve stress."

"All my gear's at the hotel."

"I have extra shorts and a towel."

Jay shrugged. "I guess I don't have an excuse."

Kurt guided them through a labyrinth of corridors and down a stairwell to a basement that had its own maze of rooms. On the way, Jay filled him in on the missing Russian physicist and the highlights of Dr. Nagorski's autopsy. "Have you ever heard of someone having a sixth finger?" he asked.

"Yeah, the last king of Greece."

"He did?"

"It's a little bump on the side of the hand, isn't it?"

"More like a bone spur. The third and fourth couriers both had one, and possibly the others. I can't be sure from the photos."

"Meaning what? They were related?"

"It's possible."

"That's a weird twist. Here we are." Kurt opened a door to reveal a room bright with fresh white paint and mirrored walls. Alongside a bench press laid an orderly row of free weights, and in a corner was a stack of red exercise mats.

The room was hot and Jay loosened his tie. "I don't think we need a workout to build up a sweat."

"All the heating for the embassy runs through those," Kurt said, and pointed to the pipes crisscrossing the ceiling.

"You set this up since you've been here?"

"Remember, I'm the *Security* Officer. Security gets anything it wants."

"It's pretty spiffy with all the mirrors."

"That's one reason why there's no money for a shower curtain."

"And no one else uses this place?"

"Maybe they're waiting for a shower curtain. We change in here."

A second door led into the locker room. Not much larger than a walk-in closet, it had two short banks of lockers separated by a bench, and a musty shower stall at the far end.

Kurt opened a combination lock and handed Jay gym shorts. "Washed recently."

"I'm glad for that."

They sat on the bench facing opposite walls and pulled off their shoes and socks, tossing them into lockers. Then they were back on their feet slipping off shirts and pants. "Now you can see the full extent of the damage," Kurt said, skipping his fingers across the shiny welts that peppered his chest. "In braille it says 'From Beirut with love.'"

They slipped on gym shorts and returned to the other room, where Kurt grabbed a couple of the red mats. "Let's spread all these out so we have plenty of room."

Soon they'd covered the floor.

"Ten minutes warm-up?"

They sat on the mats to stretch—reaching for toes, rolling heads, twisting shoulders. In the overheated room, they were soon sweaty, their backs making sucking sounds every time they came off the mats. Each knew they were assessing each other. Except for his scarred chest, the CIA man was smooth and muscled, with veins etching his ebony body. Jay was in good shape, too, though not so obsessed with exercise that he went around the world building embassy gyms. He figured he could handle anything the CIA man threw at him.

"Carl invited Mladic to a little party tomorrow evening," Kurt said. "You're expected to show up, too. He's billing it as informal cocktails with some of the Country Team. As added bait, he's holding it at the official residence."

"So he liked my idea. Do you think Mladic will bite?"

"He already did. Hook, line, and sinker."

Jay got to his feet to stretch at the waist. "Whatever the last courier brought, Mladic obviously didn't get. He wouldn't be sticking around for a cocktail party—he'd be home playing with his bomb—which means the exchange wasn't made. Whatever he had to trade must still be in his room. It's probably a suitcase full of money."

Jay laced his fingers behind his head and, pacing, flapped his bent elbows like butterfly wings. "Can you get into Mladic's room? Not you personally, but Langley. You seem to have a good network in place here."

"Anyplace else, we could bribe our way in, but not the lodge where he stays. The same manager has been running the place for over forty years, watching the same people's comings and goings—literally. Everyone assumed the KGB had installed cameras for blackmail purposes, but the manager himself never betrayed anyone. When the place was privatized, he bought it, and he's not going to start betraying his best customers now. You'd be amazed by what struggling old commies are willing to pay for a red-flocked fuck down memory lane. Ready for weights?"

"Ready."

"Three lifts each, and we add ten pounds after each round until the weights win. Where do you like to start?"

"One forty. But let's add twenty pounds to two hundred, and ten after that."

"Agreed."

Kurt changed the weights on the barbell in the bench press's rack. "I'll show you how it's done," he said and stretched out on the bench. He planted his feet on the floor and flattened his back to be entirely supported by the bench. He gripped the barbell and lifted it off the rack. He groaned at the weight and struggled to lift it once. Then he slipped both hands to the center of the bar, let go with one hand, and lifted it twice with one arm before slipping it back on the rack. Kurt smiled up at Jay, who was hovering over the rack to help him if he needed it. "See, that's how you do it!"

"Yeah, yeah," Jay said, and took his place on the bench.

The first rounds were easy, but as weights added up, they each took their time adjusting their feet and bracing their backs. Once again it was Kurt's turn. Jay stood over him, knees pressed to his shoulders, their hands next to each other's on the barbell to help Kurt lower the weight to his chest before lifting it. His arms knotted. His legs tautened. His groin bunched into a fistful of muscles. Every vein on his body bulged as he pressed it once. Twice. The third time he locked elbows and Jay helped guide it back onto the rack.

They traded places. Jay wiped his shorts to dry his palms but they were just as sweaty. Kurt leaned over him, grinning fiercely, Jay tasting his salty sweat as it sprinkled his face. Together they lowered the barbell to his chest, and Kurt let go.

Jay firmed his grip, mustered his strength, and barely budged the weight before it fell back and pinned him to the bench.

Kurt never stopped grinning.

"Sonofabitch! Get this off me!"

"Not from this angle. Bad for the back." He swung around and straddled Jay's chest. "Forfeit?"

"Forfeit!"

Shakily they managed to heave the barbell back on the rack.

Kurt raised his arms in victory and strutted a couple of steps.

Jay grabbed his ankle and tripped him. They grappled until they managed to untangle themselves and scrambled onto their feet.

They sparred like boxers, bouncing on the balls of their feet, lunging for each other, grinding the other down, entwined and rolling across the mats, wrestling to pin each other though both were too slick with sweat for a hold. Tumbling, twisting, at one point their heads clasped between the other's knees, until they fell back on the mats, breathing hard.

"Did they teach you to wrestle at Quantico?" Kurt asked.

"High school wrestling team."

"Me too. Shower time."

They picked up their towels and returned to the locker room.

CHAPTER SEVENTEEN

THE FAX MACHINE WARBLED AND lifted a sheet of paper between its rollers. Lights flickered on the dials. As the paper jerked forward, the topmost strands of the dead man's woolly hair appeared. His brow inched out, his dead eyes, his cheek with its black gash. Basia's lips curled as she remembered his vile breath when he tried to kiss her. She set aside the page as the rest of the report emerged. Kulski had summarized it, but she wanted to read Dr. Nagorski's conclusions for herself.

Basia Husarska needed a strategy. She was used to that. Communism had made stupid people stupider and smart ones dull, but shrewd ones survived on their wits. Or at least she had. Her father had been destroyed by the system, and her mother by him. Basia had grown up determined that nothing would destroy her. From an early age she learned the power of sex, even convincing her father that he had seduced her one drunken night, his deference to her whims forever sealed. Her mother gradually disappeared into the shadows of her life. Basia barely took notice of their deaths.

She had dreams beyond making the system work for her. Basia wanted out. She wanted freedom from the omnipresent hand that puppeteered their lives. Ironically, Solidarity's rise had threatened the scaffolding of escape she had constructed. The men she had loved—if *love* was a fair substitute for the word *fuck*—had fallen from their pedestals, losing their purses full of the favors they could dispense. So many had been in her control, afraid to tell their wives of their indiscretions, and infatuated with her playfulness because she did everything they could bring themselves to verbalize. Now she only had Dravko. Only he remained in her web of deceit. All her other constructs had failed.

Basia retrieved the pages that fell one by one from the fax machine, skimming them, reading again what the detective had told her about the slug from the P-83, the sixth finger, the radioactive shoes. Time, which once had stretched so uneventfully before her, now seemed her enemy. She only had as much time as it would take to trace the bullet to her. Dravko was her escape. Dravko or his million dollars, which she bet was in his steamer suitcase. Where else would you hide a million dollars in that room? But she couldn't just walk off with it. She'd be dead before she counted it. She needed more time to come up with a scheme. She set aside the autopsy report, mulling over what to tell him, what pretenses to use to get her way, because Basia Husarska would settle for nothing less.

· · ·

THE MARRIOTT'S BAR WAS ALWAYS popular at cocktail hour. More business deals were cut and clandestine affairs sealed in those ninety minutes than any other ninety minutes on anybody's clock. Basia stood in the doorway looking for Dravko. The place was lively. He usually preferred a quiet table off to the side, but that evening he was seated at the bar. The young barman was laughing at something Dravko had said when Basia slipped onto the stool next to him. "Good evening, Wojtek," she said.

"Good evening, Pani Husarska," the barman replied. "Scotch on rocks?"

"A double."

"You got it."

When he moved down the bar, she said to Dravko, "I see you dressed up for young Wojtek."

"He likes my medals."

"Be careful. They make you look rich."

"What do you mean by that?"

"He doesn't do anything for free."

"Double scotch rocks, Pani," the barman served her.

"*Dzienkuje*," she said, and to Dravko, "Cheers."

They touched glasses and sipped.

"He is beautiful," she remarked about the young barman. "I'd like to fuck him too. I'd suggest a three-way but I would probably be ignored. You haven't asked about your fourth courier."

"He didn't show. I don't have to ask. He was always adamant he would cross on Monday."

"Why?"

"He never said. But they all crossed on a Monday."

"Why did you stay?"

"To humor you."

"What are you going to do?"

"The American ambassador has invited me to a party tomorrow. Apparently the Americans want to get to know me."

"They already know you. They watch you while you're here, don't they? And now they can watch your war on the news."

"It's a private meeting at the ambassador's house."

"Ah, that makes a difference! Nobody will be watching you there."

"With the situation in Sarajevo, it will be amusing to hear what they have to say."

"The whole week could be amusing, Dravko. Stay, wait for your fourth man. I will amuse you whenever you want. And when you tire of me, I am sure it could be arranged with Wojtek, or other boys. There are so many of them, and why not?"

"I'll think about it."

"Sometimes you think too much. Act on it. Perhaps it is your last chance to have boys before you bury yourself alive in your puritanical Serbia."

"You would approve?"

"I'm only sharing you, Dravko. Of course, I will want to be amused, too."

Dravko grinned. "I'll think about it."

CHAPTER EIGHTEEN

LILKA PARKED OUTSIDE HER BUILDING. She counted four tiers of windows up and four over, picking out the square meter of concrete that constituted her balcony. She didn't see a light, but it was only twilight and Jacek might still be there. She prayed he wasn't, then admonished herself for asking so frivolously for God's intervention. If she were to have a prayer answered, it should be to rid her of Jacek forever.

In the scruffy, filthy foyer, someone had scribbled a vulgarity over an announcement for a meeting to discuss the building's "deplorable conditions of habitation." She braced herself for the climb to her floor and pulled open the stairwell's stubborn door. Stippled with cigarette butts, the steps reeked from too many men having relieved themselves, especially on the first couple of landings. At her floor, she burst into the hallway wanting fresher air, and gasped when she saw Jacek sprawled across their threshold. For a moment, she thought her prayers had been answered and he was dead. Then he reached for his toolbox.

"What are you doing?" she asked.

"What the hell does it look like I'm doing? I'm changing the goddamn lock."

"Why?"

"For security."

He got on his knees to remove the old deadbolt and she stepped around him to go inside.

He grabbed her ankle. "I don't want you touching my stuff."

She walked out of his grip. "I don't want to touch your stuff. Why do we need to change the lock for security?"

"Too many people have keys."

"What people?"

"Aleks. He's got a key."

"He's our son, and in theory he lives here."

"You don't know who he's given it to. Another one, your sister's got a key."

"She has a key for emergencies."

"Yeah, well I came home today, and your big dumb brother-in-law was here. I don't recall an emergency."

"We haven't been able to flush the toilet for two days."

"Use a bucket of water. That works."

"Tolek didn't fix it?"

"He said it needed a new mechanism." Jacek prodded the deadbolt with a screwdriver and it dropped into his palm. "I guess Mr. Scientist has been demoted to plumber if he's fixing toilets."

"You could be nicer about Tolek. He's doing us a favor. When's he coming back?"

"I told him to stay the fuck away until I said it was okay."

"Suit yourself. I'm taking a shower."

"Why? You got a date with your FBI boyfriend tonight?"

"We're having dinner."

"I told you not to see him, didn't I?"

"You told me not to bring him around."

"It amounts to the same thing. If you're seeing him, he'll come sniffing around."

Lilka went into the bedroom.

"Hey! Don't touch my things!" He scrambled to his feet. "Hey!"

She opened the closet door.

"Get away from there!" he yelled at her.

"I need some clothes."

"I didn't say you could go in there."

"It's my room, Jacek."

"Not until further notice it isn't."

"Stop it Jacek, now! I need my clothes."

Jacek approached her menacingly. Lilka waited for his blow.

"Get your fucking clothes but don't touch anything that's mine."

Lilka slid open the closet door and instantly saw the steamer suitcase

Jacek had shoved inside. Dark tan with leather straps and brass pieces, it was too handsome for something he would own. "Whose is this?"

"I said don't touch it."

"I'm not touching it. I'm looking at it."

"Don't do even that."

"You put it on top of my shoes. I have to move it."

"DON'T TOUCH IT!" he screamed.

Lilka jumped back. "What is it? You're scaring me."

"I'll get your stuff. What shoes do you want?"

"The purple ones."

"Which dress?"

"Also purple."

Clutching her purse and clothes, Lilka locked herself in the cramped bathroom. As she rearranged the stockings hanging over the tub, she heaved a dry sob and glimpsed her haggard self in the mirror. Only last night, she had believed herself to be beautiful. She clung to that memory to fight back tears. For a long time, she thought she deserved Jacek's anger and his fists, too, when he needed to lash out, because her teenage deception had contributed to the anger that ultimately consumed him.

She adjusted the water temperature, stepped into the shower, and thought about seventeen years ago—exactly half her life—when Jacek had been a catch, definitely not someone you'd push out of bed. He had mischievous blue eyes, bushy black hair, and an endearing smile. He came from a gruff family, but that didn't matter too much. He was smart and handsome. He was the boy who was going to do better than the rest. In Jacek's late teens, like his friends, he started experimenting with sex—meaning trying to score as often as a horny guy could—and he could have had any girl he wanted who was in a similar experimental mood. Lilka's friends were envious when he chose her. *You slept with him?* they asked in awe, as if he'd given her his blessing instead of the clap. She missed her next period, and in Catholic Poland, that was tantamount to applying for a marriage license.

His father was enraged that he'd knocked up a girl and ruined his chances for making a better life for all of them. One night, after too many vodkas, he chased Jacek with a knife, denouncing his stupidity, and blaming what he'd done on his movie star looks. He tripped, and a wild swing caught Jacek in the face and sliced his cheek wide open.

It ruined Jacek. His self-confidence was wrapped up in his looks. He knew the advantages of being cute as a kid and exceedingly handsome as a young man. He'd kept it a secret that he had applied to a modeling agency—it wasn't something you talked about around a garbage collector's table—but that career option evaporated. He grew a beard to cover the scar, but it didn't quite cover it all, and besides, he was one of those rare men whose looks were diminished by a beard. He knew it, and at one point shaved it off, but when he looked in the mirror, all he saw was his scar. He started growing it back the same day.

His scar is all that is left of him, Lilka thought as she dried off. While putting on her purple dress and pumps, she listened to Jacek's banging and swearing at the stubborn lock. Then he suddenly stopped. She gathered what she needed and left the bathroom.

Jacek was seated on the couch pulling at a beer. "I see 'fuck me' written all over your face," he said.

"I need a key to the new lock."

"Stay home."

"I need one for Tolek, too."

"I said I don't want him in here. Nobody, you hear?"

"Even you must like it better when the toilet flushes. Give me a key, Jacek."

He flipped one onto the table.

She snatched it.

Right after she did, he stabbed his knife into the table. "That's for your FBI boyfriend if you bring him back. He'll never fuck you or anyone else again."

She went to the door.

"What's he say that makes you want to give it to him for free? Or is it for free?"

She was in the hallway.

"Does he say you're beautiful?" he shouted after her.

She was at the stairwell.

"You think you're so fucking beautiful when you look like a fucking whore!"

CHAPTER NINETEEN

KURT CRAWFORD SLOWED AS HE passed General Mladic's lodge and kept going. A taxi following him braked and pulled up to the curb. In his rearview mirror, he observed the general, out of uniform, slip into its back seat. He mulled over the probability that the payoff for the couriers was in the general's room, and he was equally curious how Mladic might spend his sudden free time in Warsaw. Would he somehow reveal his hand in the weapons trade? Did Kurt dare offer an unrefusable bribe to the lodge's proprietor to let him in Mladic's room for five minutes?

He slowed, pretending to look for an address to keep his face turned away as he let the taxi pass him. When the driver turned onto a major boulevard, Kurt sped up and was easily able to tail him in the light traffic.

Ahead of him, Dravko had no idea he was being followed. Instead, he imagined the adoring crowds that would one day line that boulevard during a state visit and cheer his name so thunderously that the ground vibrated. Then that scene, playing like a movie in his head, became real. He saw those crowds and felt the earth move as he towered over his handsome honor guard who carried him on an open palanquin. He was searching the faces for the world leaders who were certain to be there when the taxi driver said something. The film stopped. "What did you ask?" Dravko said.

"You got a number or a name or something?"

"Wolska Street is good enough. I'll find my way."

"We're on Wolska Street. There's a lot to find on it."

Dravko, beginning to feel that *not* giving a number would draw more attention than he desired, gave his destination's address.

"*Cholera!*" the driver swore and made a reckless U-turn. "Why didn't you say you were going to the Arena? That's at the other end."

Dravko shrank back in the seat. The purplish light from passing shops gave him an unhealthy pallor. He worried the driver had seen his face too clearly and might report him, but then he remembered he could lose those fears in Warsaw. There was no longer anything to gain by reporting another's innocent misdeeds.

Over his shoulder the driver said, "I've never been inside but I take a lot of guys there. I figure I know what it's about. Is it nice?"

"I don't know. It's my first time," answered Dravko.

The driver laughed. "They all say that! I guess there's a first time for everything. Maybe I'll have to give it a try my own first time!" He pulled to the curb. "Here you are. Inside there. The door's on your left."

Dravko peered into an arcade and saw a sign for the Arena Baths.

"Bingo," Kurt said to himself as he swerved around Dravko's stopped taxi.

"Go through the arch and there's a door on the left."

Dravko waited until the taxi had driven off, and even then did not walk straightaway into the arcade. He wandered a bit, peering into shop windows, feigning interest. He tried to look inconspicuous as he checked out other pedestrians. Most hurried along the rain-darkened street, but more than one slowed his steps and cruised him—behavior that felt reckless to him. He couldn't have risked even a sideways glance in his own country, let alone a turn of the head. A rumor could topple him and put him on the receiving end of electric shocks intended to torture the queer out of him. The only men Dravko had had sex with were a few escorts procured by the lodge's discreet proprietor and a lengthening list of encounters in prison, where his gratification was another method to debase inmates who obligingly didn't survive to tell.

Kurt had pulled over and watched Dravko delay going inside. He sensed the general was building up the nerve to enter the arcade, and once he did, Kurt was right behind him. He found Dravko staring at the doorbell. "You're in the right place," he said. "At least I hope you are!" He reached past Dravko and pressed the button. A chime rang deep in the building.

"*Tak?*" a man said over the intercom.

"I'm the black guy who's been here a few times," Kurt said in English. "You'll recognize me, and I'm bringing a friend."

"I remember you. Too bad about the friend."

A buzzer sounded and they went inside and descended stairs to the check-in counter. The attendant had red spiked hair and a clinging T-shirt that left no ripple unrevealed on his sculpted young body. He set out a couple of towels and dropped a loincloth on each.

Dravko held his loincloth aloft. "I am supposed to wear this?"

"It's that or nothing," the attendant said.

"Just leave it," Kurt said. "How about a couple of extra towels? My friend is shy. Follow me," he said to Dravko. "I'll show you the ropes."

"There are ropes?"

"Not those kind! Don't get excited. We change in here."

Kurt opened the door to the locker room and followed Dravko in.

"Is this your first time here? Where are you from?" Kurt asked.

"Yugoslavia."

"You speak good English, or at least good enough to understand me."

"Thank you."

"I'm a long way from home, too, and kinda like it that way. Get away from the wife and all and have a bit of fun. I call *this* relaxation, and hell, it ain't like I'm cheating on *her*."

"You are also married?"

"You too? Shit, it's like we were destined to meet! It's safer that way, you know, sticking with married guys."

Dravko didn't know; he had entered an unknown world. And there he was, speaking to a black man, too.

"Do you always stare at strangers like that," Kurt asked, "or are you getting ready to say something?"

"Where are you from?" Dravko stammered.

"America, can't you tell by the skin?"

"By your skin, I think Africa."

"Maybe my great-great-grandfather two hundred years ago, but I'm from the land of the free and home of the Braves: Atlanta, Georgia, where there's more peach-this and peach-that than a teenager's got zits. You ever tasted peach puddin'?"

"I don't understand you," Dravko confessed.

Kurt flashed him a big, friendly smile. "Talking too fast, huh? That's what my wife says, I'm always too fast! I'll slow it down for you. What's your locker number? Isn't that how it always is: with all these lockers, they give us two right next to each other. It's like they want us to bump into each other!"

Dravko surreptitiously watched the black man undress. It startled him to be so close to one. As the clothes came off, he noticed the scars on his upper chest. When he first saw the scars on Kurt's face, he wondered if they were tribal markings, but with so many on his chest, he worried it might be a disease.

Kurt saw his worried expression and rubbed a hand over his scars. "I know, they're not very sexy. At least they don't hurt, if that's what you're worried about. They hurt ten years ago but not now."

"They are not a disease?"

"Don't worry. I'm healthy."

Kurt, naked, locked his locker and put his foot on the bench to face Dravko, who gulped at the African's solicitous pose. "Hey, take a breath. What, you've never seen a naked black man before? I'll be goddamned! That should make tonight special!"

Dravko never had seen a naked black man before, nor had he been in a place where gay sex was guaranteed, and the mere anticipation of it kept him in a state of semi-arousal. A little dazed, he stripped off his briefs without thinking to conceal himself.

"Well, aren't you looking friendly!" Kurt said.

The general held his shorts in front of him.

"Hey, there's no reason to be shy. We're all here for the same thing. But bring a towel. No need to show off to everyone. Ready?"

"For what?"

"Well, we have three options. Dry sauna, steam room, and Jacuzzi and showers. Personally, I'm up for steam."

They entered a dingy corridor and passed through a tiny bar area where a handful of men lounged around, towels and loincloths askew or missing, watching a three-way in a porn movie. Dravko paused to take a look, but Kurt said, "Let's keep going. The real thing is better. So what brings you to Warsaw? Business?" He gave a look at the general's paunch and added, "Naw, you're too trim for a businessman. I bet you're in the military. Army?"

"How did you know?"

"Army was a guess, but military for sure. Just look at you. Broad shoulders, strong arms, okay, a little soft in the gut, but you're allowed. Heck, what are you, forty-two? Forty-four?"

"Forty-four," Dravko replied, shaving five years off the truth.

"I bet your wife's a real looker, too."

"A looker?" Dravko knew his English was halting, but this man seemed to use words that came from another language. Maybe it was a Swahili word.

"Pretty, that's what I mean. Handsome guy like you oughtta have a pretty wife."

Had Ulia ever been pretty? Dravko had married her not for love but because he deemed her suitable, embodying a pedigree wholesomeness that would serve as a model for Mother Serbia. Unfortunately, she had failed to produce children. He couldn't recollect when they had stopped trying: her body, when he tried to recall it, was like a forgotten landscape seen on a foreign journey. Now he thought of Ulia always in the kitchen, skimming fat from boiling pots that permeated her clothes with rancid steam. The men in prison, too, smelled of rancid steam, and fear so pungent that only their deaths cleared it away. And now he was walking next to a naked black man who had his own smell: fecund, like plowed earth.

"Here we are," Kurt said.

The door exhaled steam when he opened it. Their lungs briefly stung from the scalding spray and their eyes took a moment to adjust. White-tiled benches rose to the right. A few blurry men were scattered on them. They picked a spot and sat a little apart. In the numbing heat, Dravko closed his eyes, and a new film started to run in his mind's eye. He was visiting his honor guard in their barracks, who were all in some state of undress, resting together on a hot summer day. When they recognized him, they cheered, and Dravko opened his eyes to realize the sound was only steam chuffing into the room.

The African had inched closer, or had he? And his towel had fallen open.

Was it the heat, or the closeness of the African that made Dravko short of breath? Beads of sweat ran down the black man's arm, and as he followed them with his eyes, he took in all of him: his hard muscles, his long limbs, his cock suggesting playfulness. He trembled when he reached to touch it. Kurt reciprocated, sliding a hand under the general's towel. Before things went too far, he said, "Let's make it special, and private. Not here. You, me, hotel."

"You don't want?"

"I want! But not here, and not so fast. Let's get you into a cold shower and calm you down."

He steered Dravko to a room with a bank of shower stalls and propped him in one. He turned on the cold water before stepping into the adjacent stall, where he could hear Dravko sputtering. He had met too many men like Mladic: uptight, guilt-ridden, married, who ventured into the clubs and other haunts of gay men, declaring their fidelity to a different manhood while seeking the very pleasures they decried. Once bedded, they were balky mates, and once mated, quick to dress and leave, slamming the closet door behind them until overcome again by unforgiving desires. He had learned to recognize these men and ignore them, unwilling to join battle with their adolescent consciousness when there were too many willing partners. But Kurt had no intention of ignoring Dravko. The general's diplomatic status protected him from search warrants, but nothing stopped Kurt from a look inside his room if invited there. And he planned to be. He would use the general's Achilles heel to make sure he was.

Kurt stepped from the shower. "How are you doing in there?" he asked and slid open Dravko's curtain. He appeared not to have moved. "I'd say you had enough." With one hand, Kurt reached for the faucet; he slid his other hand down Dravko's belly. "Rumor has it, Yugoslavian men are very sexy."

"Sexy?"

"Mmm. Let's dry off and get out of here."

The spiked-hair boy at the counter grinned at Kurt when they left. "Coming back?" he asked.

"Not tonight."

A freezing rain greeted them outside.

"My car is just there," Kurt said.

They got into it, and he started the engine. "Which direction?"

"Where is your hotel?"

"My hotel? No can do. My company rents an apartment, and I'm sharing it with someone who'd call my wife if I brought back a man for sex. Especially if I didn't share!" Kurt playfully touched Dravko. "And I'm not sharing."

Dravko pushed his hand away. "Don't. It's too public here."

"That's why I'm suggesting someplace private.

"It's impossible."

"Do you have a uniform in your room? Because I have kind of a fantasy."

The general said, "It's impossible."

"Is there a mirror?"

"A mirror?" Dravko thought about the dozens of mirrors in his room. "More than one mirror," he said.

"Then you're really going to like this. If not, we'll find a hotel room, because you, me, *somewhere* tonight."

Kurt lied, saying he found men in uniform especially sexy. Maybe the general had the same fetish, which would be fun, because Kurt liked to wear uniforms, too, and watch himself in the mirror. Dravko took the bait. Over the years the local CIA operation had learned from escorts about the mirrors and the general's strange obsession with wanting to appear to make love to himself. As Kurt hoped, he instantly saw the opportunity to turn the situation around to set up that scene.

Minutes later, they entered the former communist lodge's foyer illuminated by dusty fixtures that were missing some bulbs. The heavy-lidded hotelier stirred behind the counter and handed over a key. Blue veins traced the depressions of his bulbous nose, which he plucked with his thumb before settling back and letting his eyelids droop.

Dravko guided them around a corner and down a second hall where the threadbare carpet had been poorly repaired. Once inside the room, he relaxed and asked if Kurt wanted a scotch, and Kurt did; in fact, he needed a refill to launch into his full subterfuge. The room's red-papered walls, resplendent with mirrors of every shape and size encircling a yawning bed, so conformed to Kurt's notion of a whorehouse that he felt a pang of guilt for prostituting his sexuality, but sex was the oldest trick in the world, and he would use it every time he could when the stakes were this high. There was no moral equivalency.

Kurt didn't have to look very hard to see everything in the room. It was small and tidy. The only place to stow anything appeared to be a closet with double louvered doors. If what he was looking for was there, he wagered it was behind them.

Dravko handed him a shot of scotch. They touched glasses before knocking them back.

"Another?" Dravko asked.

"It's that kind of night, isn't it?"

Dravko poured another round.

They downed the second round, then a third, both men numbing their anxieties with liquor and using idle talk as a preamble to their little escapade. Dravko knew Warsaw well, he told Kurt, and Kurt replied that he had become a frequent visitor, too, alluding to business dealings without elaboration. No, he had never been to Yugoslavia, was it nice? Dravko waxed poetic about its sun-drenched beaches and lavender fields. His talk of home reminded him of Ulia, made more attractive—or at least more loving—by the alcohol, but Kurt steered him away from talk of his wife, knowing it would lead to guilt and self-recrimination, and likely an excuse not to consummate their encounter. The first move had to be his, and he lifted a hand to touch Dravko's cheek. Dravko flinched but didn't pull away. "You're a handsome man," Kurt said, and pulled him into a kiss. At first tentative, it became deeper, and Kurt moaned amorously. He opened his eyes enough to see the general watching himself in the mirrors. Kurt's plan should work.

He stepped back from the general. "Wait. I gotta take a piss before we get started."

He went into the bathroom and closed the door behind him. He didn't piss; he didn't need to. He hoped the general might take the hint and use the bathroom, too, so he could take a look inside the closet. He let a minute pass, flushed the toilet, and ran water in the sink.

Stepping back into the room, he said, "Next."

Dravko obliged and dutifully shut the door behind him. In two steps Kurt was at the closet pulling open the louvered doors. He spotted the steamer suitcase and lifted it to feel its heft. Roughly thirty pounds. He set it back down just as Dravko opened the bathroom door.

Kurt whirled around, holding his uniform on a hanger. "You didn't say dress whites. That's even sexier."

When they had undressed, Kurt slipped on the uniform's coat. "Pants, too?" he asked.

"Yes, but leave it hanging out."

"I can't help that it's black."

"I won't see it."

Dravko dropped to his knees to search for the perfect angle where he wouldn't see Kurt's head but only his body dressed to look like him, and of course he needed to see himself kneeling before his stand-in cock. When he found the right spot, he took Kurt into his mouth. They played like that for an hour, moving around for Dravko to find different perspectives on the same selfish orgy. At one point he landed on the idea of using a condom to make Kurt's skin appear white in the mirrors, which sent him into a frenzy that ended with his finally being spent, too. Kurt already had enough, having feigned a third orgasm, pretending to add to what had already fallen on the general's bare shoulders.

He helped Dravko to his feet. "Wow, you're something," Kurt said, already taking off the uniform. "You're more than something. Did I look like you?"

"Yes."

"Good, that was the point." Kurt got dressed while Dravko watched. "Are you staying in Warsaw a few more days. Because I am."

"I don't know."

"In case you do, I'll look for you at the Arena."

They shook hands, because some farewell was necessary, and despite what had transpired between them, at that moment any other gesture was too intimate.

CHAPTER TWENTY

BLINDLY JAY SWATTED AT THE telephone, wanting to turn off an alarm. Not until the fourth ring did he rouse himself enough to lift its receiver.

As he did, Lilka said drowsily, "It's the telephone."

"Yes, Jay, it's the telephone," Ann Rewls repeated into his ear.

"Who is that?"

"Good morning, Ann."

"Not talking?"

"I'm not awake yet. You should have room service deliver coffee if you want my complete attention."

"I doubt if that's possible at the moment," Ann said tartly.

"I hope there's a reason for this call other than harassment because I'll call security."

Lilka asked sleepily, "What time is it?"

Ann answered, "It should be about seven thirty your time."

"Seven thirty," Jay mumbled.

"Oh, I'm late," Lilka complained idly, not yet willing to scramble from bed. Lazily she draped an arm across his waist.

He said to Ann, "It must be the middle of the night there."

"I have breaking news."

Lilka had started to be playful.

"News that I need to hear right now?"

"I'm not calling to have you listen to the Noise Machine."

"Who is it?" Lilka asked, preoccupied.

"A crank call."

"I resent that," Ann said.

"Hold on," he told her, and covered the mouthpiece to say to Lilka, "I'll join you in the shower."

"What's the breaking news?" he asked Ann.

"You said you'd join her in the shower, didn't you?"

"Why do you think you know all my lines?"

"Because they're the captions on cave paintings. You thought you invented them?"

"I hope Ned's not planning on having breakfast in bed this morning, because it sounds like he might be it. What have you learned?"

"We got a direct hit on your houseboat man. The name on the envelope was easy to trace. Originally, he was—*is*—Tomasz Tomski from Chicago. He has aliases everywhere. From Tommy Turner in Las Vegas to Tommy Thompson in Atlantic City."

"What is he, a gambler?"

"With a bigamy problem. Make that trigamy. He has three wives."

"How the hell does he manage that from coast to coast?"

"Keep telling a woman you love her, and she'll believe almost anything you tell her, but you'll have to ask him how he managed the logistics. There's a bench warrant out for him in Chicago. One of the wives traced him there. He's got a string of charges against him. The latest: failure to pay child support."

"Is that extraditable?"

"What planet do you live on? That's the kind of thing that would help mostly women."

"Who's collecting his mail?"

"His mother, only not at her local post office. Apparently the family is a big name in Chicago's Polish community. His father is the King of Sausage or something like that."

"So Tommy boy is hiding out in Poland until his lawyers can straighten out his legal problems," Jay mused.

Ann unsuccessfully tried to suppress a yawn.

"Did you and Ned have a fight, is that why you're still up?"

"If you need to know, I get morning sickness somewhere between dessert and dawn."

"I bet you blame the Noise Machine for not being sympathetic enough, even though he's a direct contributor to why you have morning sickness."

"Something like that."

"Are you at your kitchen table?"

"Yes."

"I bet the Noise Machine is in the doorway behind you, waiting for you to come back to bed."

"I bet he's not."

"Okay, look."

"Okay."

"I also bet he's topless because that's how you like your men to sleep."

"I hate you for knowing so much."

"Hi Ned!" Jay said, loudly.

"Hey, Jay," he heard distantly.

"Say goodnight, boys," Ann said and hung up.

Jay approached the bathroom, thickening with anticipation, Lilka's scent still on him from their lovemaking the night before. A cloud rolled out of the doorway when he opened it. Lilka's pale body moved like a memory behind the shower's steamy glass door. He pressed himself against it, stretching out his arms. Lilka stretched out hers arms to cover his body with hers. Her breasts became white saucers for her ruby nipples. Their lips met in transparent kisses. Then he slipped into the shower. The water poured over them. He kissed his way down until he knelt in front of her. Cascading over her breasts, the water formed tributaries that joined in a river between her legs. He opened his mouth and drank greedily.

• • •

A MENU POSTED AT THE restaurant's entrance announced the cost of the breakfast buffet. Lilka fretted that Jay should spend so much, though once convinced to stay, she made it something glamorous. And it *was* sumptuous: down long tables, exotic fruits spilled from decorative cornucopias; chafing dishes offered meats, simmering porridges, and French toast, flanked by cheese rounds and mounds of biscuits and breads. Huge floral arrangements towered over the breakfasters. Lilka thought the room so elegant, she half expected paparazzi to descend upon it, snapping photos of the hungry pretenders to wealth and fame.

They ate ravenously. Outside the picture windows below them, electric trams rattled down the center of Aleje Jerozolimskie, spitting blue sparks and dispatching passengers. The sun, cresting the main train station opposite, shone as pale yellow as the marquee letters that identified it as Warszawa Centralna. People hurried up its ramp and disappeared inside its walls of black glass.

"I like to see a town wake up," Lilka said, "There is something new about each day. Do you understand?"

"Perfectly."

"Always my father walks in the morning. It is a habit for all his life. Every day he takes bread from the same shop, but always he changes how to go there to make each day a little different."

"I knew I liked your father."

"He likes you, too." She reached over and took his hand. "I am very happy to meet you."

"Me too."

Perhaps it was their glimpse of the sun that freed Lilka to talk, or the glittery breakfast room, but she did talk, about her dreams to travel, her hopes for a family, the usual things young people dream about. So she surprised Jay when she added, "The most I ever wanted was safety."

"Safety?"

"Is that the wrong word?"

"I don't know. What do you mean?"

"Before the change, nobody was safe. One day, everybody thought, it would be their turn to go to jail. My mother was always afraid, my father too, and Alina and me too. There were so many rules to break. Rules that you needed to break to survive, and always there was some-body watching. And people disappearing." Eventually she mentioned that Jacek's temper, always terrible and growing worse, made her afraid to live in her own home. "It's the opposite of what I have most wanted."

"There's really no place for you to move?" Jay asked.

There wasn't. No one had a spare room in their tiny prefabs, and to buy an apartment on the open market, well, that kind of money was a fantasy. "We make rules for living together, and Jacek always breaks them."

"Did you ever love him?" Jay ventured to ask.

"I thought yes, but we made a mistake."

"What mistake?"

"Aleks."

"Oh."

"We were too young. Too much was a struggle for us. I had to work and didn't have enough time for Aleks. He was always very shy and had no confidence in himself. That's why Jacek has been able to influence him. I blame me, too. I was too often absent for Aleks."

"Have you talked to him?"

"He is always at the river and I am afraid to go there."

"Can Tolek go with you?"

"Tolek! Oh, I forgot! What time is it?" She checked her watch and frowned. "You make me very late."

"Who wanted to make love twice?" he asked.

"You."

"Okay. Guilty."

"Now I have not enough time."

"What is it?"

"I must give Tolek a key so he can repair my toilet. It is not a nice problem to have."

"I can give it to him. He's coming about his visa this afternoon."

"I need to make a copy first," she lamented.

"I can do that, too. Where do you make copies?"

"At the train station."

"Problem solved. Give me the key and I'll make a copy."

She handed it to him.

"Now go or you're going to be late."

They kissed on their cheeks and Lilka rushed off. Jay signaled for the check and was signing it when a liveried bellhop entered the restaurant carrying an upright chalkboard on a short handle with small bells dangling from it. Passing between the tables, he twisted the handle to make the bells ring. When he drew closer, Jay saw Porter printed on the chalkboard.

"I'm Porter," he said.

"You have an urgent telephone call at the front desk."

CHAPTER TWENTY-ONE

THE DOORMAN HAILED JAY A cab and he slipped into the backseat, giving directions in bad Polish to the doughnut shop where he had arranged to meet Kulski. He puzzled over how to help Lilka, growing angry at a system that, though now dead, continued to hold her hostage. Back home he knew women who felt boxed in by lives they wouldn't have chosen, yet none had been as entrapped as Lilka, forced to remain caged with her tormentor even after she had summoned the courage to leave him.

The driver maneuvered a shortcut to avoid a one-way street and stopped in front of the bakery. Kulski stood on the sidewalk finishing a doughnut. He offered Jay the last one in his bag.

Jay took it. "What's the situation?"

The detective licked icing from his fingers. "A man went into the houseboat before dawn. He has not used the lights, but he is there still."

"His name is Tomasz Tomski," Jay reported.

"That makes sense because the boat belongs to Viktor Tomski," the detective replied. "A Polish American from Chicago."

"Must be Tommy's father. What do you know about him?"

"He's a gambler and comes to Poland many times."

"Gambling must be in the family's genes," Jay said. "Tommy's been taking lots of chances, too." He told Kulski the story of Tommy and his three wives.

"I would not have the energy for three women," the detective said.

Kulski's lookout on the bridge dropped a fishing line in the water. The morning sun had retreated behind approaching storm clouds, and he looked cold and miserable.

"How do you want to handle this?" Kulski asked.

"It's your case."

Timothy Jay Smith

"He'll be more frightened if he hears 'FBI' first."

"I'll be glad to be the warm-up act."

The gangplank, still treacherous with ice, caused Kulski to fall hard on his game leg. Rounding the deckhouse was equally challenging, and by the time they reached the door, Tommy had opened it. "Who the fuck are you clowns?" he said in English with no discernible accent. He was thirty-three going on middle aged and wore a leisure suit you'd expect to see on date night at a Chinese restaurant in Orlando.

"Are you Tomasz Tomski?" Jay asked.

"Who are you?"

"Jay Porter, FBI." He flashed his badge.

Tommy paled. "What the fuck?"

"I'm Detective Leszek Kulski, Warsaw Police."

"May we come in?" Jay didn't give him the option to say no and stepped past him into the room.

"I've done nothin' federal," he protested.

"Who said you did anything, Tommy? We just have some questions."

"I'm not answering without my attorney."

"Tommy, you're pleading guilty before being accused, that's not smart. Detective Kulski, would you like to ask your questions?"

"A man was killed three nights ago not two hundred meters from here." Kulski pointed down the river. "Just past the kiosks."

"I didn't see anything."

"So you *were* here?" Jay said.

"I wasn't lookin' in that direction."

"*Lookin'*, as in peeping through that spotting scope?"

Tommy's eyes narrowed. "You have a search warrant? I wanna see it."

"I suggest you cooperate with the local police, or they might send you home, where I hear there are three women waiting to nail your ass, and not in their usual friendly ways."

"I've done nothin' extraditable."

"I can have you deported for sexual perversion," Detective Kulski said.

Jay shrugged. "Peeping Tom, isn't that what I said?"

"What did you see, Mr. Tomski?"

Tommy sat and rubbed his face hard with a manicured hand. "It was late, and I noticed headlights coming off the main road. I'd just put out the light to go to sleep, but I started thinking about what they were probably doing out there so I got up to look."

Jay asked, "Is that a regular curiosity of yours?"

"Only because that scope is here. I'm not into peeping, not usually. It's kinda cool, though, like watching an old European film where everything's watery but you know what's happening."

"What did happen, Mr. Tomski?"

"There was two of them. They had got out of the car already. She was leading him down to the water."

"*She?*" Jay and the detective said at the same time.

"Yeah, *she*, and *he* followed her. He was limping."

"What time was it?"

"About one, maybe a little later."

"How could you see them in the dark from here?"

"The way the cars go by on the road, there's enough light. Maybe the moon was out that night too, I don't remember."

Kulski nodded. "Go on."

"I focused on her, 'cause she had stopped moving, and he was still catching up. He was limping, like I said, and wobbly."

"Drunk?" Jay asked.

"Could've been. I was still thinkin' they were, you know, going to fuck or something, only the next thing I knew, I heard a shot. For a couple of seconds I wasn't sure that it wasn't a car backfiring. Then I saw the guy fall."

"She was still downhill from him?"

"Yeah, and he was tall, too, at least six feet. He kinda towered over her."

"That explains the bullet's trajectory," Jay commented.

"What happened next, Mr. Tomski?"

"Then this other guy showed up. Where the hell he came from, I don't know, but he and the woman talked to each other, then he messed with the body some."

"What do you mean?"

"He stooped down and did something. I couldn't see what, but that's when I saw her. She was trying to light a cigarette and it was windy, so she held her lighter a long time."

"Describe her."

"She looked good in a sexy way. A brunette, I could see that."

"Age? Build?"

"Hard to say, she was wearing a long coat."

"Could you identify her, Tommy?"

"I doubt it."

"Would setting aside the bench warrant for your arrest help you recognize her?"

"It might."

"I thought so," Jay said, "and that deal's not being offered. I just wanted to know how easy it was to buy you. What was she wearing?"

"A pants suit from Saks Fifth Avenue, how the fuck do I know? I can't read labels with that thing."

"Dress, pants, coat, hat?"

"A long coat. When the dead guy was coming at her, she opened it up like he was supposed to crawl inside and get all cozy."

"What happened after the woman lit a cigarette, Mr. Tomski?"

"Another car came up. It's kind of a lovers' lane along the water. The man and woman, they started kissing then. They didn't want the other car coming any closer."

"What did he look like, Tommy? Fast, don't think about it."

"I never saw his face but I could tell he had a beard. He was a big guy, not tall like the dead guy but big. Stocky."

"What else, Mr. Tomski?"

"The other car left and they walked to her car."

"What was the make?"

"I couldn't tell. I don't know cars."

"Big? Small?"

"Smallish. Red or brown, it wasn't in the light."

"What did the man do?"

"That's just the thing. He took a suitcase out of her car."

"A suitcase?"

"It sure looked like one. And he walked away with it. From the way he was carrying it, I could tell it was heavy, but I never saw where he came from or went."

"What else did you see or hear?" Detective Kulski asked.

Tommy shook his head. "Nothing."

"You'll have to come with me to the station, Mr. Tomski, to make a statement."

"What more of a statement do you want?"

"For the record. Typed and signed."

"The hell I will without my attorney!"

Detective Kulski held out his hand. "I need to see your passport."

Tommy took it from the desk.

Kulski pocketed it.

"Hey, that's mine, you've no right to take it."

"It's insurance that you don't run away."

An hour later, Detective Kulski was typing the last words of Tommy Tomski's statement. So effectively had he layered his aliases, borrowing characteristics from one to construct another, that Jay doubted he could still recognize himself. His father had cornered the market for kielbasa in Chicago's Polish Triangle and invested in casinos. He hired Tommy to drop in on them, play their tables, and check operations. Routinely the croupiers rigged the odds in his favor. In a short time, he raked in enough money to consider opening his own casino in the family's rundown houseboat in Warsaw.

Detective Kulski handed Tommy's statement to him. "Sign, date, and put the time here."

He did, and handed it back, "Can I have my passport back now?"

Kulski looked at Jay, who shook his head. "He's too eager to have it. He'll run."

"Fuck! I'm cooperating!"

"If you need to travel, come see me. Eva!"

She appeared at the detective's door. Kulski asked her to make copies of Tommy's statement and fax one to Director Husarska. She left, taking Tommy with her to a waiting car for a ride back to the houseboat.

After they were gone, Jay said, "Looks like you've got yourself a real live witness."

"And a strange story," the detective said.

"At least now you know it's a man and a woman. A stocky man with a beard."

"Do you know how many Polish men fit that description?"

"I know one was repairing his van outside Billy's shack a few days ago."

"That's not sufficient to obtain a search warrant."

"And a tall woman," Jay said. "Possibly a tall policewoman because of the P-83. How many women in the police force?"

"Many, and a lot of them are tall."

"Then again, it might not be a policewoman at all," Jay continued. "The black market for P-83s might be small, but it still exists. I'd like to see everything collected from the murder site again. We have new information. Maybe something will click."

"It's stored at the lab," Kulski replied. "It's possible to have it here tomorrow morning."

"I'll come by early."

"Not before nine, I have rehabilitation for my knee on Friday mornings."

"Is it helping?"

"I'm walking but not much more than that."

· · ·

JAY TOOK A TAXI TO Centralna and entered the cavernous station. The whole place echoed with the voices of travelers bouncing off the glass ceiling held aloft by black iron girders. Escalators transported people into an underground mall. Jay took one and entered the maze of crowded corridors that veered off at strange angles. Flowers, lingerie, religious icons, groceries: all could be purchased in the myriad shops that displayed their wares in sooty windows. Bored shopkeepers stood in open doorways and blew smoke into the stale air. In that burrowed world, everyone's exhalations were recycled.

Jay wandered until he came to a shop identified by a sign in the shape of a brass key. A bell on the door tinkled when he entered.

The locksmith greeted him from behind the counter. His arm, in a sling, rested on the shelf of his enormous belly. He also offered shoe repairs and shines and gave Jay's shoes a questionable glance before taking Lilka's key with his smudged hand.

"Two copies," Jay said, thinking to make an extra for her.

Over the sound of the grinding machine, the locksmith wanted to know where he was from, and then if Jay perchance knew his relatives in Chicago. He didn't, and went to stand by the door to watch shoppers shuffle past. That's when Jay saw him. The man from the shack with the pinched apple-doll face was coming down the corridor.

"I'm in a hurry," he said.

Billy passed the window.

"All finished." With his good hand, the locksmith removed the second copy from the key cutter.

"How much?"

The locksmith polished the new keys with a wire brush and handed them to Jay. "Two copies."

He turned back to his key cutter just as Billy disappeared around a corner. Jay threw some bills on the counter and dashed after him.

"Wait!" shouted the locksmith, but Jay was already running. He could keep the change.

He took the corner too quickly and nearly tripped over an old beggar woman. Billy, halfway down the corridor, opened a door and went inside. Jay dropped coins in the woman's cup and went after him. He had left the door ajar, and Jay could smell stale beer even before he saw the word BAR stenciled on the window. Behind the counter, Billy was switching on neon beer signs that lit the room with puddles of color. Jay kept walking until he found an escalator that deposited him on the sidewalk outside. He gulped the fresh air hungrily, as Lazarus must have when he emerged from his tomb.

CHAPTER TWENTY-TWO

Basia Husarska stared at the door. Where was that damn secretary of hers? Kulski had called twenty minutes ago to say he was sending a fax. He had a witness, who saw the murder happen, who could ID the murder . . . *ess.* He held the gender tag back a moment, and then trumped his discovery with that revelation. The murderer was a woman. The witness was certain. Dark, sexy, she smoked. There had been a man, too, bearded, the witness never saw his face. It was a break in the case. He needed manpower to cross-check the ballistics fingerprint, assuming it was recovered, with the P-83 prints on file. Of course Basia had to agree. "Whatever it takes," she told him, and good work on narrowing it down to a woman, that left only half the human race as suspects. He hadn't laughed at her effort to joke, perhaps because she rarely did. What else did the witness say?

She lit a cigarette.

Where was that damn secretary?

What did the witness see?

Who was he?

A gambler, a fraud, a counterfeit, Kulski had told her. Some crazy story of aliases begetting aliases. A spotting scope on a moonlit night her undoing. Her destiny branded by her lighter, revealing her face to a peeper's secret pleasure. She could have screamed at the injustice of it.

Where was that damn secretary?

With the fax.

With the witness's statement.

Witness for the prosecution.

Damn if Jacek wasn't delaying the exchange. Fearful of Mladic, he wanted to be able to pretend the fourth courier had crossed on Monday a week later and that's how he came into possession of the suitcase bomb. They'd sort out some story of what had happened to delay his man. Mladic never met the couriers anyway. Jacek made the pickups and delivered the goods to Basia, who passed them on to Dravko—leaving the guileless couriers in Jacek's possession to do with them what he wanted, and he had.

Damn that secretary!

Damn that witness!

Where was that damn report?

Basia flung open her door, startling her secretary, who had raised her hand to knock on it.

"Give it to me," she said and grabbed the report from Hanna's hand.

Basia slammed her door. Skimmed the statement. Reread his description of her and was relieved it was vague. She couldn't be identified by it, and even an expedited examination of the bullet would take days. She still had time but she needed a game plan. She was the dealer in a game she had never played and she didn't know the winning cards. Was Jacek her winner? Or was he the Joker, playing everybody a fool, and mean for the sake of it? Meanness as art. But ready to split a million dollars and say goodbye on a handshake. Only they would be running from Mladic—the king and she his queen—who would have his bomb at any price.

Basia shuddered.

She needed a strategy for dealing with Mladic. In Basia's construct of her island world, he would be an infrequent interruption, coming occasionally and retreating as quickly, leaving behind nothing but stains on her sheets from trying to forestall his faltering heterosexuality. He could masquerade for others, but Basia had known him for too long. When the stunts he wanted her to perform turned demeaning, she recognized it for what it was: degradation of women as permission to desire men. Dravko's iconoclastic world was a narcissistic one. During his impromptu visits, Basia would play her roles and do her tricks, and when he left, she would gladly return to the beach alone.

• • •

THE LOCKSMITH SMILED WHEN JAY entered his small shop. "I knew you'd be back," he said. "You ran out of here so fast." He wiped shoe polish from his hands and picked a key off the lip of his cash register. "Your original."

He took the key. "Thanks."

"I saw you running after Billy."

"Billy?"

"That's what he calls himself. Fucking Russian. Illych is probably his real name. He did this to me." The locksmith brandished his injured arm.

"He broke it?"

"Twisted it hard enough. I wouldn't chase after Billy unless he's your friend."

"I mistook him for someone else."

"That's not a face you easily mistake. Looks like your shoes could use a shine."

Jay looked down. "You're right." He stepped up to a raised seat and firmly squared his feet on the brass footrests. "Where did you learn English?"

"I spent ten years in New York working for hotels."

"Why'd you come back?"

"You wanna know the truth? Every boss I had wasn't white and I got tired of working for 'em. All they wanted to do was kick my ass and tell Polish jokes. Fucking Polish jokes, like I couldn't be telling jokes about *them* all day long."

"Sounds like here you might be working for Billy."

"Fuck that. I got a small shop but it's mine, no one to tell me what's what. These guys think they can come here and take over. It's a crazy world when you gotta pay the same people not to hurt you who will if you don't."

"Did you go to the police?"

"What, and have my other arm broken? This time, the ugly man wins."

"Billy?"

The locksmith nodded. He couldn't snap the polish cloth because of his injured arm, but almost as nimbly gave a final burnish to Jay's shoes, his good elbow jabbing out this way and that. "Finished," he said, and tapped his sole.

Jay stepped down and paid him.

"Don't be going to Billy's Bar," the man warned him again.

At that moment, Basia Husarska passed his shop. The locksmith snorted scornfully. "That's where she's going."

"Billy's Bar?"

"I've seen her a few times. She's why I don't go to the police."

"Why's that?"

"*She's* police. Everybody around here knows that."

"Maybe she's working undercover."

"Sure, like the Pope is Jewish. I seen her walkin' outta here all times of day, high as a kite."

Jay followed the locksmith's advice and stayed away from Billy's Bar. If Basia were in it, she could be there for lots of reasons, and none included him. He had his doubts if any of them included police work, either. He lingered in the train station, hoping to catch a glimpse of her coming out of its catacombs. For nearly an hour he feigned an interest in magazines he couldn't read and watched updates on the arrival/departure board. Not wanting to draw any more attention to himself than he might already have, he left the central station.

CHAPTER TWENTY-THREE

THE RECEPTIONIST ADMITTED JAY TO the embassy's secured bowels. He had an overload of information to process with insufficient caffeine in his system and headed for the coffeemaker. He poured a cup and looked both ways before exiting the nook, fortunately so because Libby Barnstable came slinking around the corner looking anywhere but where she was going. Only his quick sidestep saved them from another collision.

She gave him a petrified look. "Have you seen the visa line?"

He had not; the line formed at the side entrance. "I came through the front gate," he said.

"You're undone there."

"What?"

"An epaulette, it's unbuttoned."

She craned her neck to get a look at it.

"Here, let me help," Jay said, setting his coffee down so he could fix the button on her shoulder.

Libby seemed to tremble. "Thanks. Oh, I know I'm being . . . I don't know, but nothing's going right and now this visa line! What could so many people want?" She reached for the coffee pot.

"Visas?" Jay suggested.

"I know! But so many? What do they think, America is empty?"

"Or maybe rich enough to house a few more. How about lunch today?" Libby looked panicked.

"I'll take that as a yes," Jay said. "There's something I wanted to ask you about."

"About work?" she asked.

"In a way, yes." Jay tossed a quarter into the tip can with a lonely rattle.

"The cleaning lady just collected it," she told him.

"Noon?" Jay said. Libby froze.

"Lunch, at noon?" Jay repeated. "I'll meet you in the lobby."

• • •

WITHIN FIVE MINUTES, KURT SHOWED up in his doorway. "Good morning," he said.

"Good, I'm glad you're here," Jay said. "I have breaking news."

"I've had a busy twenty-four hours, too."

"Translated, what does that mean?"

Kurt pulled up a chair. "I got into Mladic's room."

"How the fuck did you manage that?"

"That's exactly how I did it. By fucking him. Not technically, but in a manner of speaking."

"Do I want to hear the details?"

Kurt laughed. "You sure do!"

The CIA man explained how he staked out Mladic's lodge and followed him to the baths. "While we were undressing, I made sure he got a good look at all of me," Kurt continued. "He was totally dazzled by my black skin."

"By only your skin?"

"We did a little playing around and were ready to get to some serious sex when I suggested we go someplace more private. He thought I meant my room, but the general's uniform was in his room."

"Why was the uniform important?"

Kurt smiled. "I thought you'd never ask."

By the time Kurt concluded the description of his escapade—towering over Mladic in his formal uniform while he scampered around on the floor pathetically pretending to suck himself—Jay couldn't stop laughing. "That was brilliant! Good thing you knew about the mirrors."

"Good thing I knew about the ego. He's a narcissistic fuck."

"The party for Mladic at the ambassador's tonight might be a tad awkward. You're supposed to be part of the embassy team."

Kurt grinned. "I will be."

"After what happened?"

"Mladic loves me, and besides, I have a plan. Let's go talk to Carl. He has to buy into it. But tell me your breaking news first."

Jay reported on his wake-up call from Ann Rewls that woke him and Lilka, which he described only enough to suggest that any interruption was unwelcome. Then breakfast, also interrupted by a revelatory phone call: their star witness, Tommy Tomski, had returned to the houseboat. He was on the lam from three wives and a gambling habit, and telling an interesting story about witnessing a woman knock off the fourth courier. He'd watched through a spotting scope at midnight with only passing headlights for illumination. The woman looked dark and sexy to him, and he was hopeful he could ID her if they intervened in his legal problems back home. Detective Kulski had joked that even Husarska fit the woman's description.

"Does she?" Kurt asked.

"So does my ex-wife," Jay replied.

"Doesn't the P-83 point you back at the police?"

"It would, except for the fact that you can buy a P-83 at the Praga market if you flash something other than Monopoly money. Kulski doesn't like to admit it, it's a pride thing, but he's said as much. It'll be a different story if we get a ballistics match. By the way, Husarska nixed sending the bullet to headquarters for testing."

"Did she give a reason?"

"That we'd only lose two days if the local lab can't handle it. She's right, and besides, the bullet is so mangled we'll be lucky if we can match the make."

"Did Tommy see the guy?"

"A stocky guy with a beard."

"That's not very helpful."

"Especially in Poland, but it's still more than we've had. Let's go see the ambassador. You can tell me your plan for tonight on the way."

• • •

"YOU DID *WHAT*?" AMBASSADOR LERNER demanded, pacing behind his desk and coming about at the flag. "Have you any idea of the repercussions this could have on our foreign policy?" He looked at Kurt as he might a lunatic. "Now you want me to do *what?*"

"Introduce me," said Kurt. "Give me your blessing, and make sure that I have plenty of time to talk up the general."

"Damn it, Crawford! It's one thing to be . . . to be . . ."

"Gay, sir?"

"Your being gay is one thing, but to mislead a foreign diplomat—"

"General Mladic has no doubt that I am gay, sir, and no complaints."

"To search his room by . . . by . . ."

"Seducing him, sir?"

"By seducing him, and for Christ's sake quit calling me sir!" Carl sank into his chair. "So did misleading your way into a diplomat's room result in anything other than risking an international crisis if any of this is leaked?"

"I found a suitcase," Kurt replied.

"In a hotel room? Now you have my undivided attention."

"It's an unusual suitcase. It's new but looks like an old steamer trunk with leather belts and brass finishes."

"I'm waiting for the punch line."

"No punch line, except he seemed to be hiding it in the closet, and it's heavy. He hasn't unpacked it."

"So what do you guess is in it?"

"A bomb or a million dollars."

"For Christ's sake! It could be his dirty clothes," the ambassador said.

"Probably the money," Jay said. "If Mladic had the bomb, like we've said before, he wouldn't be sticking around."

"He might, now that he's apparently fallen in love with Kurt. Let's go over your cockamamie plan."

They did, and Kurt rebutted every what-if scenario they threw at him until they finally agreed that his plan might work. Carl would alert Mrs. Ambassador to a salient change or two in Kurt's biography—such as now having a wife—and otherwise they were set. Nothing in the ambassador's handshake, however, evinced confidence when they left his office.

Walking back to their offices, Jay said, "You know, your paranoia is infectious. Last night Lilka described a suitcase she thinks Jacek stole. It sounds like a miniature steamer trunk, too."

"It might not be coincidental. Making a switch using identical suitcases is Spycraft 101. No one will notice that an exchange has been made unless they actually see it happen."

"What the hell are you talking about?"

"Jacek Rypinski showed up on a watch list five years ago at age thirty-one and married. Our file doesn't show a divorce."

"Then your file is wrong."

"I'm only reporting."

"Go ahead and report."

"He'd been stopped a couple of times for possession of marijuana and was later busted for dealing. That put him on Langley's list."

"Why? You're spooks, not policemen."

"Drugs lead you to bad guys, and those are the guys we try to ferret out before they end up running whole countries. When we learned he owned a couple of trucks, right there that made it possible for him to graduate to the bigger leagues like weapons smuggling. Or nuclear smuggling."

"As far as I know, he has one van, not a couple of trucks, and zero current wife," Jay replied. "Are you still watching him?"

"Not lately."

"Who would know if he graduated to bigger leagues?"

"Internal Affairs," Kurt answered.

"You mean Minister Brzeski?"

"And Basia Husarska in Organized Crime."

"Are you suggesting there's a connection between Husarska and Jacek?"

"I'm just putting it out there to consider."

"That's pretty far-fetched when we don't really know if the two suitcases are close matches," Jay pointed out.

"Can you get inside Rypinski's apartment and take a picture?"

"Lilka isn't going to invite me home with Jacek around. Can you get back into Mladic's room?"

"Let's see what fallout there is from the ambassador's party."

They arrived at Jay's office.

"Jay, I know you're fond of Lilka—"

"I don't need the lecture."

"I think you do. You have to be open to the possibility that if Jacek is involved in your case, Lilka might be, too."

"She's not."

"Too much is at stake if she is and you're not paying attention. Husarska knew about your arrival. It would be easy enough to stage a missing suitcase, a chance meeting with a beautiful woman, and a love affair intended to derail—or at least spy on—an investigation. She has a lot of resources, spies—and, reliable rumors have it, a whole library of incriminating tapes she uses to call in chits. Apparently it's pretty extensive."

They arrived at Jay's office.

"Langley wants to isolate Mladic, stop the weapons flow, and put another foot on the neck of the mafias. They're the real security risk in this region. They could easily destabilize the whole democratic movement."

"Even more dangerous than an atomic bomb?" Jay asked.

"That's a global risk. All you have to do is look across the border and see what the mafias could do here. There have always been rackets in Russia, only now the criminals are the elite, the new *nomenklatura*, and they run everything. And own everything. From cosmetics to prostitution, you name it, the mafias are Russia's best capitalists. It's almost impossible for a legitimate business to operate. Langley doesn't want Poland sucked down the same pipe."

• • •

THE ONLY SUBJECT JAY COULD get Libby to talk about over their bowls of soup were her cats. Both strays picked up on the street. Her landlord objected until the cats started reliably catching mice. Then they became minor celebrities in the building. Over coffee, she finally asked what Jay had wanted to talk about.

"Actually, it's not about me. Have you had a chance to look over the visa application for Tolek Kuron?"

"Who?" Libby asked.

"Tolek Kuron. He applied a few weeks ago. Didn't I mention him the other day?"

"Oh," Libby said. She blew her nose in a napkin. He could see her thinking, *Is this why you bought me lunch?* But she sat up and said brightly, "Sure, I'll give his application special consideration."

Jay told her as much as he knew about Tolek, even agreed to sponsor him, not certain what commitment he had made and envisioning ending up in an INS cage.

Outside everything was wet from an earlier rain. They crossed to the embassy, where the Marine guard waved them through the gate with a friendly, "Good afternoon, Miss Barnstable." Libby blushed.

Tolek jumped up and straightened his tie when they entered the lobby. "You'll have a chance to meet Mr. Kuron in person," Jay told Libby.

Tolek looked more like a harried clerk in an ill-fitting suit than the marvel of communist resistance Jay had convinced Libby that he was. A Solidarity activist, arrested and detained under who knew what conditions; a caring father, it was clear in his application's essay on "Why I Want to Go to America" (an addendum Libby had introduced—perhaps she had initiative after all); a caring husband, too, for a wife who had succeeded professionally: these were the attributes that convinced Libby to grant Tolek his visas. She seemed stunned when a big bear of a man whose shirt stuck out even after he tucked it in rose before them.

Jay made the introductions. Of Libby, he said, "US Consul General, and of course, you know her father is—"

"Of course!" exclaimed Tolek. He flushed with excitement. "It is my pleasure, my very great pleasure." He pumped her hand.

"And mine," said Libby hesitantly, unused to enthusiastic displays.

"Miss Barnstable has approved your visa," Jay told him.

"Has Miss Barnstable approved my visa?" Tolek asked, as if responding to an instruction on a language exam: Turn this sentence into a question. Only when he had repeated it did he digest what he was saying. He expelled a few short breaths and stuttered a couple of random words. "Will Alina be surprised!" he finally managed. He flapped his arms, euphoric, ready to fly. Unable to contain himself, he embraced Libby and kissed her on the mouth. "You make me so happy! I love you!"

She fell back. "Mr. Kuron!"

"And you, Jay, you make me so happy I should kiss you, too!"

"That won't be necessary."

"It is my happiest day!"

Libby, wiping her lips, said, "Of course, there are still formalities."

"Procedures," he translated for Tolek, with an eye on Libby. "Mere formalities, right, Miss Barnstable? He can buy his tickets?"

"For my son, I thank you," interjected Tolek. "'Those who desire to give up freedom in order to gain security will not have, nor do they deserve, either one.' Thomas Jefferson."

Astonished, Libby asked, "You know Jefferson?"

"I know all the presidents! The capital for every state!"

"He does," Jay confirmed.

Libby, clearly impressed, raised her chin and said, "Mr. Kuron, let me welcome you to America."

He bowed, gentlemanly. "Thank you."

She then excused herself, walking backward away from them before turning and scuttling off. Tolek stood there grinning.

"So you are really going to America," Jay said.

"I am! Can you believe it? My son will know the kind of freedom I have only imagined. And now I want to announce to Alina that we have visas! Thank you. You have helped so much."

They shook hands.

"Wait, I have Lilka's key. I made her two copies." Jay pulled them from his pocket but couldn't find the original. "Somewhere I have it," he said.

"It's okay, give it to Lilka. Or send it to me in America!"

CHAPTER TWENTY-FOUR

D RAVKO PEERED IN THE MIRROR, fishing for the nose hair that was tickling him, and finally managed to pluck it. With manicure scissors, he snipped away the hairs sprouting from his ears and ran a safety razor around the edge of them. His grooming complete, he stepped back to admire himself. Power had appeal, and he felt spotlighted that night. He'd been invited to the American ambassador's residence for an off-the-record tête-à-tête. That could only mean one thing: the Americans were acknowledging that he was going to achieve Serbia. He'd be both her mother and founding father, and the Americans, always so reluctant to support ethnic independence movements, were finally acknowledging the inevitable: President Dravko Mladic.

A final pat of his hair, a last sweep at dandruff, and he turned off the bathroom light. In the mirrored bedroom, Dravko knew precisely where to stand for his reflection to ricochet and spin long chains of his likeness as far as his eye could travel. Slowly he turned, dazzling the room with his bright-shining medals. In the many mirrors, he tried to see himself all at once, to see the whole Dravko, and what he saw satisfied him. Pleased him. He was ready for the world.

He lifted his arms and, watching in the mirrors, briefly danced with himself before leaving the lodge. The proprietor bid him good evening as he passed the reception desk, and in those spare words, Dravko thought he detected a glimmer of congratulations. Proudly he hitched up his trousers, slipped into the waiting taxi, and gave the driver the address for the American ambassador's residence. How had the invitation read? "An informal cocktail at the Residence." Dravko knew the doublespeak of diplomatic sidestepping to decipher what lay behind the invitation: the siege of Sarajevo had sent the Americans clamoring for a meeting. They were the first to recognize his certain destiny, as would the whole world when it learned he had the bomb. When next he made this trip it would be in a motorcade. He leaned back in the seat, imagining the evening ahead, the whispered innuendos, the suggestions that as soon as he is president... The film inside his head started again. The streetlights were his klieg lights, passing headlights the flash of cameras, the taxi a limousine to his inauguration. The faxed invitation in his pocket his acceptance speech. Dravko smiled in the dark, enjoying the practice run.

• • •

JAY HAD ARRIVED AT THE ambassador's residence needing a drink. Now he was swirling the ice in his second scotch while telling Kurt and the ambassador about his encounter with the locksmith. They were in the library, which was lined with bookshelves tall enough to require stepladders. "That puts Basia in Billy's Bar, and Billy was at the mechanic's shack," he told them.

"For Christ's sake!" Carl broke in. "Do I need to remind you that you are here to assist the police, not investigate them? You're suggesting one helluva conspiracy. The next thing I know, it'll involve the Pope!"

"It probably doesn't go any higher than a minister," Kurt suggested.

"For Christ's sake!"

Kurt had been watching out the window and said, "Mladic is here, and he's dressed for the occasion. Formal whites. He must be in good shape to heft around all those medals."

Ambassador Lerner chugged what remained of his drink. "Don't break any laws, because neither of you has diplomatic immunity. Now I'm going out there, and hope to God I'm not starting World War III."

• • •

UNCEREMONIOUSLY DROPPED OFF, DRAVKO BLINKED in the drizzle, confused by the lack of crowds. It took him a moment to remember the taxi ride was only a practice run. He faced the ambassador's house, encouraged by its stately columns. A worthy residence. He mounted its steps and rapped on the door with its lion-headed knocker.

A maid—he guessed a Filipina, or some female from another one of those maid-exporting countries—ushered him into the foyer. As she took his overcoat and cap, he felt he was in a place where he belonged. Seconds later, Ambassador Carl Lerner appeared and held out his hand.

"I'm glad we have this opportunity to meet, General Mladic."

The two men shook hands.

"It is my pleasure, Ambassador."

"On a cold night like this, I imagine you could use a drink. Scotch, isn't it?"

"You're very well informed."

"We Americans like to know our friends. I've invited some staff to join us. We'll have our private conversation later."

Dravko followed the ambassador through double doors into a banquet hall, where the conversations stopped as all heads turned to assess him. Their expressions were gloomy, certainly not the cheering, applauding supporters he had imagined, and for a moment he wondered if he had been lured into a hostile meeting, until the cocktail chatter resumed with good-natured laughter. With a clap on his shoulder, the ambassador steered him to his heavyset wife, whose blue eyes twinkled with permanent surprise from too many facelifts. In an English he could barely understand, she begged his indulgence and introduced him around the room. He spoke briefly to a man dressed as a racing jockey who insisted on speaking French, though he was neither French nor a jockey but director of America's development program. When Dravko remarked he thought that America was developed already, the development man's wife brayed at his remark while surveying a tray of canapes. Next he was introduced to a younger woman with fleecy hair who nervously jammed her fingers into the many pockets of her attire, reminding him of squirrels looking for nuts they'd secreted away. She ogled his medals.

"Now Libby, don't hog the general," the ambassador said as he approached them. "I want him to meet someone."

They turned to see Kurt Crawford.

All the blood drained from Dravko's face.

"General Mladic, I want you to meet Kurt Crawford. He's a

businessman visiting us here in Warsaw. I thought you two might enjoy a discussion of common interests."

Kurt extended his hand.

Memories of the African's hands came flooding back as Dravko grasped his paler palm.

"This is a coincidence," said Kurt with a crooked smile.

"You've met before?" asked the ambassador.

"The general stopped me to ask directions on the street. Do you remember?"

"I remember you," Dravko choked out.

"Our small world keeps getting smaller," said Carl. "And our time shorter. Would you gentlemen please join me in the library?"

A minute later, the ambassador poured shots of scotch while he said, "I hope straight up is good for everyone. I refuse to dilute this scotch with ice or water." He handed out the short glasses. "Cheers."

"Cheers." They all lifted their glasses.

"So, General Mladic, as I said, our time is getting shorter too, so let's get down to business. On the record, I want to say that the United States government officially protests your country's siege of Sarajevo and we stand with the international community in condemning attacks on innocent civilians. Off the record—and the rest of this conversation will be off the record—we must be pragmatists and look beyond the war at who will be able to be left in charge. We believe that will be you, General Mladic, in a very big way, and we can help you."

"Help me how?"

"We're used to riggin' horse races in Texas. If we're betting on you, we want to make sure you win, and hopefully win by more than a nose."

"I am afraid my English is not good enough to understand," Dravko confessed.

"Kurt, maybe you could step in here."

"What Ambassador Lerner is trying to say is that we expect you will be the president of Serbia," Kurt said. "That makes our president want to be friends with you. President to president."

"You are inviting me to the White House?"

"That will come later," the ambassador answered. "First you have to win a war or two, and that's where Kurt comes in. He has an interesting proposition for you. The bottom line, General, is that we want this horse race in Bosnia to be over."

"But you need the right firepower," added Kurt, "convincing firepower. Are you with me?"

Dravko was. The scotch had the effect of clearing his head and blurring over language gaps. "You are offering me American weapons?"

"I will excuse myself and let Kurt discuss the details," replied the ambassador. "You understand, General, that protocol forbids my discussing these matters personally." With that, Carl closed the door after him.

Kurt burst into muted laughter. "Can you goddamn believe this? It looks like you could use another drink. I could for damn sure!" He retrieved the bottle from the bar. "Goddamn!"

"You did not plan this?"

"*Plan* this? Hell no! I don't mind saying, though, I was glad to see you when I walked in tonight. I always prefer doing business with a friend."

"What is your business? It has not been explained."

"The dirty shorts of American foreign policy, that's my business. I'm a weapons dealer for Uncle Sam. I make sure that American weapons get where they're needed no matter what the public or piddling-assed Congress thinks. No money up front, no problem if you slip on the payments. When Uncle Sam picks a winner, like you, he makes sure that he wins."

"Me?"

"Apparently the American brass like your style. They know you've got a setup with PENZIK and things are moving south without a problem. No road bumps, only sleeping policemen. We want to piggyback on what you've got in place and keep using your network."

"My network?"

"It appears to be operationally seamless. You haven't had a bust yet, have you?"

"A bust?"

"I didn't think so. Your whole operation is smooth, Dravko. Can I call you Dravko?"

"Yes."

"You should be proud of yourself."

"I am."

"And for good reason." Kurt flashed a seductive smile. "You were goddamned good last night, too. I have some pictures in my head that I'd like to copy."

"You can do that?"

Kurt laughed. "You have a good sense of humor, don't you? Maybe we could have a rerun of last night. Copy *that*. You and me."

"You are suggesting—"

"Only if you want. No pressure. I don't usually combine business with pleasure, but for you and a rerun of last night, I'll make an exception."

"Yes."

Kurt smiled. "I guess it doesn't get any more affirmative than that. So about our business."

"The weapons?"

"That's another affirmative. Of course, you need time to make a list. There are issues of compatibility, redundancy, firepower. Battlefield strategies."

Kurt reached to pour the last of the scotch into their glasses. His silk shirt stretched over his sporty body and revealed the impression of his nipple. Dravko put a tentative finger to it.

"Aren't you the daredevil, but I like it." Kurt slipped his hand under the general's white coat to pinch his nipple in return. "How about tomorrow, Mr. President? Same place, same time, same shower?"

The emotions that coursed through Dravko! They tipped him into whitewater, threatening to drown him in eddies where he had never swam. He had never been infatuated before. He had never experienced those palpitations of the heart, that shortness of breath, the arousal of anticipation. He had dared touch the African in the ambassador's library!

Jay knocked on the door and swung it open.

The general jumped at his intrusion.

"Excuse me. I thought the ambassador was in here."

"There you are, Porter!" boomed the ambassador, coming up behind him. "You're as hard to catch as a greased turkey on Thanksgiving." He poked his head into the library. "Are you gentlemen done talking business? Because you are barricading the best scotch in the house. What Bitsy serves at these parties is swill."

The ambassador pushed Jay into the room. "Let me introduce FBI Special Agent James Porter."

"FBI?" Dravko stuttered.

"Relax, he didn't say tax man," Jay said and shook the general's hand. Next he introduced himself to Kurt, pretending they had not met before.

"Mr. Porter is here on a murder investigation," Ambassador Lerner said.

"Murder?" asked Dravko, still unsettled.

"It's not confidential, is it, Porter?"

"Not once the newspapers printed the story. I've got it here." Jay pulled a newspaper clipping from his pocket and unfolded it to reveal a headshot of the fourth courier that clearly showed his wounded face.

Dravko instantly recognized Sergej Ustinov and took an unsteady step.

Kurt put a hand on his shoulder. "Steady there, General. But I agree, that's gruesome enough to make you lose your cupcakes."

The general regained his composure. "Cupcakes?"

"He's the fourth victim," Jay informed them. "All killed the same way. The face is cut, and then bang! A shot to the heart."

"When is the man killed?" asked Dravko.

Jay smiled. "Where were you Monday night?"

"Monday night?"

"It was a joke, General."

"The man is not dead?"

"Oh no, he's dead. Very dead. In fact, he's the fourth dead man. But I can say no more than that about the case."

"Gentlemen, my wife is waiting to bid General Mladic goodnight," the ambassador said. "When I say, General, that I hope all our plans work out, I cannot be more sincere. Kurt has our confidence, of course, and as the senior American diplomat in the country, I am speaking for the President of the United States."

He held the library door open for Dravko to lead everyone out.

CHAPTER TWENTY-FIVE

B ILLY'S WOMAN WIPED THE BAR with a scowl. *You watch yourself.*

Basia's laughter floated away, boomeranged back to make her laugh again.

Jacek doesn't like his women too free.

Her head swayed to music only she could hear.

Who gave her the shit?

She recognized Jacek's voice.

And opened her eyes just as his slap stung her.

"Let her be," Billy's woman said.

"Fuck you, woman! You dragging that sourpuss around like the mop you never use."

Basia held a hand to her jaw. "You sonofabitch."

"How much did you sell her?" Jacek asked Billy, who was behind the bar washing glasses.

"Ask her."

"I'm asking you."

"She'll tell you if she wants to."

"I told you not to be coming here without me."

"I was waiting for you," Basia said.

"You came early to score."

"What if I did?"

"I told you, you coming around for stuff is fucking with my business. Nobody wants a cop around, not even a turned one."

"Our business is almost over," she sneered.

"What're we waiting for? I bet he has a suitcase full of money in his room."

"I saw it. It looks exactly like all the other couriers' suitcases."

"Then fuck it, let's just take it. The old fuck at the front desk will let you in his room."

"I've told you, double-cross Mladic, you end up eating your own guts."

"He doesn't even have to know. You carry one suitcase in, the other suitcase out, and Mladic won't know until he opens it up. Fuck, that might surprise him. Boom!"

"Let's solve another problem first. Did you bring it?"

Jacek reached into his coat and handed her a gun.

"Does it have a history?"

"You think the seller's going to tell me if it's hot?"

"Give me another shot, Billy," she ordered.

"Take her home, Jacek. I don't want her puking on my floor."

Basia got to her feet. "I'm not going home with him."

Jacek helped her into her fur coat. "That's it tonight? Just the gun? Not even a thank you?"

"Thank you."

"You can't do better than that?"

"What do you want, a blow job in the toilet?"

She walked out of the bar.

• • •

THE CAR KEPT FOGGING UP, and Jay and Kurt cleared small patches on the windows to see if anything was happening. The icy rain pinging on the car's roof made it almost impossible to hear what the other said without shouting, and the whole point was to not make themselves obvious. Up the street, the hotelier briefly opened the lodge's door and a square of yellow light fell into night. "You think Mladic will take the bait?" Jay asked.

"We threw too much his way for him not to do something."

"I'd like to have seen his face when you walked into the room. Do you think he bought your story?"

"He wants to believe it."

A car turned the corner, went a block, and turned again. "Male driver, Warsaw tags," Jay reported and checked his watch. "It's been over an hour."

"He's inside sweatin' over something," Kurt said, "and I'm hoping it's over me. I'm counting on fucking with his head enough that he makes a wrong move."

"Watch it," Jay alerted him. "Someone's coming up behind us."

An old woman in a rain bonnet tugged a reluctant dog along the sidewalk. She stopped at their bumper and encouraged the dog to do his business. Another car turned into the street; its headlights illuminated their interior. "Shit," Kurt murmured, and they hunched lower.

"*Chodz! Chodz!*" the old woman commanded. She yanked on the dog's leash as they retreated down the street.

The men sat taller. The other car was turning the corner.

"Red?" asked Kurt.

"Or reflection of the taillights," Jay replied. "I can't tell."

They sat and waited, and nothing happened. Finally Jay asked, "If you're so well-adjusted to being gay, why tell Mladic you have a wife?"

"To put him at ease. Closeted guys like to think their occasional dalliances are just that, dalliances, nothing defining. Even when they get their butts plugged, they still want to believe they can walk away straight."

"You think he'll show at the baths tomorrow?"

"The guy trembles every time he's near me. You don't get that excited about someone and turn down sex. What's your take on him now?"

"You saw his expression when he looked at the newspaper," Jay answered. "He recognized the courier."

"Now are you convinced that he's involved with the murders?"

"I'd like to have the one thing that's missing: evidence. Look ahead."

A woman, shielded by a wide umbrella, stopped on the corner. She crossed the road and approached the lodge. Her steps were cautious, uncertain, teetering on high heels as she dodged puddles. She made a blurry reconnaissance of the street and rang the lodge's bell. The hotelier swung open the door, throwing a rectangle of light over her. She faced the street to shake out her umbrella, and in that moment the light revealed her face.

"Fuck!" Jay exclaimed.

"You know her?"

"That's Basia Husarska."

• • •

A THIN STREAM OF SMOKE rose from an ashtray in the overheated foyer. By rote Basia drifted toward Dravko's room as the sleepy-eyed hotelier took in the open fur coat kicking at her ankles. Slowly the gray opiatic miasma in which she was traveling started admitting colors. Her heel snagged a tear in the carpet and she steadied herself with a hand on the yellow wall. She knocked on Dravko's door, uncertain how she had made it there from Billy's Bar, only vaguely recollecting his summons on the telephone: "You must come immediately."

Basia stepped into the room.

Dravko slapped her hard. She fell against the bureau, pressing a hand to her jaw.

He knocked back a swallow of scotch.

His reflections in the many mirrors spun around her. "You sonofabitch," she snarled at all of them.

"You're double-crossing me," Dravko accused her.

Basia pulled herself together. "What are you talking about?"

"Sergej Ustinov is dead. I saw his autopsy photos."

She sat on the loveseat and wrapped her fur cocoon-like around her. "Give me a drink," she said and lit a cigarette.

He plunked down the vodka bottle and handed her a glass. She poured a shot with a shaky hand and downed it. "It's Jacek who's double-crossing you. He took the bomb."

"What's he want?"

"The million dollars."

"What million dollars?"

"The million dollars in your fancy suitcase that your dead man told him about. I was going to warn you."

"Don't lie to me."

"I swear it's the truth. Jacek is a little crazy. He cuts them, do you know that?"

"I saw what he did to Sergej."

"I've been afraid to tell you." Basia willed her eyes to tear up.

"You're a mess tonight." He knocked back another shot. "The other three are dead, too."

"I know."

"Did you kill them?"

"I gave them to Jacek. He wanted them."

"He wanted them?"

"I didn't ask the details."

"Did he tell you he planned to kill them?"

"Why would I care? Three less witnesses and they all saw me."

"I should have been told," Dravko complained. "Where's the bomb?"

"Jacek has it. Your man Sergej was drunk and told him about the million dollars. He killed him and took his suitcase. Is it really a bomb?"

"Yes."

"An atomic bomb?"

"Yes."

"You are Mad Max."

Dravko ignored her and asked, "What is Jacek's plan?"

"He's going to wait until Monday and contact you, pretending Sergej crossed a week late."

"Why does he play such a game with me?"

"I told him, bring the bomb and you'll give him the money. I told him you don't fucking care about the couriers, but he's afraid that if you know he took it, you'll kill him."

"I will kill him, as soon as I have the bomb."

All of Basia's deceits caught up with her in that room. Dravko's threat to kill Jacek might as easily have been directed at her. She had connived, whored herself, and done anything she needed to do to survive communism's misogyny and deadening mediocrity. The Soviet Woman was expected to be even more tedious and cowed than the Soviet Man. Eventually, Basia's determination to survive (albeit with some flair) had become its own end and turned her heart cold. In that room, she had one more charade to play out.

She reached for Dravko's hand, pulled him to the loveseat, and put his meaty hands around her neck as if he were strangling her. "You won't abandon me, will you? There's nothing left for me here except probably prison." She pressed on his hands. "Kill me now, if you're not going to take me with you."

Dravko hardly heard her. His reverie started when he knew the bomb could be retrieved, though now, thanks to the African, he would have all the weapons he needed. American weapons. The bomb, of course, would be his *coup de grace*. So engrossed was Dravko in such thoughts that he hardly noticed when she fiddled with his belt buckle and unzipped him, freeing him, and speaking to his desires as her lips closed on him. "You still want Basia," she murmured, but it was not her lips he wanted. He screwed his eyes tight, and in the blackness he felt the African's lips on him. It was the African's tongue that teased him and made his legs tremble. It was for the African that he cried out.

• • •

TOO LONG IN THE PARKED car, they risked discovery, so they left to find a bar without waiting for Basia to emerge from the lodge. Was she involved in Mladic's weapons smuggling, or the murders, or both?

Or were they only lovers? It seemed unlikely but not impossible. At the very least, Kurt was certain, she had helped Mladic move his guns over the borders. Tommy's account implicated her as well—the long coat, the small, possibly red car. Long into the night, they mulled over scenarios that condemned and then exonerated her. They were still spinning webs of coincidences when Basia left the lodge. A moon broke through the clouds and she lifted her bruised face to it. The wind blew raindrops from the trees, sprinkling her face with the tears she wouldn't cry.

CHAPTER TWENTY-SIX

EVA NERVOUSLY BIT HER LIP. "I am so sorry, Pani Husarska. Was Detective Kulski expecting you?"

"I thought so."

"He has rehabilitation on Friday mornings."

Basia managed a withering smile. "I am unfamiliar with his schedule."

"I was only trying to explain."

"I will wait in his office."

"But Pani Husarska . . ."

Basia closed the door in the girl's face.

Of course she knew the detective's schedule. That was precisely why she was there. She took a drag on her cigarette and noticed his No Smoking sign. She looked for a place to extinguish it and stuck it in the soil of a potted plant. Its lipsticked filter could almost be mistaken for a red bud.

The secretary peered in.

Basia swung around, clutching her shoulder bag. "What is it?"

"Does Pani Director want coffee?"

"Yes, please," Basia said, dispatching her.

The door closed and Basia crossed to the closet. Its handle gave way. If Kulski's gun was inside, he had left it unsecured, contrary to regulations. A common oversight that Basia counted on that morning. She patted down his jacket and felt the heavy bulge of his holster. Quickly she removed the gun, exchanging it for the P-83 in her purse. She closed the closet.

Jay walked in, startling her. Her heavy makeup failed to conceal the bruise on her jaw. "Good morning, Pani Director," he said brightly. "The fur was a good choice today. There's a cold wind outside."

Her deer-in-headlights gaze gradually hardened into a glare. "I am waiting to speak with Leszek."

"About our case?"

"We have many cases, Agent Porter."

"I'd be interested in hearing about them."

"Leszek reports that you are making progress," Basia said.

"Every day, another small step."

"Then you believe you will identify the murderer?"

"We have a witness."

"I understand he is not reliable."

"His character, no, but his eyes are pretty good."

"And your mad Russian, Agent Porter, have you identified him?"

"Only as a dead man. You're right, the Russians are not so helpful."

Basia made a point of glancing at a wall clock. "I have waited too long."

"Detective Kulski should be here in ten minutes. We have an appointment."

"I, too, have an appointment. Goodbye, Agent Porter."

He stepped aside to let her out the door. "Director Husarska, by any chance do you know General Dravko Mladic?"

She hesitated. "What is his name?"

He repeated it.

She considered it and said, "It is not a Polish name."

"Yugoslavian. He's head of their state security. I suppose that means secret police."

"Why should I know him?"

"I met him at the ambassador's last night. He seemed to know you."

His lie was a gamble and it paid off. Basia paled and said, "Perhaps his name is familiar."

Again she turned to leave.

"Did you meet him at Piła?" Jay's question was another stab in the dark.

Basia rocked on her heels. Her eyes burned into him. "What do you know about Piła?"

"It has quite a reputation," Jay replied. "For a long time, it was—and maybe still is—the best police academy in the East bloc for learning how to conduct undercover investigations. It makes sense you would go. General Mladic mentioned it, too." He had not. Jay had read it in Kurt's dossier on him.

"It was a long time ago," said Basia.

"Just curious." He smiled benignly.

"You are too curious, Agent Porter."

With Basia in retreat, he quickly scanned Detective Kulski's office, wondering about her real purpose for being there that morning. If things were disturbed on his desk, he couldn't know. The rusty red butt of a cigarette caught his eye, and he plucked it from the pot and dropped it in a pocket. He would bet money that it was Basia Husarska's.

Kulski entered, limping badly.

"Did you have an accident?" Jay asked.

"It always hurts after rehab. Where is Eva?"

"Making coffee, I think. Director Husarska was here."

"She was?"

Eva entered carrying a tray with two coffees. "Where is Pani Husarska?" she asked.

"She left for another appointment," Jay said and took a cup when the tray was offered.

"I'll take hers," Kulski said. "She must have forgotten that I have rehab on Fridays."

"I reminded her," Eva said on her way out.

Kulski sat and stretched out his painful leg. "The laboratory has sent the evidence. It is trash, I think. Eva will show you the examination room. We have plastic gloves for you. Do you have news?"

"No new news." Of course he did, certainly suspicions and speculations, but nothing he could report to Kulski. He was suspect by association. The more the noose fit around Basia Husarska (and she had given it her own hardy tug by denying an acquaintance with Mladic), the more suspicious he had to be of anyone around her. Of course, she might have had an altogether different assignation at the lodge—they could not with certainty say which room she had visited—but that was an evidentiary argument, and they were running on intuition. Jay's intuition said to trust that Kulski was on their side. His training said to wait for proof.

Kulski suggested, "If you are ready, I will have Eva show you the way. She is single, you know, and a very sweet girl."

"I'm sure she is, only I've met someone else. Another sweet girl. Poland seems to be full of them."

"She made me promise to say something."

Eva led the way to the evidence room. He sensed her nervousness but had no flair for flirting that morning. His thoughts were far from her shapely legs, though not so far that he didn't notice them. She left him alone in the room with four wooden boxes on a table. To their left was a stack of butcher-paper squares, to their right a collection of tweezers, magnifying glasses, and feather brushes. He pulled on rubber gloves and flipped open all the boxes. In one was a shoe, curled with age and mildew. Another held a plastic bag with three spent condoms, two so rotted the pleasure was long forgotten. A third contained two dozen or more cigarette butts, the fourth a stubby metal pipe. Kulski's men had collected everything within a five-meter radius of the body, and anything else they found nearby that potentially related to the crime. Trash indeed.

Jay spread a sheet of butcher paper on the table and gingerly dumped out the collection of cigarette butts. Immediately the smell and taste of stale ashes assailed him. He spread them out with tweezers.

Two matched. He placed them side by side.

He pulled Basia's butt from his pocket and placed it alongside them.

They all matched. The same brand. The same color lipstick.

He placed the three cigarettes in a clear plastic bag and debated what to do. If he suggested DNA testing at headquarters, would Kulski be obliged to notify Basia? How to suggest it without confessing his suspicions of her? And if Kulski and Basia were in cahoots, what then?

The detective entered the room.

Jay decided to trust him and showed him the cigarettes he'd bagged. "Looks like the same smoker to me. Same brand, same lipstick. She was hanging around a long time on a cold night."

"Tommy said the woman was smoking."

"If we get a DNA match, it might help us later."

"Can it be done in Washington? We haven't such labs in Poland."

"Will you need to clear it with Director Husarska?"

Kulski handed back the baggie. "She can only say yes."

"Good. They'll be in DC by tomorrow. I've been wondering, Detective, how do you think the couriers have come to Warsaw? Airports are too secure and a bus too slow. Trains?"

"From the border it might be a bus or a train. Or a private driver."

"Which it probably is, if it's a smuggling operation. But if somebody did get off a train from Russia, he's probably hungry or used the john, and maybe somebody remembers seeing him."

"It's a good suggestion."

"May I ask you a personal question?"

"Of course."

"I've met someone whose son has a problem with drugs. Heroin. Is there a way for him to get help without getting into trouble?"

"I must ask. It is a new problem for us, too. We expected only miracles, never so many problems. There is a price to freedom, isn't there?"

"Is it freedom or capitalism, Detective? The drug dealers are motivated by greed; freedom only makes it easier for them to operate." Jay crumpled up the butcher paper and discarded it. "I'm finished here."

CHAPTER TWENTY-SEVEN

L ILKA, HURRYING, TRIPPED AND STUMBLED into the arms of a teacher leaving his classroom. "Oh Mr. Czarniecki!" she cried. "Are you all right?" She reached out to steady the ancient professor.

"Are you still running through the halls, Lilka? Let me guess, you're late."

"For Tadzu's recital! I don't want to miss the start."

"Then take off your shoes and run like you used to!"

Lilka laughed brightly. "I'm too old for that now. Are you coming?"

"Much more slowly, my dear, much more slowly."

Lilka bounded up the stairs two at a time, just as she had when late for class, which was almost always. The double doors to the music room stood open to reveal a piano on stage before a dozen rows of collapsible chairs. Wooden buttresses added grace to the otherwise simple room. When a student herself, Lilka had loved to stand in the hall and listen to the orchestra practice. She tried to learn the violin, until the neighbors' complaints embarrassed her into quitting, but she never lost her love of music. After her classmates finished practice, she would come into this room and in the silence summon their perfect measures and rousing choruses.

Alina beckoned her from near the front. "Scoot over," she said to Tolek when Lilka came up. "Let her sit next to me."

"Isn't this exciting?" exclaimed Lilka. "Tadzu, having his own recital!"

Alina squeezed her sister's hand. "I'm so nervous!"

"And there are so many people. Like he's a rock star!"

"Maybe in America," scoffed Tolek.

"*Then* would you approve of his playing piano?" Lilka asked.

"I approve of his music."

"Not as much as you should," Alina said, knowing she was taking a chance with Tolek's mood.

He raised his hands in mock surrender. "Not the Wolnik sisters ganging up on me again! I give up!"

They all laughed.

"We have visas for America," Tolek said proudly.

"Alina told me. Are you really going?"

At that moment, the music instructor appeared on stage. He ran a finger under his collar as he waited for the audience to hush. "We will be starting in ten minutes. My apologies for the short delay."

"I hope nothing is wrong," worried Alina.

"Nothing is wrong," Tolek assured her. "In fact, it's a relief—I need to find the WC."

He made his way to the aisle and left the women.

Lilka squeezed her sister's hand. "I'll be so lonely without you."

"I never thought it would happen," sighed Alina. "Why should America want Tolek?"

"Because he's the most wonderful and loving man on the planet."

"He is, isn't he? But that wasn't a job category on the application."

"You're lucky, Alina, yet you always worry, I don't know why. Going to America, now there's a dream the whole world dreams, and you're unhappy! Be happy!"

"You're certainly cheerful," said Alina. "Is it because of Jay? He's very nice."

"Did you think so?"

"He likes you."

"He treats me nice."

"Oh Lilka, wouldn't it be wonderful if you married him and moved to America, and we could be together!"

"We can't both leave Mama and Papa."

"I wish it were you going and not me. I can imagine you happy in America. You would like the excitement."

"Alina, you are going to be sad in America, aren't you? Now I feel guilty asking Jay for his help."

"You didn't, I did."

"Can't you tell Tolek you really don't want to go?"

"Do you think I haven't? It's been his dream forever. I married him knowing that."

"Does Tadzu want to go?"

"He's afraid Tolek will make him quit his music."

"He wouldn't, would he?" Lilka sensed her sister's reluctance to answer. "What is it, Alina?"

"Tadzu's teacher thinks he will be ready for the competitions in a couple of years. He won't have the same chance in America."

"Tolek always says there are so many more opportunities there."

Alina sighed. "So Tadzu will have the opportunity to become an astronaut. I am not sure that I want my son flying to the moon."

Lilka laughed. "Is that Tolek's newest idea?"

"It might as well be, he asks so much of Tadzu. He's only a boy. If only Tolek understood better. If he *heard* his music, the way I do. He plays only for his father. If they've argued, I hear his anger, and if not, then his love. He continues his conversations with his father on the piano, saying what he can't say because he's still just a boy, only Tolek doesn't hear it. He's not listening."

"He only wants the best for Tadzu."

"I don't argue that the boy should try to be the best, only he has to be the one who chooses what he does."

Lilka sighed. "I'm worried about Aleks. He hasn't been home all week. I think he's at the river, but you know Jacek, he won't tell just to be mean. Alina . . ." Lilka's voice cracked, and she found a tissue in her purse. "Aleks is using heroin."

"Oh no!"

"Jacek told me."

"Of course he would tell you that, anything to hurt you."

"I'm afraid to go to the river to look for him. Those dogs . . . and I hate that man Billy!"

"Tolek can go with you."

"Do you think he would?"

"Would I what?" asked Tolek, returning.

"Help Lilka find Aleks."

"I didn't know he was lost."

"Be serious," Alina chided him, "she's worried. Maybe you could take her to the mechanic's shack tomorrow. She thinks he's there."

Tolek begrudgingly accepted the task. "If you remember the way."

The music instructor reappeared and the audience hushed. "Ladies and gentlemen," he addressed them, "this is a very special evening for our school, and for our fine young maestro, Tadzu Kuron. It is Master Kuron's first public recital, and we have no doubt that this very, *very* gifted young man will play before many audiences in his lifetime. Are his parents in the audience?"

Shyly Alina raised her hand.

"Stand! Stand!" he prompted, and Alina and Tolek stood to polite applause. "You should be immensely proud of your son. And now, I will let Tadzu Kuron speak for himself. Or rather, *play* for himself."

The boy approached the piano bench. He took a short bow, using the moment to scan the audience and find his parents. He quickly averted his eyes; the smile he had for them was a private one. He sat at the piano and stared at the page of music propped before him. A last cough, a cleared throat, a chair's squeak. The crackle of a candy wrapper. Tadzu arched his hands over the keyboard, and when the audience stilled, he started to play. The boy paid little attention to the printed music, having memorized the piece, a favorite Mozart sonata of his father's. He played passionately and confidently. He played with his heart, and Tolek heard him. Tears came to his eyes. One spilled down a cheek, and then another. The women, too, had to dab their eyes, hearing Tadzu's love song.

CHAPTER TWENTY-EIGHT

THE STIFF WIND BLEW SPRAY across the abandoned promenade. A beer sign banged against the side of a kiosk. Basia drew her coat tighter. Ahead of her the dimly lit houseboat rolled in the water. She balanced herself using the gangplank's guide ropes and managed to reach the tilting deck. She came around the deckhouse windows. Inside, Tommy was getting stoned and didn't see her. He jumped when she knocked, quickly snuffing out his joint.

He came to the door and opened it wider when he saw it was a woman. Her open fur revealed breasts pressed into something low-slung and legs still good enough for black mesh. He had made love to far less sexy women.

"Are you Tomasz Tomski?" Her voice was hoarse, seductive. She strutted into the room. "Your uncle thought you might be getting lonely."

Tommy couldn't take his eyes from her. "My uncle?"

"Perhaps I got the message wrong."

"You're in the right place."

"Then come here." Basia opened her arms to embrace him.

He slipped his hands under her coat. "What's your name?" he asked.

"Charon."

"Karen?"

"Close enough."

He fondled her.

She pretended to enjoy it. For a moment.

Then pulled Kulski's P-83 from her purse and, to Tommy's eternal mystification, shot him between the eyes.

A clean black hole.

The back of his head dropped like a smashed melon.
She discharged a second shot into an easy chair.
Then dropped the gun over the rail and fled.

CHAPTER TWENTY-NINE

THE POLISH BOYS WERE SO much freer than Dravko had ever have imagined boys could be. They were men to be sure, but their lack of inhibition in the steam room, indeed their playfulness, revealed youthful indiscretion. Their easiness of purpose, and frank lust for it, unsettled Dravko at first, as if by proximity their sinfulness might taint him, or mark him; yet they bore nothing that damned them. Gradually he grew accustomed to their inquisitive stares and adjustments of a towel for his benefit. They were harmless passes, baited hooks designed to snare the hungry fish, not the merely curious.

Sex had always been a guilty affair for Dravko. Like his youthful peers, he had craved an introduction to its mystery; yet once experienced, he fretted that he had missed something. All that preambled hoopla for a bestial—and, if truth be told, messy—act, his first time consummated at nineteen with a neighbor's wife twice his age. With his rite of passage, Dravko could more easily conjure the sex act and daydreamed about his male friends in lovemaking's rigor, the panting and humping and sweating, the clenched buttocks and rising shoulders of ejaculatory abandon. Never once did he imagine the sighing, satisfied girls; never once their painted fingers pressed to a lover's back, their rumps rising in exhilaration, their sweet whispered words commanding more. At school, and later in military training, he observed his friends in the gymnasium, and it was images of their downy asses and pendulous manhoods that he took to bed at night and woke with in the mornings. Yet his father, church, and god all condemned him each time he muted his satisfied cries, tissues in one hand, his cock in the other. They condemned him each time he imagined a man naked. The curves of their buttocks or bulges were enough for Dravko to dream of acts each sufficiently reviled to forever damn him. His guilt tortured him.

The door opened, and the African emerged from the roiling steam, a shadow taking form as it drew closer. He sat next to Dravko, untucking his towel in an easy movement and draping it between his legs. Other men, seated on the tiers of white tiles, stared curiously before resuming their conversations.

"Hello, General." Kurt dropped a hand on his thigh. His long, exploratory fingers made Dravko shiver. "I was hoping you'd be here."

The general's hand tentatively touched Kurt where his towel revealed a stretch of black thigh.

"You are shy, aren't you?" Kurt's fingers felt his hardening cock. "But not *that* shy. Maybe we should take care of that before we talk business."

They tucked their towels at their waists and left the steam room. Kurt led them down a short hall lined with cubbyhole rooms. Dimly lit, they were all taken by pairs of men in such varied positions it seemed to Dravko that the secret pornography of his mind had come to life; as if the acts he alone had imagined were being realized on a stage. He trembled, overwhelmed by his power to shape reality, for Dravko had no doubt that these men existed because of his dreams.

"Looks like a full house," said Kurt, breaking into his thoughts. "Let's try the showers."

Dravko followed him to the shower stalls.

The water ran over them. Kurt readied his prey, for Dravko was prey: a *something*, not someone, to outmaneuver until he could pounce. After some short-shrifted foreplay that employed a bar of soap, Dravko acquiesced when Kurt turned him to the wall, aware of his intent. "This might hurt at first," he warned, but pain was a door to Dravko's ecstasy. He let Kurt stretch his arms into a cross and barely whimpered when he entered him.

Kurt moved gently in him and Dravko gasped with pleasure. He put his mouth to the general's ear and said, "Now let's talk business."

"Wha-a-a-t?" Dravko replied in a pinched voice.

Kurt maintained his slow, steady rhythm. "We want to help you. *I* want to help you, but I need to know who to work with here."

"It's impossible." Dravko could hardly breathe.

The African, pressing deeper into him, sent a shock wave through him. "We can help you, General, you heard the ambassador."

"Help me . . . help me . . ."

"That's right, General, help you. Only we need to know the contacts, the routes, the weapons you want."

"What I want . . ."

"Did you make a list?"

"No-o-o."

"What do you want?"

"I. Want. This."

"I want it too. That's why I want to help you." Kurt slowed his thrusts; he needed information, not satisfaction. "Bombs, tanks, the same stuff America uses, they're all yours. But I need a way to get it to you. Who can I trust? Who, Dravko, *who*?"

"Br-zes-ki."

"Brzeski? Jan Brzeski, the Minister?"

"Ye-es."

"Who else?" probed Kurt. "There must be someone else I can trust."

Dravko had lost the willpower to speak.

"Do you want me to stop?"

"Don't stop!"

"Then tell me, who else?"

"Hu-sar-ska." The African drove each syllable from him.

"Basia Husarska?"

"Ye-es."

His confession was complete.

Kurt slipped from him and out of the shower. Dravko slumped rapturously into a crouch. The African's seed swirled at his feet before the water carried it away.

CHAPTER THIRTY

T HE EARLY MORNING FOG RISING off the black river blurred the blue revolving lights atop the covey of police cars. An ambulance crew fastened straps around Tommy for his last ride and carried his stretcher back across the gangplank. A solitary siren emitted a low growl like an animal warning off another. Detective Kulski stood on the boat's rocking deck. Tommy had been shot dead. So had his chair. The overstuffed leather upholstery had slowed the bullet enough for it to be retrieved intact. The bullet to Tommy's unintact head would no doubt be deformed from rearranging his skull.

"Who reported it?" Jay asked.

"A woman," answered Detective Kulski. "She didn't identify herself."

"Who did she talk to?"

"That's the strange thing, she called the station in Konstancin."

"Where's that?"

"South, perhaps ten or twelve kilometers."

"Maybe she lives there."

"She said she'd been walking her dog when she heard a shot."

"That's a long walk," Jay agreed. "Someone wanted us to know Tommy was dead. Who knew he was a witness?"

"It was no secret."

They watched the forensic crews finish up, the police photographers pack up, the first of the police cars leave.

"It's the bullet," Jay said. "*That's* the setup. The bullet in the chair. The killer wanted us to find it."

"It is possible to shoot the chair in a struggle," responded Kulski.

"But not shoot someone smack dab between the eyes. Tommy wasn't expecting it. My guess is that you'll find the gun right here over the rail." They both looked into the water swirling around the boat's hull. "It's down there. I'd bet on it."

Kulski said, "I'll have the river searched." He snorted at nothing in particular and limped away, careful on the gangplank where icy patches lurked.

Jay followed him to shore.

• • •

JAY FOUND KURT WAITING FOR him at the Marriott.

"It looks like you've been up all night," Jay said.

"I could say the same for you."

"Let's get some coffee."

They took a pot from the hotel restaurant and found a table on the mezzanine balcony. Jay reported Tommy's murder as he poured coffee. "Nice clean shot right between the eyes. Left his brains all over the floor."

"He wasn't under protection?"

"Kulski pulled surveillance because it had been there only to report if Tommy came home. He'd taken Tommy's passport to keep him from running."

"You're sure Kulski's a good guy?"

"Do you know something?"

"Absolutely nothing. Yet."

"Quit looking. You're wasting your resources."

"So in Tommy's case, who do you notify as next of kin? Wife one, two, or three?"

"Beats me," Jay said. "What do *you* figure when the only witness turns up dead?"

"That the murderer knew he was a witness, and that points back to the police, too. Is that what you're thinking?"

"I'm thinking Basia Husarska," Jay replied and told him about the cigarette butts. "It'll be another three or four days for the DNA results."

"You don't have to wait. She's guilty," Kurt said, and described his night with Mladic at the baths.

When he concluded, Jay said, "You play rough, don't you?"

"My motto is *caveat amator.* Lover beware. If God made me gay, why not use it? It's a tool, and I might as well have fun while using it."

"What do we do now?" Jay asked.

"Do you want to go to Kulski?"

"And say what? 'I've got three cigarette butts and a confession from a deranged narcissist?' Plus, what if Kulski *is* involved? Then we've exposed ourselves and we're dead."

"It's all linked, isn't it?" said Kurt. "PENZIK and the murders. Mladic and the weapons. Langley's always assumed some of the supposedly good guys are involved, it makes sense it's a minister. It would take someone with authority to get trucks carrying weapons across borders without being searched, and with Husarska as a helping hand, that's a winning team."

"Almost foolproof," Jay agreed. "For her, it might've been, except for smoking too much."

They heard a ruckus and leaned over the rail. In the lobby, two luggage carts had collided, and the bellhops argued as they realigned their loads. "I sure would like to get my hands on those suitcases," Kurt remembered.

"Yesterday at the train station, I counted at least a dozen suitcases with leather straps and brass finishes."

"Yeah, but they haven't ended up in your girlfriend's apartment or Mladic's hotel room. I have a hunch about these suitcases. And I have a hunch that Rypinski is the man with the beard, and that he's connected to Mladic."

"How?"

"Through Husarska. Probably her connections."

Jay laughed. "A nice little package if we could prove it. The only problem, we've no evidence that they know each other. We don't even know if Rypinski has a beard."

"Lilka's never said?"

"Nothing about a beard." Then Jay told him about the bearded man at Billy's shack. "The locksmith said that Husarska frequents Billy's Bar. If Rypinski uses Billy's garage to work on his van, maybe that's the connection between her and Rypinski."

"I'd like to tail her, but that's your call," Kurt said.

"She'll probably recognize your regular spotters."

"She's never seen me before."

"You don't exactly blend in."

"I can put my elbows next to hers at a bar. It's a great place to pick up information if you stay tuned. Do you know where she lives?"

Jay described her pink apartment building and made an effort at directions before Kurt left to find Basia Husarska.

CHAPTER THIRTY-ONE

JACEK HAD NOT COME HOME the night before. Lilka woke up to a blessedly peaceful apartment. She treated herself to a bubble bath and a lingering breakfast, though she still jumped at every sound, fearful of an ambush. When she emerged from the bedroom after getting dressed, he was there, his back to her and dancing a step or two.

"Zip zip zip!" he said and whirled around to face her. He was sweating. With the knife in his hand, he made a slashing motion, as if carving a Z across her chest. "Zip zip zip!"

Lilka screamed and fell back.

"I told you not to go in there."

Zip zip zip.

He broke into a lunatic's grin.

Zip zip zip.

"Leave me alone, Jacek," she pleaded.

He lunged at her and pressed the knife to her cheek. "I should have done this a long time ago."

"I'm not the one who cut you." Lilka whimpered, certain this time he would do it. He laughed and pushed her away.

Trembling, Lilka gathered her things to go to work. Purse, coat, hat: she was ready to flee.

"I'm going away," he told her.

She started to open the door. He slammed it closed and leaned on it. "You answer me when I talk to you."

"You didn't ask me a question."

"Ask me how long I'm going away for."

"How long are you going away for, Jacek?"

"Forever."

She glared at him.

"Isn't that the answer you want to hear?"

"Let me pass. I'll be late."

"Answer me, isn't that want you want to hear?"

"I don't believe you, you're drunk."

"Answer me!"

"Yes, it's true, it's what I pray for every day. Now are you satisfied?"

He stopped her from opening the door. "We aren't finished talking. I'm answering your goddamn prayer, you can give me two minutes."

"What's this about? Has something happened to Aleks?"

"This is about you and me, not Aleks!"

"You *are* going away, aren't you?"

"Forever starts today." He laughed bitterly. "You and I haven't talked, Lilka, for a long time. Almost never. Not since before Aleks, and before this." He ran the knife down the side of his face.

"You know that never mattered."

"It mattered to me, and it did just what Daddy wanted, to turn me mean like him. I know it. I'm not so stupid that I don't know it."

Jacek stumbled to a cabinet and brought out vodka. He took a long pull from the bottle. Lilka knew his temper too well and shuddered as he drank more of its reliable fuse.

"I was handsome, wasn't I? You remember?"

"That never changed."

"Daddy took that from me. People started looking away from me. I had nothing left, only what was inside, and that wasn't good enough."

"You had me."

"You hated me from the start. Blaming me for Aleks, blaming me for this."

"I blamed *me* for what your father did," said Lilka.

"That's the only reason you stayed. Love didn't count for anything."

"I'm going to work," she said.

Jacek crossed the room to block the door again. His swift steps echoed the younger man he had once been, earnest and self-assured. He had been full of swagger, even obnoxiously so, but that didn't detract from his staggering good looks. Every girl wanted him except Lilka, whose lack of self-confidence prevented her from imagining that any man, and certainly not the handsomest boy in school, would desire her. But Jacek ultimately pursued her. A last conquest. His flattery, exploiting her low self-esteem, led to the one night that changed everything that followed. He was right. Love had never entered into their relationship.

He said, "Sometimes I see with a clarity, do you understand that?"

She nodded.

"Answer me! I can't hear a fucking nod!"

"I think I do."

"That's better. I've waited seventeen years for you to start talking to me. I'm trying to say goodbye, but you're not listening, and suddenly I realize, that's been our big problem. You talking and not listening for seventeen years. That's one of those moments of clarity. I'm seeing lots of things for the first time, because maybe it's the last time."

"You're not making sense."

"I'm going away, Lilka, that's all the sense you need to know. I've been waiting for a break and I got me one. One last delivery and then I'm gone. I'm disappearing down the escape route. It's your break, too, and Aleks's. You want to know another moment of clarity? I see my father and I see me and I see Aleks, and I see the same man. Aleks is in trouble all right. I got him there and I can't help him. I don't want my boy cut like me, and I'm bound to do it."

"Where are you going?"

"Now you're asking too many questions."

Lilka tried to get past him. "May I leave, please? I'm already late."

"That's your goodbye?"

Suddenly furious, Lilka lashed back. "You expect me to miss you, ask you to stay, *cry*? I've cried every night for seventeen years, sometimes for you, mostly for me. Have we had one happy night? You want me to miss you?"

He lunged at her with the knife, but stopped short of stabbing her. "Zip zip zip!"

She escaped out the door.

His lunatic laughter continued until Jacek could no longer hear her steps in the hall. *So that's the thanks you get for being decent to a bitch*, he mused. Wasn't he being decent when she walked out on him? That was a mistake. Lilka was always making mistakes. They'd started their marriage with a mistake, one he could've fixed if she hadn't concealed her pregnancy from him. Soon enough their parents had to be told about the baby. In a drunken temper never before so violent, his father had pulled a knife and, in a single, damning flick, cleaved Jacek's cheek. Their hurried wedding was festooned with recrimination. Jacek's bandages came off later, the stapled wound the first scar on their marriage, and the one most picked at.

He went into the bedroom to check the suitcase. *That bitch better not have messed with my stuff.* She hadn't. He went back into the living room and spread the contents of a satchel on the table. He got his spoon and needle ready, but decided to wait before trying the new Afghan shipment. He needed a steadier hand and clearer head than heroin for his next task and opted for a shot of vodka on his way to the bathroom.

Once there, he unpacked a sack from the pharmacy, placing shaving cream and a straight razor on the back of the sink. He found a pair of scissors in a drawer and attacked his beard, sending clumps of wiry black hair into the basin until he reduced it to stubble. Then, slowly, he shaved with the razor. Jacek was in no hurry. He knew what he was uncovering. Unearthing. The archeology of his failed life. After passing over his scar, he could see, in the thin residue of the shaving cream, the pockmarks of his stitches. He rinsed his face. There was still stubble in the deeper depressions. Jacek sensed that he was perched on the cliff of his final downfall. He had wanted to see what had landed him there. And there it was, a railroad track of stitches with a red line running through it, polluting half his face.

He slammed his fist into the mirror and broke it.

Sucking on a cut knuckle, he returned to the living room, poured a glass of water, and sat at the table. He pinched some white powder from the Afghan shipment, put it in the spoon, and mixed it with a little water. He heated it with a lighter until the instant it started to bubble. He loaded the syringe and set it aside. Using his teeth and one hand, he tied a tourniquet around his other arm to make his vein bulge. He emptied the syringe into it.

Clarity rode the heroin's first fast-breaking wave. The prickly points of Jacek's life came into focus. His accusers, and those he would accuse, popped into view like picture flashcards. His own face was among them, a fiery red scar burning through his beard. He decided that he should've cut Lilka. She was responsible for that devil on the flashcard. She was the seductress who hid the baby until things had gone too far. Then the opium's second surge toppled him with its numbing claw. He relaxed into its sure serenity, void of judges, responsibility, motivation. That was part of his clarity, too. Jacek had opened a hatch into a world where there was no remorse.

CHAPTER THIRTY-TWO

KURT CRUISED PAST BASIA'S PINK building a couple of times. Her sporty red car sat at the curb. He could find no vantage point from which to watch inconspicuously. Hell, to be inconspicuous he'd have to leave the country. He had never experienced such frank curiosity about his color. If an exotic animal wandered down the streets, he doubted the Poles would react any differently. Sometimes he liked the attention. Right then he wished he were white.

In a neighborhood coffee shop, he eavesdropped on conversations, surprised by how many words he understood for having the same Slavic roots as Russian. All those hours standing guard in Moscow had paid off. He settled his check, drove back by Basia's place, saw her car was still there, and circled the block. When he came back to her building, it was gone. He glanced each way down empty streets.

Kurt checked his watch: four o'clock. Early for cocktail hour, but he doubted if Billy stood on propriety, if that's where she was going. There or Mladic's lodge were his only guesses. He swung around in the direction of the train station and navigated the neighborhood streets with a map spread on his lap. When he reached the main road, he gunned the motor and accelerated over the bridge. Yanking his car into a hard left to beat oncoming traffic, he bounced into the Marriott's circular driveway to a chorus of angry horns. He left it running for the valet and dodged back across the busy avenue and up the ramp to the station.

He reconnoitered the vast hall's layout, determining it had too many entrances for him to cover all at once. He decided to hang near the escalator that descended into the underground mall, going through a charade of checking his watch and the departure board, ever-alert to anyone who could be Basia Husarska.

From across the cavernous hall, Detective Kulski had seen Kurt come into the hall. A black man in Poland was a magnet for the eye. He tried not to stare as Kurt walked by.

From inside his booth, a vendor said, "That's something you don't see every day."

Kulski showed him the artist's sketch of the fourth courier. "You ever seen him?"

"Sometime last week, starin' at me from right over there." The vendor pointed to his newspaper rack. "Front page."

A wise guy. Kulski smiled his amusement. "Before that, in the land of the living, did you see him?"

"I figure I did."

"Did you think to call the police?"

"No offense to you, you showed me your badge first thing. Most of the time, the police just come sniffing around. If I tell 'em I saw the dead man, they'll start asking why I run with crooks. That's all the excuse they need to ask for more payoffs. I can't afford to have the cops going to the bank for me."

Kulski had a pad and pen ready. "This won't cost you anything. Tell me what you saw."

The black man walked by again, consulting a schedule and watching destinations change on the departure board. He carried no luggage, Kulski noticed, and wondered if he was having trouble deciphering the foreign words. But he had no time for anything else; he had a witness.

"I sold him stamps," the vendor told him. "He came up to me and handed me an envelope, and says he wants a stamp."

"Where was it going?"

"Moscow."

"Do you remember the name or address?"

"It's lucky enough I remember Moscow. Most days I don't remember morning to night. Sitting in this box all day, it's a life best forgotten."

"Yeah, yeah, be a philosopher another time. Was he alone?"

"You see how much I can see? He coulda been holding Madonna's hand and all I'd see was his ugly face."

"So you got a good look at his face?"

"Enough to see he was ugly. And no missing his breath. His tongue must've fermented. I saw him coming up, he'd been standing over there." The vendor stuck his hand out his window and pointed. "Where the bums sleep. You see that cardboard?"

"Did anyone else see him?"

"Look, the guys here, we don't grab beers at the end of the day and talk about who buys what newspaper. If the other vendors were my friends, I'd shoot myself. I know what they got to talk about. Nothing, same as me. I show my wife the day's take; if it's enough, she puts out. It's good for another day."

"All right," Kulski said. "I understand, you and the other vendors did not discuss the matter. What exactly did happen?"

"Like I was saying, he handed me a letter and said he wanted a stamp. I told him I don't sell stamps for letters, only for postcards, so he asked how many postcard stamps it would take. Am I a post office? He told me to give him five stamps."

"Postcard stamps?"

"That's what I said, isn't it? Five of 'em, stuck all over the envelope. I told him he could mail it over there."

Again a hand emerged from the kiosk and directed the detective's gaze. From the same direction, a woman approached. Director Husarska. Her long coat swayed seductively as she approached, her heels going clickity-clack. She wore dark glasses. Her fur and whole demeanor screamed "high-class whore." Kulski assumed she was working an undercover assignment. She had spoken of them, and he turned away so as not to blow her cover. She passed him close enough he could smell her smoke.

The black man, too, saw Basia coming, watching her over the fold of a newspaper that he likely couldn't read. When she disappeared down the escalator, he replaced the paper and casually followed her. Friend or foe, Kulski had no way of knowing.

"I'm telling ya, I need a bigger window," the vendor complained. "Not for my health, for the view. Even a blind man's got eyes for her."

"You've seen her before?"

"Not often enough."

"How about on the night you saw the dead man?"

"Do I look like a guy who keeps a diary?"

• • •

AMAZING, KURT THOUGHT, HOW SO many men could smell a sexy woman coming, and none ever tired of watching one pass. As a ship makes a wake, Basia rippled through the crowded underground passageways, and he only had to track the turning heads to know he was close behind. Kurt didn't understand the hungry, sly words cast after her, but he could guess their meaning. For something men always talked about, they had mastered only a limited vocabulary for women.

Shops were starting to close for the day. The lights in their windows flickered off, withdrawing their contribution to the corridor's already dim illumination. The stretches of shadowy interludes grew more frequent the deeper Kurt followed Basia into the underground labyrinth. When she entered Billy's Bar, he kept walking. He went to the end of the corridor and turned back.

Billy was sneaking something into Basia's purse when he entered the bar. He took a seat two down from her and ordered a beer. Billy, so ugly he looked contagious, handed him a bottle, and Kurt wiped its rim clean. Billy's woman came from behind a curtain and wanted payment. Leave the man alone, Kurt figured him to say, and she shuffled off to dance with a broom.

"English?" Billy asked. He meant his nationality, what not language he spoke.

"American," Kurt told him.

Basia set her empty glass on the bar. "Give me another drink."

"Can I buy it for you?" Kurt asked.

Billy slid a glass across the bar. "You don't have to, she's paid in advance."

"I'd still like to buy you a drink."

"That's sweet," she said.

"You speak English, too?"

"You are surprised?"

"I don't speak Polish."

"You are a capitalist, why should you speak Polish?"

Kurt laughed.

"You think I am funny?"

"Aren't you trying to be?"

"Most men have no humor. Are you here on business?"

"For a couple of days," Kurt replied. "I'm staying across the street."

"At the Marriott, and you came to Billy's for a drink? Did you hear that, Billy? He's staying at the Marriott and thinks this dump has more class."

"He can pay for class there if he wants. Here he gets beer."

"Here's got prettier women," Kurt said, flirting.

Basia laughed. "Isn't that sweet? Here, sit here." She tapped the stool between them.

Kurt slipped over.

"I've always been curious about black men," she confessed. "Maybe later you can take me to your hotel."

Kurt hadn't expected her quick come-on, and he replied lightheartedly, "It might cost more than I have on me, unless you take traveler's checks."

Basia glared at him. "You think I am a whore?"

"Aren't you?"

She slapped him.

At that moment, Jacek entered the bar. "Are you making new friends again, sweetheart?" He slung his satchel onto the counter.

"I'll put that back here for you," Billy said and tucked the bag under the bar.

He asked Basia, "Who's your nigger friend?"

Basia tapped out a cigarette. "He might understand you."

"Do you speak Polish?" he asked Kurt in English.

"Sorry, pal."

"I didn't figure as much. You're in my seat."

"It looked empty."

"Not after I walked in."

Kurt managed a smile. "That's cool, I don't think the lady likes me anyway." He slipped back to the third stool.

"That's just her way of saying hello, isn't it, babe? She likes it rough."

"I like it different."

"Is black different enough?" asked Kurt.

Jacek grinned lewdly. "That'd be different, wouldn't it?"

"It would," she said, "only not tonight. Excuse me."

Basia slipped off the stool and went down the hall to the WC. Her slick leather miniskirt attracted light until she disappeared.

"You two are friends, I take it," said Kurt.

"Something like that. What makes you interested?"

"I got eyes, don't I? What's her name?"

"If she wants you to know it, she'll tell you."

Billy told him, "It's Basia."

"It's a pretty name."

Jacek replied, "She's not responsible for it."

"She's got a pretty face, too. I've got a friend who says we're responsible for our own faces after thirty. You ever hear anyone say that?"

Jacek's whole body knotted up. "You talk of my face? I am responsible for it?" He slipped his hand into his coat pocket.

Billy shot an arm across the bar to restrain him. "It is a joke, yes?"

"Look at my face," Kurt said. "Of course it's a joke."

Basia returned to her seat. "What did I miss?"

"I'll let your friend tell you. What do I owe you?"

"Four hundred zlotys," Billy told him.

Kurt gave him a five-hundred bill. "Keep the change. Nice meeting all of you." He walked out of the bar.

Jacek said to Billy, "Let's settle up now. The stuff's in my bag."

"Is it good?"

"Very pure."

Billy's woman wiped down the bar with a wet cloth. "Go in the back, Billy, and taste it."

He took Jacek's bag and went behind a curtain.

"What the fuck, bitch!" Jacek snapped at Basia. "I walk in here and you're almost between that darky's legs!"

"I'm trying to keep him off guard."

"You'll keep any man off guard with your knee on his cock," Billy's woman said.

"Piss off! He's been tailing me."

"What the fuck are you talking about?" Jacek asked.

"He drove past my building this morning."

"You sure it was him?"

"How many black men live in my neighborhood?"

Billy came back to the bar. He showed Jacek the dollars bundled in his satchel. "You see this, baby?" Jacek said to Basia. "In case Mladic doesn't come through with the million, we got enough to get away and set ourselves up anywhere we want."

"I never said I was going anywhere with you," she said.

"I know. I'm going with you. You got a villa someplace already picked out?"

"Mladic will kill you."

"Not if I kill him first. And that reminds me," Jacek said to Billy, "don't plan on coming to the shack any too early tonight."

"Is that the solution you've been thinking on so hard?" Basia asked. "Killing Mladic?"

"There'd be no witnesses. We'd have the money. Who's to know?"

"The whole fucking world, that's who will know. You don't kill a man like Mladic without someone asking questions."

"We'll be heroes if they ever figure out who did it."

"When are you planning to do it?"

"Tonight," said Jacek. "I'll get the suitcase. You call and tell him to meet us at the shack."

"What about the black man?" Basia asked.

"If he's still tailing you, we'll let Mladic have some fun with him first. I've got tools he can use in the shed."

"You got it all figured out, don't you?"

"Going away with you is my chance, too. I figure I'm out of chances here."

"That's not especially persuasive."

"Tell Mladic to meet us in an hour. That'll give you and me a little time."

A minute later they rode up the escalator. Basia crossed the great hall for the exit while Jacek stayed back. He immediately spotted the black man pretending to read headlines at a newspaper stand while obviously watching for her. He started following her.

Detective Kulski also saw Basia aiming for the exit and the black man fall in behind her. Was he part of an operation? *Probably not*, Kulski thought. He was obviously a foreigner, and it dawned on the detective that he could belong to one of the mafias trying to infiltrate Poland. Kulski sensed danger to Basia. Had the tables been turned and she was being chased? He would be remiss if he didn't act. He stopped the black man at the door and flashed his badge. "Police. Your ID, please."

Jacek walked out of the station laughing.

CHAPTER THIRTY-THREE

J AY CIRCLED THE BLOCK A third time. A guy, slouched in a car up the street from Dravko's lodge, hadn't budged. Jay assumed he was Kurt's man, watching Mladic while Kurt himself was tailing Director Husarska.

He checked the time. Lilka would be at work for another half hour. He pulled over to look at a map.

The background check Kurt had run revealed an address for Lilka. Twenty minutes later, Jay stood outside her building trying to guess which apartment might be hers. She had only mentioned that she lived on the fourth floor with a permanently out-of-service elevator. All the small balconies had different items on them, but Lilka never mentioned if hers had plants, or a drying rack, or the small table with a single chair. He squeezed the key in his pocket, knowing she was at work but clueless whether Jacek might be home. He had to risk it.

Lilka had described living in an apartment building, not a hideous prefab concrete monolith that leached sweat marks like armpit stains and smelled as unpleasant. He found her name on a letterbox so he knew he was in the right building, but when he had climbed to the fourth floor, he discovered there were no names on the doors. Only letters above them, eerily reminiscent of prison cells. Then he remembered that Jacek had changed the lock. He looked for the shiniest doorknob.

A woman cracked her door and asked, "Who do you want?" It was in Polish, but the meaning was clear.

"Well, you see . . ." he stammered. "English?"

"Yes, I am a translator." Agnieszka stepped into the hall.

"I am a friend of Lilka's and, um, she asked me to come by and check on something. The toilet. She's worried her brother forgot to fix it."

"Brother-in-law."

"Right."

"Tolek didn't forget. He was here."

"Right. Well, since Lilka asked me to check, and I've come this far . . ." Jay brandished the key. "I might as well check myself."

"It's F. The door at the end."

"Right, thanks." He took a couple of steps, and turned back to ask, "Is Jacek home now?"

"No, and don't let him catch you." Agnieszka shut her door.

The tumblers in the new lock turned soundlessly and Jay swung the door open. The apartment was dark. "Hello!" he called and turned on a light. Quickly he scanned the place: bedroom left, kitchen right, bathroom tucked in a corner. It had a tidiness that belied the disharmony of what Lilka had told him of her life. Pictures stuck to the refrigerator's door drew him into the kitchen. Among them, the bearded man he presumed to be Jacek was the man he had seen working on the white van outside Billy's shack. Instantly it confirmed his theory of the triangle between Mladic, Basia, and Jacek. All the evidence he needed was inside that apartment.

The telephone rang once and fell silent. Had it been a signal? It rang again, and he lifted the receiver without speaking.

"You must leave immediately." It was the neighbor woman with the lisp. "Jacek's van is in the parking area. He's already out of it."

Jay replaced the receiver. Automatically his eyes read the numbers scribbled haphazardly on a list pinned to the wall. He saw "BH" next to Basia Husarska's telephone number. It was proof of their collusion. He ran into the bedroom for the suitcase. It was heavy, and as he was pulling to untangle it from Lilka's clothes, he had the passing miserable thought: how could she not know about Jacek's business when the suitcase was in her bedroom closet and Basia's number on their telephone list?

Jacek said from the doorway, "Don't touch the latches. They're set to make it explode."

Jay looked up into Jacek's gun. Past its nozzle, he saw the grisly trail of botched stitches on Jacek's clean-shaven face. "Why'd you shave your beard?" he asked.

"What's it to you?"

"It won't keep the witness from recognizing you."

"Your witness is dead."

"How do you know?"

"I know. Now pick up the suitcase nice and easy by its handle and walk out."

Jacek followed him with the gun poking his back.

"Did Basia Husarska tell you she killed Tommy?" Jay asked.

"I should shoot you now."

"Then you'd have to carry this down yourself."

"Who do you think carried it up? Why, is it heavy for you? I thought FBI like Superman!"

"Too bad about the elevator never working. Not just about lugging a heavy bomb upstairs, which must have been damned inconvenient, but tomatoes can be heavy, too."

"Communists make everything bad. Now capitalists make everything bad."

"Will Mladic make everything good, Jacek?"

"Good for me."

"You think he will let you live?"

"Shut up!"

Outside, Jacek guided them to his white van. He opened the cargo door. "Get in."

He did. Jacek slid the door shut and locked it. Not a pinprick of light penetrated the pitch blackness. His eyes had no light to get used to. The engine started, and Jacek jacked up the music until the sides vibrated. He shifted into gear and bounced over the curb leaving the parking lot. His unanticipated turns sent Jay tumbling until he managed to brace himself with outstretched legs between the tire wells. The van's shock absorbers had long been shot, and each jarring pothole or bump vibrated through the cold metal floor and up his spine. He had no way of knowing where they were headed. His guess was the shack. He rummaged in his daypack for the walkie-talkie. It was easy to turn on and its tiny green light was enough for him to make out the walls of the van.

He pressed the first button. A burst of static. He pressed the second. "Graceland? Can you read me? This is Cher. Graceland, this is Cher. Can you read me?"

• • •

THE SECOND BURST OF STATIC woke Millie up. It took her a moment to realize it wasn't coming from the television but the duty officer's radio. She was always willing to volunteer whenever someone was needed, and that night an embassy wedding was preoccupying all the young people. It took her a moment to realize that someone was trying to talk to her. It was Kurt Crawford, he said, or no, he was saying she should contact the black man. He sounded like the other man. The Potter man. Crawford. Crawford. And how to remember? Before she had a clue-minder for Crawford he was saying shack shack shack shack shack . . . And she wrote down sugar. Sugar shack! She could remember that. But *why* did she write it down? Sugar?

• • •

BASIA SAT IN HER CAR, legs tucked beneath her, wrapped in her fur. It was cold, and her breath had condensed on the windows. Occasionally she drew a hand across the driver's side window to peer at the dark shack, silhouetted by lights on the far side of the river. The rain had stopped and sky had cleared, and the full moon made brief appearances through branches swaying in a rising wind. The dogs skulked about her car, growling, occasionally pouncing at her door, and each time they did, Basia cringed. She saw a light flicker in the toolshed, but no one heard her call for help. She was trapped.

She turned on the radio, found a blue note. Showtime coming up, she thought. How would it play out? Basia didn't know herself. Was Jacek right, would killing Mladic set them free? Or was Mladic her best protection? Dravko thought he could forget her, would like to think he was through with her. She doubted it. He'd come for her on her island. How long would the sex hold Jacek? She couldn't squeeze him tight enough to keep him from eventually running. It was a moment of clarity, like Jacek sometimes talked about: the obvious truth becoming truly obvious.

Where was he?

The sonofabitch said he'd be following in ten minutes with the suitcase. With Dravko's bomb. Could it be possible?

Basia disliked this part of getting high, the coming down, the thinking part. She wanted another fix. She thought: I have no one to bid goodbye. Family had ceased to matter, and friends were fickle, political, nonexistent. Had she become such a deviant that she had no friends, only partners? Sex partners. Crime partners. Where was the trust of friendship in these?

Through the trees she saw the van's approaching lights. The dogs bounded to it and barked furiously until it bounced to a stop. Jacek got out and kicked them back, and they slunk away to snarl in the shadows of his headlights. Basia rolled down her window.

"You could've waited inside," he said.

"Your fucking dogs wouldn't let me out of the car."

"I had 'em chained earlier. Aleks must be here. They won't bother you now."

She left the car. "I told Mladic an hour."

"Good, we can play first." Jacek opened the passenger door and gently lifted the heavy suitcase to the ground. He grinned. "Our ticket to hell."

"I need a fix."

"I figured on it. I pinched some from Billy's shipment. It'll cost you." He pulled her into an embrace and kissed her. A beggar, she returned his passion.

"I need it now, Jacek." She meant the drugs.

"You better start acting like you like me more, or I might be the one leaving you. You don't have a substitute for nothing."

"You won't leave me. You need me to keep Mladic from killing you."

"We're killing him, remember?"

She asked, "How do you propose we get to the island? We need Mladic for that."

"We don't need him for anything. We've got a hostage."

With that, Jacek flung open the cargo door and shone his flashlight in Jay's face.

Basia peered at him disbelievingly. "You are a fool. This changes everything."

The dogs edged closer, hanging in the shadows like Cerberus, sniffing curiously with growls caught in their throats. Basia and Jacek exchanged angry words. His flashlight bounced around the black sky like klieg lights on opening night. He made sure Jay didn't move— rather, his gun did—and when he waved him out of the van, he indicated Jay should carry the suitcase inside. The dogs nipped at his heels and Jacek kicked them away. Jay took another step and they attacked. One caught his cuff. The other bit into his wrist.

Basia screamed.

Jay dropped the suitcase.

Jacek shot the black dog. The gray mutt crouched in terror and tried to bolt. Jacek clipped it. Whimpering, it crawled away where it could be heard but not seen. Jacek spotted it with his flashlight on the shack's threshold and shot it again.

Jay stepped over the gray dog to open the door. Jacek flicked the switch for a bulb on a cord that dimly lit the nearly bare room. As Basia adjusted the kerosene heater, Jay could not know what was to come. He could not have predicted the revelry.

• • •

DRAVKO SPENT THE DAY IN bed splicing film. Two movies ran simultaneously in his head: *Dravko the President,* and a porn flick starring the African. He tried to weave these into a single, plausible script, but he didn't succeed. They told stories of such different men that he must have been miscast in one. He replayed last night in freeze frames. The black man riding him. Dravko pressing against him, whipping his head in unfamiliar ecstasy. He whispered names. They were ripped from him: they were not. Forced from him: not. Raped: not. They were gifts to the black man. Thank-you names.

Basia called. Jacek wanted to make the exchange. Tonight, in an hour, at the shack. Dravko checked his lists of flights. Midnight to Paris with a morning connection to Belgrade. Perfect.

He straightened his cap. Lined up his epaulettes. Aligned the rack of medals on his chest. The hotelier telephoned to say his taxi had arrived.

Dravko walked out, carrying his steamer suitcase, feeling like a million dollars.

• • •

"May I please practice now?" asked Tadzu.

"Your father hasn't finished eating," replied Alina.

Tolek said, "Go ahead, son." Since the recital, he'd been more lenient with the boy, even encouraging him to practice more. He scarfed down the last of his meal.

"It's the last of the sausage," Alina reminded him. "Eat slower, you'll enjoy it more."

"I'm enjoying it enough. I told Lilka I'd be ready when she got here."

"You've at least five minutes."

"Time to finish the potatoes." He helped himself. "It's all good, honey."

"Do you have to go, Tolek?"

"I promised Lilka."

"But it's started to rain again."

"Her boyfriend's responsible for getting our visas. I owe her a favor."

Alina started to carry plates to the sink. "That shack frightens me."

"Is that what has you worried? Come here." He embraced her. "It's only an old bait shack."

"Then why is Lilka scared to go there?"

"She's scared to go alone."

"See, I told you!" Alina pushed him away. "All this talk of moving, and changes . . . it's unsettling, Tolek, it makes me nervous. I feel all jittery inside."

He took her back in his arms. "Why do you worry so much? What ever happened to make you so afraid?"

From the street, they heard a horn toot.

"That's probably her," he said.

"Be careful, promise me?"

"I promise."

"Don't forget your hat, it's raining."

In the living room, Tadzu's playing reached a crescendo.

"I'll be back before he's done."

Alina took his hands and kissed them. "I'll wait up."

Lilka tooted the horn again.

Tolek gave his wife a quick kiss. "I love you," he said, and was gone.

Outside, he found Lilka waiting by her car. "Will you drive?" she asked. "I'm just a bundle of nerves."

"Sure."

Tolek leaned into her car and pushed her seat back before getting in.

"I'm sorry. I forgot to move it for you," she said.

"No problem."

"You're just a big friendly bear, aren't you, Tolek?"

"Grrrrr!"

He pulled away from the apartment block.

"I'm so grateful, Tolek, for your help. Did Alina tell you that Aleks hasn't been home for a week? I'm all jittery."

"So is Alina. It must be a sister thing. What exactly did Jacek say this morning?"

"That I needed to protect Aleks, or he would cut him. Why would he say something like that?"

"He's never gotten over his own cut, has he?"

"There's nothing left to Jacek but his scar."

Tolek tried the defroster again. "*Cholera!*"

"I'm sorry it's broken. Oh Tolek, please hurry! I'm so worried."

Soon they crossed the bridge to follow the river drive on the Praga side.

Lilka reached to wipe off Tolek's side of the windshield. "I know it's a left turn," she said. "Can you see?"

"Barely. I think we've gone too far."

"We need to hurry."

"I am hurrying. You need to tell me where to turn. Cars are flashing their lights at me."

Lilka peered at the black forest along that stretch of the river. "Thank goodness there's a moon tonight."

"What's near it?" he asked.

"I thought you said you knew it?"

"It was a bait shack then, with nothing much else around."

"There's a nightclub now. You turn just past it."

"A white building? That must be two kilometers back."

"How did we pass it?" moaned Lilka. "I was looking for the lights."

"It must be closed."

"On Saturday night?"

"Out of business. Like everything."

"Turn back, Tolek."

"Where can I?"

"There must be a place up ahead. Oh hurry, Tolek! I feel something is wrong."

• • •

BASIA NEVER TOOK OFF HER fur while fucking. She was the animal she wore—wild and voracious—and Jacek, sweating and grotesquely bald, stalked her. A trickle of hair disappeared beneath the waistband of his black jeans. Perched on a sturdy table, she wrapped her legs around him and teased his zipper down. Then she let him take her.

Jay, tied to a straight-backed chair, was the only audience for their coarse coupling. It was their second go at it. For the first round, she held onto the back of Jay's chair while taking their pleasure. The Afghan shipment had an edgy eroticism, they said in words he didn't speak but understood.

Jacek punched a button on the radio and bar music swooned into the shack. He swung around a second straight-backed chair and sat in it backward, facing Jay, lewdly grinning. Basia stepped up behind him and ran her fingers through his hair. She had a knife in her other hand. "Let me have it, babe," he said.

She dropped it in his hand.

He leaned forward to press it to Jay's face.

He tried to avoid it, but there was only so far he could wrench his head.

"Don't move, it'll make it worse," Jacek warned him.

"Is this where you brought the others to kill them?"

"Sitting in your chair."

Slowly he dragged the knife's down Jay's cheek, scoring but not slicing it. He only knew he'd been cut by the trickle of blood on his face.

Jacek set the knife on a table. "There's more to come." He turned and closed his mouth on Basia's breast.

When Dravko entered, that was how he found them.

He stood in the doorway in his formal whites, ablaze with medals, curious until he recognized Jay. His expression slackened with uncertainty. He set his suitcase next to its twin.

"Someone's outside," Basia cautioned.

Everyone froze just as a woman yelped with fear. Jacek reached for his gun.

Outside, Lilka called tentatively, "Aleks?"

Jacek threw open the door. "What the fuck!"

"Why are the dogs dead?"

"You get out of here now!"

"She wants to see Aleks." It was Tolek.

Lilka saw Jay tied to the chair. "Oh my God! Jacek, what are you doing?" Tolek went to help him.

"Stay away from him!" Jacek waved the gun menacingly.

Tolek picked up Jacek's knife and started cutting Jay loose.

"I said get back!" Jacek aimed for him.

"Jacek, no!" Lilka screamed.

His shot hit Tolek square in the chest. Tolek looked surprised before folding at Jay's feet.

"Tolek!" Lilka ran to him.

Jacek pointed his gun at Dravko. "Don't move. Get the money," he said to Basia.

Lilka cradled her brother-in-law. "You've killed him. You've killed Tolek. Why? *Why?*"

"I told you, get the money!" Jacek barked again.

"You can take the money," said Dravko.

"Get his suitcase!"

Basia didn't move. "Is there an island for us, Dravko?"

"You're coming with me," Jacek said. "Remember?"

"Where can you go that Mladic won't find you?" Jay asked.

"Shut up!" Jacek shouted.

"He'll kill you, too," Jay said. "After he tortures you."

In a flash, Jacek was behind him, the gun pressed to Jay's head. "I'll shut you up!"

"*Nooo!*" Lilka screamed, and flung herself on him. The gun clattered on the floor.

Jacek tried to push her off him. "Get away!"

"Let her go." The voice came from the doorway.

Aleks had a steady gun trained on Jacek.

"You wouldn't dare," Jacek sneered.

"You killed my dogs."

Jacek swept up his knife, grabbed Lilka from behind, and pressed it to her throat.

"Let her go," said the boy.

"When I'm out of here."

"If you get a shot, take it," Jay told him. "Shoot him. Do you understand?"

The boy nodded that he did.

With his arm around her neck, Jacek dragged Lilka to the suitcases. "Pick it up!"

"Which one?"

"Which one has the money?" he asked Dravko, who pointed to it.

"Pick it up!" he yelled at her.

Lilka managed to grasp its handle. "Please, Jacek, you're hurting me," she cried as he dragged her to the door.

He stepped backward over the threshold and tripped over the gray dog's body. The weight of the suitcase set Lilka off-balance as well, and she fell to the side, exposing him.

"Shoot him!" Jay shouted.

Jacek's body convulsed from the shot from Aleks's gun. He fell out of the light, made a gurgling sound, and was quiet.

Lilka fell to her knees next to Tolek. She wept uncontrollably. The boy knelt and embraced her. "Mama," he said, "Mama . . ."

Still tied to the chair, Jay watched helplessly as Basia and the general fled with the suitcases. He heard their car drive off. "Untie me," he said, but Lilka was sobbing too hard over Tolek's inert body to pay any attention, and Aleks didn't budge, keeping an arm draped around her shoulders. "I have a walkie-talkie in my pack. Just press the button for the embassy."

"That won't be necessary." Kulski stood in the doorway.

Kurt Crawford stepped around him. "What the hell happened?" He picked up the knife and used it to free Jay's hands. "Is that Rypinski outside by the dog?"

"Yes."

Kulski tested Tolek for a pulse. "I am sorry," he said to Lilka, and she collapsed in Aleks's arms.

Jay rubbed his wrists and summarized what had happened. "They're ten minutes ahead of us. My guess is that Mladic will head for the airport and take the first flight to anywhere."

Kulski said, "I'll wait for the ambulance, then go to the director's apartment."

"I need your car keys," Jay said to Lilka.

"Tolek had them."

Jay searched Tolek's pockets. His heart ached at this death and the terrible news it would be to Alina. He imagined Lilka's tears were as much for her sister as for Tolek, and for their son.

"I'll drive," Kurt offered. "You already look like roadkill."

◆ ◆ ◆

Basia turned onto a service road that rose through the snowy park to the zoo. She pulled over and cut the engine and lit a cigarette.

"What are you doing?" asked Dravko.

"Smoking." She pressed the lever to open her window. It glided down. Somewhere nearby, a monkey howled.

"We haven't time," he said.

"I suppose you have a plane to catch." She flicked an ash. "Did you remember to buy my ticket? I thought not."

"Why did you decide to double-cross me?"

"I let Jacek think that. It was never true." It was only a half-lie; in truth, Basia hadn't known what she was going to do until it was done. "There is no island, is there, Dravko? No villa."

A lion's roar answered her, setting monkeys to chattering. Brisk winds carried their exotic sounds across the park. They seem to come from as far away as Basia wanted to go. "There was a time when we shared a dream, wasn't there?"

"There was a time," he admitted.

"You made me dream your dreams, Dravko. I look into your eyes and I can see your world."

"If only you could."

"I am in your film, Dravko. I hear the crowds cheering for you."

"You hear the crowds?"

"I hear them. Take me away, Dravko. Take me with you."

"It's time to go," he said.

"That's no answer."

"You know why I can't."

"I've heard your speeches." She blew smoke into the night. "So my purpose is served and you have your bomb."

"You have the money. You can buy what you want, your villa or anything."

"Except sanctuary. Where can I run and be protected?"

"I have no place for you."

"Not even a beach?"

"Not even a beach."

"So it is finished." Basia tossed out her cigarette, started the engine, and continued up the hill. Her headlights caught the startled eyes of caged animals.

"They might be looking for my car already," she said.

"Are your police so efficient?"

"It can be so."

She pulled behind a taxi stand.

He went to the back of the car and opened the trunk to the twin suitcases. They fled from the shack in such haste he had not paid attention to which side he placed the suitcase with the bomb. Basia had to point it out.

"Are you sure?"

She thought so. He grappled to lift it from the snug compartment and snagged a latch on the trunk's lip.

"Stop!" Basia cried.

Dravko froze. "What is it?"

"There's a trick to the latches. Sergej told Jacek, they're set to detonate it."

He eased the suitcase to the ground.

"How does your film end, Dravko?"

"Now I am ready for the end," he answered.

"Then you haven't watched it?"

"I come to a point where I am on a platform and the crowds are cheering. I rewind it, and watch to that point again. It is always the same, except each time the crowds are larger, the cheering louder, like I am getting closer to that moment."

"Next time, watch it to the end," Basia said. "I'll be there, and the boys will be, too. The dark passions, Dravko, you cannot tame them."

They had been lovers, but were less practiced in their affections. They had no more words for each other. Not goodbye, nor a parting embrace. Dravko touched his cap and walked to a waiting cab.

The driver, impressed by his fine white uniform, jumped out to help load his suitcase. "Where's the gentleman going?"

"The airport," said Dravko, "and hurry, my flight leaves in thirty minutes."

Basia watched the taxi pull away. Oncoming headlights silhouetted Dravko in the backseat. He never turned back to wave.

CHAPTER THIRTY-FOUR

NOTHING ABOUT LILKA'S CAR WORKED. Its clearance was too low, the defroster was broken, acceleration was more a state of mind than fact. Kurt stalled twice when he pitched into potholes. They shared curses that served as prayers as they willed the engine to turn over. It did, and he gingerly navigated the rutted track past the nightclub. They had lost another ten minutes.

He pulled into traffic.

Kurt glanced over at Jay, who held a wad of toilet paper to his cheek.

"I should take you to a hospital."

"It's not deep."

"It doesn't matter. Cheek wounds bleed a lot."

They rode in tense silence, impatient as seconds added up to minutes.

"How did you know to come to the shack? The duty officer?"

"That was Millie last night."

"Millie?"

"She called me but couldn't remember why. She'd written down Mr. Potter and sugar."

"You figured out Billy's shack from sugar?"

Kurt shook his head. "Never crossed my mind," he said. "I had Mladic under surveillance. When his taxi turned into the nightclub, my guy let me know. You'd described Billy's shack as being past the nightclub, so that's when I knew the clue was for you: Mr. Potter at the sugar shack. I called Detective Kulski. You had said you trusted him and I didn't have a choice."

Kurt told him how Detective Kulski detained him at the train station, explaining it was a random security check, but Kurt felt it was intended to let Husarska lose him. Kulski was a common name, but Kurt was certain he was the detective on Jay's case when he saw him limp away. When Millie telephoned, he had no choice but to contact him even if he was in cahoots with Husarska. "Fortunately he wasn't," Kurt concluded. "He picked me up and you know the rest."

The international terminal loomed ahead of them. Kurt swerved to a stop and they jumped from the car before its engine had stopped gasping. A security guard blew her whistle and gave chase. They crashed through the terminal's doors, searching the crowd for the general's white uniform as they raced for the gates. On the departure board, Belgrade wasn't listed. Where could he be going? A world of destinations was possible, but boarding lights flashed only for Paris and they ran for the gate. At passport control, Jay flashed his FBI badge without waiting for clearance, and more guards gave chase.

The last Paris-bound passengers passed through the gate and the attendant locked the glass door. She yelped in alarm when she saw Jay's bloody face. Mladic was the last to board a shuttle bus. Jay shook the door's handle and shouted for her to open it. Mladic heard the commotion and looked back, recognizing Kurt. Their eyes locked.

Kurt pulled a newspaper out of a trashcan and held it up for Dravko to see. He flicked his tongue, and pantomimed sending lewd kisses, while pointing to the paper. His message could not have been clearer: Kurt would out him. The general visibly paled as the bus pulled away.

By that time, the security guards chased them down. They raised their arms to be led away.

Shakily, Dravko mounted the steps to the airplane and stowed his suitcase in the overhead compartment. Did he require anything? the flight attendant asked. Would he like to remove his hat? A drink, perhaps champagne before takeoff? He waved her away and sagged into his seat.

Wearied by his narrow escape, his eyes closed and his mind drifted. Again he saw Kurt's last kiss—the flick of his pink tongue especially lewd in the circle of his black lips—and his pale palm pressed to the glass door as if ready to pull him off the bus. Dravko jerked awake. He was sweating. He asked for water. It refreshed him, and he sat back, closing his eyes again.

The film in his mind began to play. From boyhood achievements to military adventures, his biography unfolded, the story of his inexorable rise. Dravko missed his airplane's takeoff; he was so engrossed in a battlefield scene that he mistook the engines' roar for army tanks. As surely as the plane's lift, Dravko treaded an upward path, accumulating medals and honors, power, and faithful followers. He reached the point in his film where he stood on a platform surrounded by an honor guard and the crowds roared his name. At that point, he always rewound the film to hear the cheering again, but that time he let it run on, ready for the rest of his story. The camera panned the crowd. What was that? They were holding up newspapers! They weren't cheering but jeering him with words taken from the headlines. The African's headlines. Words of unworthiness. Scandalous words. Immoral. Too late, he tried to stop the film, to rewind it, but it jammed and burned from the center, shriveling away to reveal a final flick of the African's tongue.

Dravko cried out and bolted from his seat. Other passengers, curious, stared at him. They leered, it seemed to Dravko; they already knew his dirty secrets. *So this is how it will be*, he thought, *the shame of revelation*. His destiny derailed by the dark passions that had bidden him to sow his own ruinous seeds. An anguished noise rose from his throat as he pulled his suitcase out of the overhead bin. Vaguely he heard admonitions not to do that, please sit down, did he have a medical problem?

He plunked the suitcase in the aisle, which brought a sudden hush. Someone cried out, "He has a bomb!"

They knew his power then. They, too, shared his destiny, and before their anxious faces could turn to hatred, he released both latches.

Lipstick tubes exploded into the aisle. They bounced off armrests, rolled under feet, scattered everywhere. A nervous laugh became infectious and spread through the cabin. He heard their mockery and collapsed on the suitcase, losing his cap to reveal his thinning hair. A flight attendant helped him up. He wept as she fastened his seatbelt.

CHAPTER THIRTY-FIVE

BASIA HAD TURNED ON ALL the lights to reveal her world, her end of the rainbow, her pot of gold: her corner apartment. For all her dreams, she had traveled no farther than that table, those chairs, her bed, and the knickknacks that made the place personal. All so pathetic, too, those knickknacks and make-do furnishings. How far she was from the glamorous beaches she had imagined. She tried to pinpoint when her life had become so shabby and couldn't. It had crept up on her.

Dreams forestalled.

Dreams denied.

Time up.

Needle, spoon, lighter. She placed them on the table. She had escaped that world often, the needle her joy ride, and yet had failed to plan her final escape beyond trusting in Dravko's protective shield. It had become so complicated, the tangled murders and double-crosses within double-crosses, that to sort through them took an effort greater than her weariness allowed. It was over.

Spilling half of Billy's powder into the spoon, she dissolved it with water, loaded a syringe, then repeated the process with what heroin remained, adding it to the same syringe. She put the lethal needle on the bedside table before dimming the lights and slipping a tape into a VCR player that projected a film on the wall of Dravko fucking her, both much younger and he in dress whites, on the loveseat at the former KGB lodge. She toasted their lovemaking with a bottle of scotch and swigged from it before turning her attention to the suitcase. A million dollars, was it possible? How ironic if true. How much it would have meant at one time. A million dollars, it was another life. It was everything, and anything, and more, and yet now it could buy her nothing that she needed. Her certain capture and imprisonment made it worthless. She had purchased her freedom at the cost of it.

Basia undid the leather straps on the suitcase. She had a passing thought: what if she had confused suitcases with Dravko? This could be the bomb. Annihilation in a nanosecond had a certain appeal.

She popped the latches and opened it.

"Oh my God, Dravko, it *is* a million dollars," she said aloud.

He had stuffed the bag with lopsided stacks of dog-eared dollars. A couple tumbled to the floor. Basia pulled out more, slipping off their rubber bands. She whirled around, scattering the bills. She opened her coat—she was still naked except for the fur and heels in which she had fled the shack—and showered herself with money while twirling in a little girl's fantasy of dancing on streets paved with gold.

The blue flashing lights on police cars appeared at the end of the street.

Basia stopped her dance.

It was time.

She scooped up a pile of money and flung it over her bed. She flung a second unceremonious armful, and a third. Her buzzer rang insistently. She fell into her bed of money and picked up the syringe. She heard the downstairs door break open, the pounding footsteps on the stairs and boots kicking her door. As the wood cracked, she found a vein and emptied the syringe.

Before the angels fluttered beside her, she heard Dravko in the film cry out her name one last time.

"Basia!"

CHAPTER THIRTY-SIX

J AY AWOKE THE NEXT DAY to discover it was already afternoon. He wondered why no one had called before he remembered he had unplugged the telephone, at what time he couldn't say. He hadn't managed to undress unless taking his shoes off counted.

He called room service for coffee and took a shower. He scrubbed the dog bite on his wrist and tried to keep the bandage on his face dry. The slice was clean, he remembered the doctor saying. He had sutured it with butterfly bandages as carefully as if using a needle. "There won't be a big scar," he assured him. "No one will notice it." Jay wondered how much might have been different in so many lives if Jacek's scar had been as easily erased. Had his viciousness been driven by it, or was he such a swaggering sonofabitch that he would have ultimately ended up at the same dead-end? It didn't really matter why. He'd ended up there.

Jay tried reconstructing the prior night's events. Kidnapped by Jacek and brought to the shack. Tied to a chair, his face cut, forced to watch a constantly repeating sexcapade. Tolek's death. The chase to the airport, Dravko escaping in the bus, Kurt and himself helpless to stop him. Arrested themselves, but treated respectably after a telephone call to Detective Kulski, which ended with a police escort to a medical clinic to treat his wound. Somewhere in the night, he was returned to the hotel.

He heard the porter's knock at the door and answered. He carried a tray to a side table, poured the coffee, and laid back a napkin to reveal breakfast pastries.

"Is your telephone not working?" the porter asked, handing him a stack of messages.

"I unplugged it." Jay signed the check and tipped him.

"Thank you, sir."

When he left, Jay went through his messages.

Kulski: *Please come at your convenience.*

Ambassador Lerner: *Expects you at his house at 16h.*

Kurt: *Confirmed physicist had two suitcases.*

His father: *Call your father.*

Lilka hadn't called. What would she have said?

He regretted abandoning her in such distress the night before. He was eager to know what happened after he left her at the shack with Detective Kulski. He had coffee while he dressed quickly and took the pastries to eat in a taxi. Speeding across the Poniatowski Bridge, he craned his neck to glimpse Tommy's houseboat farther downriver.

• • •

DETECTIVE KULSKI OFFERED HIM COFFEE from a thermos. "I thought you might need a cup of American coffee this morning," he said before launching into the aftermath of his departure from the shack the night before. He sent officers to Basia's flat, but they arrived too late. She had overdosed while sprawled on a bed of money with nothing but a fistful of greenbacks to cover her shame. "She stopped breathing before they reached the hospital. Also, we arrested Billy last night. We found many drugs at his bar. Of course, it will take more time to collect all the evidence."

"It's all there," Jay assured him.

"We also have more evidence about Tommy's murder," Kulski said. "A gun was found in the river under the houseboat."

"Let me guess, it's yours."

"How did you know?"

"Director Husarska was setting you up. She probably took it the morning you were at rehab. She knew you'd be gone and you wouldn't take your gun with you. I guess Tommy died in vain."

"If I had given him back his passport, he wouldn't be dead." Kulski shook his head regretfully. "It is also too bad that Pani Husarska is dead. I know she was not a good woman, but I think necessity made her that way. Or started her to be that way, and then it became a habit."

"You have a kind thought for everyone, don't you, Detective? You should have been a priest."

"It was my mother's wish." He handed Jay what appeared to be a receipt. "This was found in her pocket."

"What is it?"

"For cleaning her coat."

Jay smiled when he understood. "Of course, the fourth courier bled on her. They were embracing when she shot him. That's why the fur went missing for a day."

"There were many clues, yes?" the detective asked. "After the facts are known, a lot more is obvious." He sipped his coffee. "Also, I questioned Pani Rypinska."

"Lilka? How is she?"

"I think you say, in a shocked state. She will come tomorrow to make a statement."

"Where is she?"

"My wife took her to her sister's last night."

"Your wife?"

"I could think of no other way. I thought it better for her to go with a woman, and not a policewoman."

"And her son, Aleks?"

"He ran off. Here is her sister's number." The detective handed it over. "She will need to stay there until my team finishes in her apartment. It might take another day."

"That's understandable."

"I also have teams in Mladic's hotel room and Pani Husarska's apartment."

"Sounds like you've got it covered."

"It's a big case. You will also need to make an official statement."

"I'll prepare something in advance and set up a time with Eva for tomorrow."

"Good." Kulski poured off the remaining dribble of coffee between their cups. "Unfortunately that's all there is."

"That's fine. I have to go. I've been summoned to the ambassador's."

"He must be pleased."

"Perhaps. Or we might get sent to the guillotine for the scene we created. Thanks for intervening with airport security. Otherwise, I would probably be in jail right now."

"It only required a telephone call."

"That you could make but I couldn't. Also, I think your doctor did a good job on my face. He said the scar would be barely noticeable. I'm curious, why did you stop Kurt Crawford at the train station?"

The detective reminded Jay that it had been his suggestion to canvass the station's vendors, and he was glad that he'd made it because Kulski hit pay dirt. The night Ustinov was murdered, he purchased stamps at a magazine stand to send a letter to Russia. "Whatever he had to mail, it seemed important to him. He put extra stamps on it to make sure it arrived."

"He had some last words for somebody," Jay said, "even if he didn't know that they were his last words."

"I was talking to the vendor when I noticed Mr. Crawford come into the station," Kulski continued.

"Why? Because he's black?"

"Yes, it's true. We see so few black people in our country."

"That's what he tells me."

"He pretended to read the newspapers, but I sensed he was waiting for something to happen. As soon as he saw Pani Husarska, I knew he had waited for her. He followed her into the underground, and later when she was leaving the station, he was still following her. I thought she might be in danger."

"Did Kurt explain his business?"

"Not at the station. Later, going to the shack, he told me enough to understand it is secret."

"What I said about the bomb is also confidential," Jay said.

"I understand. How long will you stay in Warsaw?"

"Only two or three days. Long enough to make a statement and go over any last details and wrap things up. My older son has a Little League game at the end of next week and I want to go to it."

"Little League?"

"Baseball for kids. His team is in the regional championships for middle schoolers."

The detective smiled. "So we are both proud fathers of sporty children."

"Yes we are, and I'm going home to tell mine. They're both going through a hard time because of the divorce."

"It's hard on kids."

"It wasn't my choice. I'll get the results of the DNA tests on those cigarette butts to you as soon as I have them. I'd bet a million dollars that they're Director Husarska's. If they are, they put her at the exact spot of the crime, and Tommy's statement says he saw her toss at least one cigarette away." Jay stuck out his hand. "Good work, Detective Kulski. Case closed. You broke up a drug ring and solved four murders."

"Only with your help."

"As I recall, I was the one who needed help."

"Did I tell you that I knew her brother-in-law?"

"Tolek?"

"We were in the same prison camp. He was humorous. People smiled when they saw him. His funeral will be Tuesday. It's sad when a good man is killed unnecessarily. And just after he was granted a visa to go to America."

"If you hadn't stopped Mladic, he would have kept trying until possibly millions of good people were killed."

Kulski said, "I don't feel like a hero."

• • •

THE MAID ANSWERED THE DOOR and escorted Jay into the ambassador's library. Kurt was already there, browsing the books on a corner shelf. "How's the FBI feeling today?" he asked.

"Like roadkill resuscitated. What's the ambassador thinking, do you have any idea?"

"I haven't seen him."

"I just left Kulski," Jay said. "He's got his evidence guys going over Jacek's apartment and Mladic's room. Do you think Carl's going to bust our balls?"

"He should give us fucking crowns but I don't know what he's going to say. Langley's ordered me home tonight. The director wants to know why a senior Yugoslavian official had to be removed in a straitjacket from an airplane in Paris blubbering my name."

"No shit. Mladic cracked up?"

They high-fived each other just as Ambassador Lerner entered. He scowled. "You gentlemen seem to be in a good mood for having had a very eventful night."

He opened a cabinet and lined up three glasses and poured heavy shots of scotch. "I just got off the telephone with the secretary of state. He wanted to be briefed on the situation. I told him what I knew, which is very little. Cheers."

"Cheers." They drank.

"I think my last words to you were 'don't break the law.'"

Like scolded schoolboys, Jay and Kurt started to mutter apologies until Carl held up his hand. "Stop right there. Congratulations from the secretary of state. You're responsible for Mladic's arrest, and probably averting an eventual global catastrophe. Now tell me what happened."

For nearly an hour they wove a devious web of smugglers, cops, and politicians, and when they were through, all agreed they thought they knew most of the story. There were loose threads, to be sure: the identity of the couriers, their exact cargo, and the whereabouts of the uranium and detonator. Kurt reported Mladic's indictment of Minister Brzeski's involvement in the weapons smuggling racket, but with Basia dead, no one remained to corroborate it, and Carl hardly relished pursuing the matter given the circumstances by which Kurt had extorted the confession from the general.

"Mladic was arrested when his plane landed in Paris, but the authorities aren't certain what to charge him with," the ambassador said. "No one has ever tried to bring down a plane with a suitcase full of lipstick tubes."

"Unfortunately there *is* a missing portable bomb," Jay reminded them. "Dr. Ustinov defected with two matching suitcases, one presumably the bomb. Mladic and Jacek had matching suitcases, but it turns out neither was a bomb. So there must be a third matching suitcase somewhere."

"That's not a very comforting thought," the ambassador said.

"Especially since portable means it could end up anywhere in the world."

The maid interrupted them. "The Yugoslavian ambassador is on the telephone, sir."

"I'll take it in my study. When you finish your drinks, gentlemen, please find your own way out. I expect I will be on the telephone a long time."

The ambassador left and Kurt retrieved the bottle of scotch. "A short one for the road."

Jay held out his glass.

"How much longer are you staying?" Kurt asked.

"I'm assuming three days. I need to make an official police statement and wrap up some other things."

"Rypinska?"

"She's included in other things."

They knocked back their drinks and collected their coats.

"You did all right for the FBI," Kurt said.

"And you? Better than expected for Langley. That's good, if we end up working together on another case."

• • •

ALL THE WAY BACK TO the hotel, Jay debated when to call Lilka. The message light on the telephone in his room was flashing, and he eagerly pressed the playback button. It was Ann Rewls haranguing him for not returning her calls. Where the hell had he been? He should call her immediately. The telephone rang, and Ann Rewls in person started boxing his other ear.

"This is unfair," he moaned. "I don't need you in stereo." He turned off the answering machine. "I assume this isn't a social call. Do you want to go first?"

"I'm only checking in with you."

"Why? Is Ned snoring?"

"That too."

Jay recounted his last twenty-four hours as if they belonged to somebody else. He knew they didn't when Ann reminded him, "Don't forget you need rabies shots. You should start those today."

"You know how to cheer a guy up."

"It's because I'm concerned."

He went into the bathroom and splashed cold water on his face, careful not to wet his bandage. The ringing telephone called him back into the bedroom.

"Hello."

"I left a message to call me. Didn't you get it?" It was his father.

"I thought I should wait until you were awake. Has something happened?" Jay asked, dreading bad news.

"Yes, something has happened. Cynthia's not going to fight you on custody. I faxed my photos to your lawyer, who faxed them to her lawyer, who saw the marijuana and apparently advised her not to fight for full custody or she might lose altogether. Apparently courts are pretty strict about things like that, and in this case, it turns your working for the FBI from a liability to an asset."

"So your photos are legal evidence?"

"They're pictures I took of my grandsons. When I got home, I noticed all the other stuff. Or so that's what I said."

"That's very clever, Dad."

"I didn't study rocket science for nothing. Your lawyer says you might win full custody, if you ask for it."

"I don't want to do that to Cynthia. I'm not trying to punish her, and the boys need a mother as much as they need a father."

"You could remarry."

Jay laughed. "Let's not rush the courses, Dad. I'm wrapping things up here. I'll be home next week for Martin's Little League game."

"Good."

"Give Mom my love."

Jay hung up and sat on the edge of the bed pondering the new reality that soon he'd be spending time with his sons. A father again. He had almost resigned himself to rare sightings as his boys grew up, and even to the possibility that his ex-wife might steal them away to California, wedging a whole continent between them. Apparently neither bleak prospect was going to come to pass. He took a deep breath and felt a lot of sadness leave him.

He returned to the room and drew the curtains to block the last of the day's light. He kicked off his shoes, sat on the bed, and pulled out the telephone number Kulski had given him. He dialed the telephone, hoping Lilka would answer.

She did, in a voice so filled with tears that he choked up, too.

"When can I see you?" he asked.

CHAPTER THIRTY-SEVEN

Spring arrived overnight. Bulbs had sprouted in the dark earth, trees had new leaves, and the sky cleared to pale blue. Even flowers had miraculously bloomed. Or had Jay simply not noticed the spring's colorful onslaught through the miasmic haze of his investigation?

Lilka had asked for a normal day, not one filled with tears, though she knew she'd cry when they finally said goodbye. They met at the park near the embassy, and after a couple of long hugs and sniffles, she wanted to show Jay the palace. Lilka took delight in its ornate rooms filled with furniture fit for a king, for indeed Lazienki Palace had been a royal summer residence. Though badly damaged by fire, the building had survived the war, not for reason of German benevolence but in a rare moment of Teutonic inefficiency: the Nazis had completed the task of drilling holes to place explosives in the marble walls, but too late to set the charges before the advancing Russians overran them. Lilka knew her history, and she told Jay popular anecdotes of the people whose portraits lined the walls: the prince who had a penchant for prostitutes, the prostitute who had a penchant for kings, and the king who had a penchant for the prince. Jay laughed at every story.

Outside, the sun reflected on the palace moat. They watched two boys chase ducks down its bank, making them waddle faster, while the boys' mothers smoked and gossiped at a nearby table.

Lilka took his arm. "You miss your sons, yes?"

"Yes, I miss my sons. Those boys are about their ages."

"Aleks came home last night."

He squeezed her hand. "Good."

"I am very happy."

"Me too."

"We will take tea, yes?"

He smiled. "We will take tea, yes."

They followed paths through the palace's gardens. Peacocks pecked at the hard ground. Twice Jay acted the fool by cavorting in front of them to try to make them display their tail feathers, but apparently he was the only male prepared to display himself that afternoon.

Soon they came to a café, squat and prefabricated, out of place in the park's woods with its bold yellow-and-red strips of plastic siding. The interior was surprisingly pleasant. The cheerful proprietress waved them to a table by the window. Without being asked, she carried over a large kettle and poured tea for both of them.

Lilka wrapped her hands around the cup. "The tea is very special here," she said. "You can smell the earth in it."

Having earth in his tea wasn't exactly appealing to Jay, and he gave the dark brew a more discerning look. Indeed there were a few specks of something floating in it, but he trusted that the water had boiled long enough to sterilize almost anything. He took his first tentative sip, and couldn't wait to take a second. It was like a hot mulled wine, only better.

"I am glad to meet you, Jay."

"Me too."

"My life is different because of you."

"Mine too."

"I was afraid to lose Aleks forever. Now, with Jacek gone, I think there is a chance for him. I left Aleks alone with Jacek too many times. He was a bad influence."

"I'm worried Cynthia is becoming a bad influence on my boys, too."

"You must convince your wife—"

"*Ex*-wife."

"—that you need to spend more time with them."

"Supposedly she's agreed to let them live with me half the time."

"Oh, Jay! I am happy for you!"

"It hasn't happened yet. We still need to finalize it in court."

"Tell the judge you want your sons to grow up to be like you, not Jacek."

Jay chuckled. "She won't know who Jacek is."

"Every judge knows a Jacek. More than one." Lilka reached for his hand. "If you come back to Poland, you will come back to me?"

"That's an easy promise to keep."

They kissed across the table, paid their check, and left.

"Alina is waiting for me to help prepare things for the funeral."

"I wish I could have saved Tolek," Jay said.

"It's the saddest for Tadzu." Lilka nodded. "His father loved him so much, and now he's gone. Oh, look." Lilka stooped at a rose bush that already had buds. A couple had opened, and she plucked one and gave it to Jay. "The first rose of the spring. It's beautiful, isn't it?"

"Like you," he said.

Arms around each other, they walked to the main road. Jay waved down a taxi.

Lilka turned and asked, "Tell me, Jay, if things were different, would you love me?"

"I do love you," he said, and they kissed a last time.

Then she was gone, in the backseat of the taxi, tears streaming down her cheeks as she waved goodbye.

EPILOGUE

NATALYA'S STOUT LEGS STRUGGLED UP the last flight of stairs. She stopped on the landing, lowered her travel bag, and pulled up her stockings. She fluffed her hair. Her sister, three years older, had always been the smarter of the two, with her Moscow friends and newer fashions, and Natalya didn't want to appear frumpy when she first arrived. How many years had it been since she had seen Olivia? Five? The stairs still smelled of the same stale cabbage. She wondered again at her sister's urgent summons. Olivia had refused to say anything over the telephone, only that she must come to Moscow.

As Natalya knocked on the door, she half-imagined Sergej opening it, thinking that to be a trick he might pull. Since his disappearance, she had thought she had seen him so many times. She had never realized how many men resembled him in Kosmonovo. But it was only Olivia, her hair bundled into a netted bun, who answered the door. Her skin smelled papery when they embraced. She sniffed the hallway as if ferreting out spies and hustled Natalya inside.

"What is it, Olivia? What is so secret?"

Her sister withdrew a book from a shelf and removed a letter she had concealed in it. She handed it to Natalya. "It's from Sergej."

Natalya sat heavily in a chair and turned the envelope in her hand.

"It's must be very important to have so many stamps," remarked Olivia.

"He sent it from Warsaw."

"Open it, Natalya."

She did, and when she shook out the letter, a claim check came with it. She unfolded the single page:

My loving Natalya,

You are surprised to hear from me, ha! You think I am in the grave.

I am not, I am with my sons, three of them. Or I shall be. I have sent them ahead of me. Does that surprise you? All those years they bred me, never telling me that I had conceived children, but I learned. I learned! My sixth finger, that harmless nub, was the giveaway. They bred for recessive genes, thinking in them lay genius, can you imagine such stupidity? But you cannot, you are too smart, that is why we were paired. I have come to love you, if too late. Like a bird in a cage left open, I took my chance to escape. I have joined the birds in the forest, ha! Our baby, our little Davy Crockett, I have left for you. I have carried it to safety and hidden it. I know what they will do, how they will hound you until you are no longer. Use this, Natalya, to save yourself. It is worth the whole world to them. Ha!

Your Sergej

Natalya examined the claim check. It had a number. Nothing else to identify its origin. "My Sergej," she sighed, "he was always so crazy."

Timothy Jay Smith is a writer of fiction and plays. His ceaseless wanderlust has taken him around the world many times. En route, he's found the characters that people his work. Polish cops and Greek fishermen, mercenaries and arms dealers, child prostitutes and wannabe terrorists, Indian chiefs and Indian tailors: he hung with them all in an unparalleled international career that saw him smuggle banned plays from behind the Iron Curtain, maneuver through occupied territories, represent the US at the highest levels of foreign governments, and stow away aboard a "devil's barge" for a three-day crossing from Cape Verde that landed him in an African jail.

His novel *Fire on the Island* took the Gold Medal in the 2017 Faulkner–Wisdom Competition for the Novel. He won the Paris Prize for Fiction (now the Paris Literary Prize) for his novel *A Vision of Angels*. His novel *Cooper's Promise* was called "literary dynamite" by *Kirkus*, which selected it as one of the Best Books of 2012. His stage play, *How High the Moon*, won the prestigious Stanley Drama Award, and his screenplays have won competitions sponsored by the American Screenwriters Association, WriteMovies, Houston WorldFest, Rhode Island International Film Festival, Fresh Voices, StoryPros, and the Hollywood Screenwriting Institute. He is the founder of the Smith Prize for Political Theater. He lives in Nice, France.